LAW AGAINST LAW

"You there, on the trail," a voice boomed from the rocky hillside above them. "Raise your hands! Don't try to make a run for it. We've got you surrounded."

The three prisoners stuck their hands high in the air; Sam raised his hands slowly, chest high, as he searched the hillside and saw a tall figure standing atop a rock with a rifle aimed down at him. A few yards on either side of the rifleman stood another gunman, each with a rifle raised and ready. Sam was certain there were more than these three—other gunmen up there out of sight. These three had revealed themselves as a show of force.

"I'm Arizona Territory Ranger Sam Burrack," he called out. "Who are you, and what's your business here?"

"I'm sheriff's deputy Denton Shenny," the rifleman called out. "These men are my posse. We've been following an assassin's trail out of Mesa Grande. Now show me a badge, slow-like," he said in summation.

"[Cotton's] works incorporate . . . pace and plot in a language that ranges from lyric beauty to macabre descriptions of bestial savagery."
—Wade Hall, *The Louisville Courier-Journal*

"Gun-smoked believability . . . a hard hand to beat."
—Terry Johnston

MESA GRANDE

Ralph Cotton

A SIGNET BOOK

SIGNET
Published by the Penguin Group
Penguin Group (USA) LLC, 375 Hudson Street,
New York, New York 10014

USA | Canada | UK | Ireland | Australia | New Zealand | India | South Africa | China
penguin.com
A Penguin Random House Company

First published by Signet, an imprint of New American Library,
a division of Penguin Group (USA) LLC

First Printing, January 2015

Copyright © Ralph Cotton, 2015

Ⓟ REGISTERED TRADEMARK—MARCA REGISTRADA

ISBN 978-0-451-47156-7

Printed in the United States of America
10 9 8 7 6 5 4 3 2

For Mary Lynn of course . . .

Prologue

Nothing had moved down on the sand flats for over an hour. But that didn't make Arizona Territory Ranger Sam Burrack trust this scorched stretch of badlands any more than he would trust a sleeping rattlesnake. The men he'd been following had ridden out onto a stone shelf covered with dried mesquite and spiky cactus and disappeared. Only two things they could have done, the Ranger reasoned to himself. They could have abandoned their horses and climbed down a steep hundred feet of broken rock, or they could have lain down and taken cover, hoping he'd either give up the hunt or come riding in blindly.

Not likely they would leave their horses, though, he further deduced—not with only one man tracking them, not up here in Apache country. These two didn't spook that easy. They were there, lying in wait for him. He was certain of it.

He squinted and looked all around the terrain from under the brim of his lowered sombrero. Midmorning sunlight blazed white and sharp above him. His black-point copper dun stood with its head poked inside the thin shade of an upreaching saguaro cactus twenty feet away. This was a waiting game, he reminded himself, no two ways about it. Sooner or later the desert would force him or the two outlaws to make a move.

That's how it works. So be it. . . .

He scooted back and stood without stirring up any dust. He stepped over to the dun, loosened its reins from the saguaro and led it over into the fuller shade of the boulder. Keeping an eye on the stone shelf, he took the canteen from his saddle horn, poured a few drops of tepid water onto his palm and pressed it to the dun's muzzle.

The dun took the water, licking at his palm and butting his hand when it realized his palm had gone empty.

"Easy, Copper," he whispered, and he patted the horse's warm neck. "This won't last much longer."

He sat down quietly in the sand and relaxed there for almost another hour, sided against the large boulder, his Winchester across his lap. He stiffened and laid his thumb over the rifle hammer when he heard a voice suddenly call out from the stone shelf.

"You over there," the voice said. "What say we call this thing a draw and we all go our way?"

Sam didn't reply. If this was an attempt to find out if he was still here, answering would remove any doubt. He sat listening, hoping the dun wouldn't make any sound that might give him away.

"Did you hear me over there?" the voice called out, not sounding any closer. Not yet anyway. But that would come once these two got tired of standing in silence in the scalding desert sun. "We know you were following us. . . . We saw your dust. So you just as well admit up to it."

Sam listened and leaned back against the boulder. He would know when the two stepped into sight.

"See? We're businessmen out of New Mexico, the two of us," the voice said. "I'm Halberd Tacker. This is Ernst Yunt. We figure you to be a highwayman, out to rob us—not that we are carrying anything of any great value. Being just honest businessmen, we worry about that sort of thing all the time. Things being as they are."

The Ranger almost smiled to himself. He kept silent. Waited. Listened. He heard the sound of their horses' shoes clack on the sand-dusted stone shelf.

Any minute now. . . .

He cocked the rifle hammer too quietly to be heard. The copper dun stood looking down at him as if knowing what was afoot.

"The thing is," a second voice called out, "we're willing to pay you something for allowing us to pass through here unharmed. That's how things are done, ain't it?" the voice asked innocently. "You tell us—we don't know."

Only the sound of a passing wind whirred through the rock passes, echoing through the shelf as if it carried the voices of mournful spirits.

Finally the Ranger heard the second voice say in a half whisper, "Hell, he's gone, Rollo. I ain't standing here all day like some damn fool talking to the wind."

"Jesus, Cero, use my name, why don't you?" the first voice said, sounding put out by his companion.

"I'm telling you it doesn't matter," said the second voice, a voice the Ranger now realized belonged to Cero Atwater, an outlaw he'd come to know over the past year. "Whoever it was is gone, unless he's some sun-struck idiot."

The first voice, belonging to Rollo Parker, cursed and grumbled under his breath.

"You'd better hope you're right, Cero," he said. "If we get jumped, I am holding you accountable."

The Ranger stood up silently, slowly, his back against the boulder and listened as boot steps and horses' hooves moved closer.

"Accountable, hell," Cero said, sneering, the two of them leading their horses on the narrow sandy path around the edge of the boulder. "If there was anybody up here, don't you suppose we'd've known by now?"

Here we go, the Ranger said to himself, his rifle in both hands, braced, ready. He saw the toe of the boot nearest him reach into sight. *Now!*

"It makes no sense to me," Rollo Parker said. "That man would track you this far, then not be here when—" His breath cut short and exploded from his lungs as the Ranger's rifle butt smacked him hard in the sternum. *"He-eeg,"* he expelled painfully as he dropped to his knees, bent double at the waist and resting his forehead on the dirt. *"Heeeg!"*

Seeing his partner go down, Cero Atwater tried to make a move. His hand snatched at the butt of a Colt holstered on his hip. But as it came up, the Ranger's rifle butt swung hard again. Cero bellowed as the rifle cracked against his gun hand, sending the Colt flying away and causing the gunman to fall to his knees beside his cohort. As the gunman tried to struggle up from his knees, Sam swung the rifle butt again and clipped him across his jaw. Atwater collapsed backward, his legs folded back under him like some broken marionette.

There, now. . . .

Sam kept the two covered with his rifle. But after a moment, realizing that Atwater was knocked cold and Parker was having a hard time catching his breath, he stepped forward and raised Parker by his collar.

Parker gasped again as he straightened onto his knees. His hat brim stood flattened up in front; dirt clung to his forehead. He gripped his chest with both hands and continued making hoarse guttural sounds.

"Breathe deep, Parker," Sam coaxed, holding him up by his collar. "That's it. Draw some air in." As he spoke, he leaned his rifle against the boulder, reached down and took Parker's Remington revolver from its holster. He shoved the gun down into his waistband, then picked his rifle up. Seeing the outlaw gaining his balance on his knees, Sam stepped back and looked down at him.

"You all right?" Sam asked. A few yards back, the two outlaws' horses stood watching, only having spooked a little when the Ranger sprang out and made his play.

Parker wheezed and gasped, his hands still tight on his chest where his ribs met.

"I'll . . . do," he said weakly, his voice coming out as if being squeezed through a small funnel. Then he added with a trace of sarcasm, "Thanks . . . for asking."

Sam only nodded.

"Wipe your face," he said, gesturing his rifle barrel at Parker's watering eyes, the string of saliva bobbing from his chin.

Parker lifted one hand from his sternum and wiped his face with his bandanna.

Sam stood watching quietly, letting the outlaw collect himself a little. Parker looked around at Cero Atwater lying limp and still in the dirt beside him.

"Is he . . . dead?" Parker managed to say, his face still bluish red, his eyes swirly and running.

"I don't think so," Sam said. "But he went out awfully easy for a man his size." He looked closer at the knocked-out gunman. A fly circled down out of nowhere and walked around the edge of Atwater's ear. Atwater didn't move.

"Can I—? Can I check . . . and see?" Parker asked, still struggling for air. Without waiting for the Ranger to answer, he turned and leaned in close to Atwater. Sam's rifle barrel poked in between the two and guided Parker back from his unconscious friend.

"I'll check him," he said. He stepped in and pulled the folded outlaw forward onto his limp knees. Atwater managed a short groan. Sam turned him loose. Released, the outlaw flopped back into the same position and dust billowed around him, but before he hit the ground, Sam jerked a small derringer up from behind Atwater's gun belt. He gave Rollo Parker a dark look as he stepped back and shoved the little gun down into his vest pocket.

"Is this how's it's going to be with you?" he asked.

"I didn't know . . . it was there, Ranger," Parker said. "I swear I didn't." He flinched and held his free hand out as if to ward off another blow from the Ranger's Winchester.

"I'm not going to hit you, Parker," Sam said. "But if you go for a gun, knife, anything at all, I *will* put a bullet in you. You've got my word on that."

"All right, *all right!*" said Parker, his hand still raised protectively. "We've run our . . . string out with you, Ranger. "We're not going to try nothing. Right, Cero?" His breath was coming back to him. He tossed a sidelong look at his knocked-out partner. Atwater still lay sprawled and limp, his half-crossed eyes staring off into the sunlight. "Well . . . ," Parker said with exasperation, "if he could talk . . . he'd tell you the same thing. We're played out here."

"Good," said Sam. He stepped back, took his canteen from his saddle horn and stepped forward. He uncapped the canteen and poured a short trickle of water onto Atwater's face. Nothing. Then he stooped and reached over and adjusted the outlaw's hat brim down over his brow to keep his eyes out of the sun. While Parker watched, Sam took a pair of handcuffs from behind his back and snapped them onto Atwater's wrists. "Let him sleep while we gather your horses," he said.

"Where we headed, Ranger?" Parker asked, pushing himself to his feet, holding out his wrists.

"First stop, Mesa Grande," said the Ranger, closing another pair of cuffs around Parker's wrists.

"Mesa Grande's a far ride from here, Ranger," Parker commented, staring at his cuffed hands.

"It is at that," Sam said. He gave a thin, wry smile. "But it'll give us a chance to talk some.

Maybe you can think of something I might want to know—something that might get you and your partner here a shorter sentence once I tell the judge about it."

"Hey, I don't jackpot nobody, Ranger," Parker said, as if a bad taste had just come to his mouth.

"Suit yourself, Parker," Sam said quietly.

"I sure as hell will," said the outlaw. "I'd rot a hundred years in Yuma Prison before I'd gullet-up on a trail mate. The judge can kiss my saddle-burnt behind."

"*Hmmm*. Kiss your saddle-burnt behind . . . ," Sam repeated as if committing the words to memory. "Right before his gavel falls I'll tell him you said that," he said coolly. "He'll likely appreciate your being so bold and direct. It's not always that a man comes before the bench with a—"

"Now, wait a minute, Ranger . . . *Jesus!*" said Parker, cutting him off. "There's no cause in you saying something just to make the judge break ugly on us. Me and Cero here are likely enough to get the short end of the stick as it is. This being the first time either one of us has been caught."

"If this is all new to you," Sam said, "let me tell you that anything you say to me will be told to the judge." He stared at Parker. "You might want to weigh your words, even show some cooperation."

"Let me get this straight . . . ," Parker said, appearing to have a hard time understanding. "You're saying that anything I say to you is going to be held *agin* me in court?"

"Yep, that's how it works," Sam said.

"Hell, that's not fair!" said Parker. "What kind of fool law is that? What about freedom of speech?

What about me being free to say anything I want to any time I want to say it? This judge sounds like a crooked rotten son o—"

"Easy, Rollo Parker," said the Ranger, stopping him in the middle of his rant. "Didn't you hear me? Everything you're saying right now I'll be telling the judge."

Parker stopped and stared, stunned. After a tense pause he let out a breath.

"All right, listen, Ranger," he said. "What say we wipe the tabletop clean and start all over?" As he spoke he made a circular motion with his cuffed hands wiping his words from the air. "I know I said some things I never should have said. Let's just forget I said anything. Can we do that?"

"That all depends," Sam said. "Let's see how well we all get along on the trail."

"Yes, let's do that, please," said Parker. "You know all me and Cero did was sell some horses to the wrong caliber of men and deliver them at a time when those men were off robbing a store."

"Sounds innocent enough," Sam said wryly. "Now, that's the way you want the judge to hear it."

"Think so?" said Parker, weighing it in his mind.

"I know so," Sam said. "He'll see that what you did was provide fresh getaway horses. But he'll consider your version of it."

"Are you joshing me, Ranger?" Parker asked.

"No," Sam said. "But in the end I think you two will most likely winter in Yuma, learn some masonry skills there."

"Busting rocks," Parker mumbled to himself. "Damn it to hell."

PART 1

Chapter 1

Mesa Grande, Arizona Territory

Sheriff David "Bronco Dave" Winters worked the ramrod on the barrel of his cap-and-ball Army Colt and seated the final lead ball into the cylinder. Once the gun was loaded, he kept its hammer at half-cock and shoved a fingertip of pasty cornmeal batter down over the front opening of each chamber. The cornmeal paste, once dried, served to keep a loose spark from igniting all the other chambers at once, causing a dangerous chain fire and making the gun blow up in his hand. With the ball of his thumb he pressed a firing cap onto each of the gun's six iron nipples.

This being the seventh cylinder he'd loaded, he left the cap in the gun, spun it and lowered the gun's hammer between two chambers for safety. Then he laid the big gun aside. Hearing a dark chuckle coming from an occupied jail cell, he looked up and saw the bushy-headed prisoner, Sherman Geary, standing with his hands wrapped around the bars, grinning at him. Geary's eyes looked huge behind a pair of thick eyeglasses.

"Holy Joe and Mary, Sheriff," Geary said. "That's *forty-two shots* you've made up. Are you expecting a war to break out in Mesa Grande? Who are you scared of?"

Sheriff Winters eyed the prisoner, his bruised forehead, his swollen right jaw. Then he turned his gaze to his battered desk. Six extra cylinders he'd just finished loading stood shiny and black, with the same dab of cornmeal batter drying in their chambers.

Scared? Ha. . . .

"There's a saying, Sherman," the sheriff said. " 'I'd rather *have it* and not need it than to need it and not *have it.*' "

"Yeah? Well, here's another saying for you, *Bronco Dave*," said Geary, taking on a darker tone. " 'Let a man out of his cell, and he'll whop you worse than you've ever been whopped in your life.' "

"Never heard that one," the sheriff said, going along with him.

"You've heard it now," said Geary. "Let me out, I'll show you how an ass-whopping works." His eyes loomed large and swirly.

The sheriff gave a half smile and shook his head.

"Sherman, Sherman," he said in a patient tone. "If I had a dollar for every time you got drunk and tried to *whop* me, I wouldn't need this job." He paused and then said with a level gaze, "How's the welt across the back of your head coming along?"

Geary's hand went to the back of his sore head.

"You never hurt me none, if that's what you're thinking."

"That's too bad," said the sheriff. "I'll remind myself to swing a little harder next time."

Seeing the sheriff start to stand up from his desk to go make his rounds, Geary shook his cell bars with both hands.

"Come on, let me out of here. I'm sober now. Look at me," he said.

"I don't have to look. I can tell when you're sober," the sheriff said. "When you stop talking about fighting me, you'll be sober. Right now you're still drunk. I don't want you falling off your horse and breaking your neck on the way home."

"Damn it," Geary grumbled, turning away from the bars. "I swear to God, if I don't whop you senseless, there ain't a dog in Georgia."

The sheriff just shook his head, use to it.

On the corner of his desk lay a rawhide bandoleer with six empty compartments for the extra cylinders he'd loaded. He picked up each cylinder one at a time, inspected it and placed it into its respective compartment and closed the flap and snapped it shut.

There. . . .

He hefted the bandoleer on his hand, looking at the cylinders. If he found himself needing a fast reload, here they were, loaded, capped, ready to fire. He would unpin the barrel from the gun's frame, slide off the empty smoking cylinder, slide on a loaded one, replace the barrel, set the pin and be back in the fight. He could do the whole thing in less than thirty seconds if he had to. Twice in his life he'd *had to*, he reminded himself. He caught a glimpse of those times, dead men, both white and Apache lying all around him, the battle still raging . . .

He hoped he'd never *have to* again, he told himself, rising from the chair. He picked up the Colt lying on his desk and holstered it before he carried the heavy bandoleer to the gun rack and hung it from a peg.

"Geary, can you eat something?" he asked the prisoner. "It might help sober you up."

The prisoner didn't answer. Instead he cursed and flopped down onto his cot.

"You need to send that ol' smoke wagon to the Colt factory," he called out to Winters. "They'll convert it to a *modern-day* gun for you for seven dollars—send you a box of bullets to boot. No real lawman carries a cap-and-ball. It's an embarrassment. Makes you look like from the days of—"

"Suit yourself," said Winters, cutting Geary short. "I'll bring you some food anyway, if your jaw's not too sore to chew."

"Don't worry about my jaw," Geary snapped back. "Worry about your own when I get out of here."

Sheriff Winters stepped away from the gun rack and picked up the loaded repeater rifle leaning against his battered desk.

"Any fool needing forty-two pistol shots is in worse trouble than he knows," Geary called out.

"You might be right about that, Sherman," the sheriff replied, levering a round into the rifle chamber. He smiled thinly. "But that's why God made the Winchester." He added a warning. "Don't be smoking while I'm gone, Sherman. Town can't afford to build a new jail. I'd hate to throw you in the smokehouse next time you get your bark on."

Geary didn't answer.

With the rifle hanging in his left hand, Winters took his Stetson and the cell key from a peg beside the door. He snapped the large brass key ring at his waist, placed the Stetson atop his head, adjusting the hat brim to the time of day, and opened the door into a white glare of sunlight. But before he could close the door behind himself, a bullet slammed into his chest, flinging him backward into his office and over the top of his desk.

His rifle flew from his hand; he left a bloody smear across the desk, clearing it of paperwork and incidentals, and landed broken and unconscious against a row of cell bars as the sound of the shot echoed along the street.

"Lord God!" Geary shouted. Springing up from his cot, he leaped over to where the sheriff lay sprawled. He adjusted his glasses quickly as if not believing his eyes. Flattened down on the floor lest another shot ring out, he reached through the bars and shook the downed sheriff by his shoulders.

"Sheriff! Wake up!" he shouted. Rolling the sheriff onto his side, Geary saw the gaping hole in his chest, the pool of blood forming and spreading on the dusty floor beneath him. "Don't you die, Sheriff, damn it! Don't you die!" he shouted, seeing frothy blood rise and fall in the sheriff's open lips.

"Hel—help me . . . ," the sheriff murmured in a waning whisper.

Help you . . . ? Geary looked at the blood pouring from the sheriff's chest. Then he shot a glance toward the open door, seeing people gathering in the street and looking all around.

"Lie still, Sheriff," he said, even though the wounded lawman wasn't moving. Geary ran his right arm through the bars and took the cell key from the sheriff's belt. "I'm out of here sooner than you thought."

In an alleyway across the street from the sheriff's office, two gunmen stood staring out from behind a stack of empty shipping crates. Erskine Cord, the one holding the fifty-six-caliber Pryse & Redman custom English rifle, gave a short chuckle as he and his younger nephew, Ozbourne Cord, watched the stunned faces of the townsfolk who stood looking all around in the wake of the loud rifle shot. Doors trembled; windowpanes shuddered in their frames.

"They're a bunch of sheep, Ozzie," said Erskine Cord. He spat and hefted the smoking double rifle in his hands. "I could shoot a half dozen more before they ever figured where we are."

"I'm game for it," said Ozzie, sounding excited at the prospect of watching any number of people fall broken and dead in the dusty street. He grinned and fanned his hat back and forth and put it back atop his head. "Give me the gun and some cartridges, Uncle Erskine. I'll shoot a few." He reached for the smoking big game rifle. But Cord pulled the rifle away and gave him a look.

"I don't kill for the fun of it," Cord admonished, his grin suddenly replaced by a somber stare. "Only a sick-headed fool kills for free. He looked his younger partner up and down with a disdainful stare. "Do you understand that?"

Ozzie turned somber too, looking a little embarrassed.

"Yes, I do understand, Uncle Erskine," he said. "I just figured, if you meant it, I'd go right along with it, just for practice so to speak—"

"Good. Now we understand each other," said Cord. He handed the young man the rifle. "Here, you can carry it all the way back to camp. Mind you don't get it wet crossing the creek."

"I won't get it wet, Uncle Erskine," Ozzie said, taking the big rifle and holding it to his chest. "I'll hold it over my head when we cross."

"All right, let's split up and get out of here," Cord said. "I'll meet you at the camp." He nodded back toward the street. "Curland will be showing up here any minute to save the day." He glanced toward the street that was now filling with townsfolk. "Just between us, Curland makes me want to puke—likes his men to call him Mr. C." He saw three men running through the open door of the sheriff's office. He gave a sigh. "But he's the customer—the man with the money."

"Yep," said Ozzie, " 'the man with the money,' " he parroted. "You explained all that to me."

"Too bad somebody don't want Curland killed

too," said Erskine Cord. "I'd give them a half-price special." He gave a dark half grin.

The two turned and walked away along the alley to a telegraph pole where they had hitched their horses. Once mounted, they rode away in different directions. On the street the gathered people turned their eyes to the sheriff's office as a carpenter by the name of Harold Flake reappeared at the open doorway and stood shouting, waving his hands.

"The sheriff's been shot! Somebody get the doctor, quick!" he shouted.

"Is he alive?" a voice called out from the street.

"I don't know . . . just barely, I think," Flake shouted, seeing two townsmen already running along the street toward the doctor's office a block away. "For God sakes, hurry up! He's bleeding something awful!"

Sheriff Winters faintly heard Flake's voice.

"I'm not dead . . . ," Winters managed to whisper in a weak raspy voice.

"You will be, though, if you don't shut up and lie still," Sherman Geary said, pressing his wadded-up blood-soaked shirt down on the sheriff's open chest wound.

Kneeling beside Geary, a teamster, Ison Prine, pushed both palms down atop Geary's bloody hands.

"I'll help you," he said.

But the quarrelsome Geary would have none of it.

"Help how, by mashing him into the floor?" he barked.

He butted his head against the teamster's shoulder, getting him to back off. He kept his hands pressed firm on the sheriff's chest.

"You're still drunk, I see," Prine observed.

Geary shot him a cold, hard stare through his blood-smeared lenses.

"I'm only trying to help you," Prine said meekly, knowing how wild and violent Geary could get when he had even the smallest amount of whiskey in him.

"You can help by getting the hell away from me and keeping your loud mouth shut, Ison!" he shouted. "Where the hell's Doc Young anyway?"

Prine looked at the open cell door, the key still in it. He looked Geary up and down, Geary shirtless, covered with blood to his elbows, his face and chest blood-splattered and dripping from before he'd gotten the flow under control. His thick eyeglasses were blood-smeared from where he'd wiped them on his bare shoulder to clear them. He leaned on his hands, pressing his shirt down on the wound as firmly as he dared.

"Jesus, Sherman," said Prine. "He's lucky you was here, else he would already bled to death."

"Yeah, *real lucky*," Geary said with stewing sarcasm, staying the flow of blood on Sheriff Winters' chest. "You want to do something, damn it? Take these glasses off me and wipe the blood off. I can't see shit." He cocked his head toward the teamster and let him remove the eyeglasses. Then he looked around over his shoulder toward the open front door, batting his weak eyes. "Flake? Where the hell is Doc Young?"

"Here he comes," said Flake, backing away from

the doorway as he waved the running doctor
toward the office. "Hurry on, Doc," he shouted.
"He's in an awful way!"

On the floor, the sheriff opened his eyes slowly
and gazed up at Sherman Geary, seeing that
Geary held his bloody hands down firm against
his chest wound.

"Hang on, Winters," said Geary. "Doc Young is
here."

Other townsmen came into the office right behind
the doctor. They gathered around and watched as
the doctor dropped onto his knees and slung open
his medical bag. He quickly stripped off his wrin-
kled linen coat and rolled up his sleeves, all the
while looking closely at the downed sheriff and the
amount of blood surrounding him on the plank
floor.

Reaching a hand down under Winters, the doctor felt warm blood pumping from the hole in his
back with each beat of the sheriff's heart. He pulled
his hand out and studied the thick dark blood
running from the tips of his finger.

"He's a bad bleeder and he's hit bad clean
through," he said to no one is particular. "I need
every towel and cloth you can rustle up." He
looked somberly at Sherman Geary and nodded,
as if to confirm his findings. Then he looked up
at two townsmen standing nearby as he wiped his
bloody hands on a cloth someone pitched to him.

"We've got to get him to my office. Somebody
run there now, get the stretcher leaning against
the wall of my surgery room."

"Doc, is he—is he going to die?" Ison Prine

asked, leaning down, staring at the sheriff's pale ashen face.

"Ain't we all?" the doctor said gruffly, placing his hands down over Sherman Geary's on the sheriff's chest.

Chapter 2

From his office window above the Old Senate Saloon, Joseph Curland checked his pocket watch as he looked down at the crowd gathered out in front of the sheriff's office. Beside him stood the French-Canadian gunman Denton Shenny. A moment earlier when the sound of the rifle shot resounded along the street, the saloon had fallen silent below them. Within seconds, they'd heard Curland's *segundo*, Bob "Duck" Duckworth, bounding up the stairs. He'd stopped and stood pounding on the door.

"I heard the shot, Duck," Curland called out through the heavy pounding of fist on wood. "What happened?"

"A whore just run in and said the sheriff's been shot, Mr. C!" shouted Duckworth!

"Oh my God, Duck!" Curland shouted back as if stricken with pain. He turned and gave Shenny a grin. "I'll be right down, soon as I get my trousers on."

"I'll be waiting for you at the bar," said the burly Kentuckian.

As Duckworth's heavy miner boots rumbled

down the stairs, Curland and Shenny turned back
to the window and looked down.

"Is Duckworth going to cause me any trouble,
him being your second in charge?" Shenny asked.

"Bob Duckworth's my second, only because he
does what I tell him," Curland replied. "He might
not like it, but he'll go along with it."

"And if he doesn't?" Shenny asked.

Curland turned his eyes to him for a moment
but didn't answer.

They waited and watched as a crowd tightened
around the front of the sheriff's office. They only
gave each other a look as two men ran from the sheriff's office to the doctor's office over a block away.

"What the hell?" Curland said under his breath.
They stared in silence until only seconds later the
same two men ran at a fast clip from the doctor's
office carrying the folded stretcher between them.

"Why are they running?" said Shenny. "Who's
in that big a hurry over a *dead man*?"

"Shhh," said Curland, engrossed in the scene.
"Pay attention here."

Shenny gave him a fiery stare, but then he
clenched his teeth and turned his eyes back down
to the busy street. They watched in silence as the
crowd parted and the two townsmen raced inside
the sheriff's office with the folded stretcher.

"Sweet Holy Mary and Sue!" Shenny said quietly. "This can only mean one thing."

"I know, damn it," said Curland. "It means Winters is still alive." He took a deep breath, shoved his
watch into his vest pocket and smoothed his hand
down over it.

"Not a doubt about it," Shenny said. The two continued to stare down, knowing that had everything gone as they'd planned, Dr. Young would have walked out onto the boardwalk, coat and hat in hand, shirtsleeves rolled up and bloody, and pronounced the sheriff dead, no questions asked.

Instead here comes a stretcher? A stretcher for God sakes! Curland said to himself in disbelief. He and Shenny both watched the scene playing out beneath them.

Off to one side of the crowd, the two saw Sherman Geary sitting on the edge on the boardwalk, shirtless, his bloody forearms dangling over his knees. A lit cigarette hung between Geary's bloody fingers. Two townsmen stepped away from the crowd long enough for one of them to pat Geary's bare blood-splattered shoulder. The other extended his arm down to shake Geary's hand. But Geary showed the man his bloody hands, declining the man's offer.

"They're congratulating Geary? *For what*?" Curland said, amazed.

"Beats me, Mr. C," said Shenny. "But it looks like this fool wants to shake his hand." He gave Curland a puzzled look. "What's happened down there?"

"I don't know," said Curland, "but I'm going to find out." He turned away long enough to take his derby hat and his swallowtail coat from a coatrack. "If this *rube*, this *bummer*, this *saddle trash* has somehow foiled our plan, I will choke him to death, *personally*, with my own bare hands. I'll kill him, drag him off somewhere and set fire to his body."

As he shoved his arms into his coat sleeves, he looked back down out his window in time to see Ison Prine waving the onlookers out of the way, clearing a path for the doctor and the townsmen.

"Whoa, look at this," said Shenny.

Curland slumped as he saw the stretcher come through the door, the sheriff lying flat on it, the doctor hurrying along beside him. He saw the sheriff move his head back and forth weakly as if trying to focus on the gathered crowd. He saw the crowd part again, letting the stretcher bearers and the doctor through their midst.

"Of all the blasted luck." Curland closed his eyes for a moment, shook his head and took a deep breath.

"Not so fast," Shenny said, "you saw all the bloody bandages on Winters' chest. Just because he's alive now doesn't mean he's going to pull through this." They looked down as the stretcher bearers bounded away along the dirt street, some of the crowd running along behind them. "You're a gambling man. What were the odds of a man living through a rifle shot like that—straight through his body?"

"Very slim odds," said Curland, calming down and considering the matter. "You're right," he added, setting his hat atop his head and adjusting it. "We have to stick to our plan. Even if he were to live, he'll never wear another badge in this town. He'd be lucky if he could ever feed himself again." He smiled a little. "There's always something to be thankful for," he said.

"Call it a bright cloud on the horizon." Shenny grinned. "Be glad you didn't pay Cord and Ozzie the full amount they charged for killing him. If Winters lives, those two assassins will have to either finish the job or forfeit the other half of their pay."

"I'm already considering that," said Curland. The two stopped at the door while he examined his face in a mirror. He ran a fingertip across his thin sharply trimmed mustache and gave the mirror his best smile and a tilt of his head. "Either way we're going to be all right," he said reassuringly. He gave himself a wink in the mirror, then turned and walked out the door.

Shenny hurried along beside him until they descended to a lower landing where the stairs forked. "We'll split up here," said Curland, nodding toward the stairs leading down to a side entrance. "Give me a few minutes, then show up at the sheriff's office. We'll get this thing set up, no matter whether Winters lives or dies."

"I'll be right along," Shenny said. He tugged at his hat and started to hurry on down the darkened stairwell. But he stopped a step down and turned and looked back up at Curland, touching his battered Stetson brim. With a slight nod of his head, he said, "I'm looking forward to working with you, Mr. C. Once I'm in office, we're going to make lots of money together."

Curland nodded, smiled and touched the brim of his flawless derby in return. "Yes, we are *indeed*."

When Curland swung open the Old Senate Saloon stairwell door and walked briskly across the sawdust floor, Duckworth swung away from the bar and walked right beside him. He hiked his gun belt up as they walked and kept a thick palm resting on the butt of his holstered nickel-plated Remington.

"Last word we got, the sheriff won't live the day out," he said sidelong to Curland, the two of them moving quick.

Curland's face looked concerned and troubled, but purely for the sake of appearance.

"How *the blazes* can something like this happen, Duck?" he said sidelong, the two of them out of the Old Senate and headed slantwise across the street to the sheriff's office. "This is the nineteenth century, for God sakes."

Duckworth noted something in his boss's voice that didn't strike him as sincere. But he kept quiet and walked on.

"Damned if I know," he said quietly, his open palm still riding atop the Remington's ivory butt handles. He looked back and forth half menacingly at the remaining spectators out in front of the sheriff's office, giving them cause to back away.

The two walked onto the boardwalk, through the lingering onlookers and into the open office. Sherman Geary watched them from behind his thick eyeglasses, then stood up from where he sat smoking and walked in behind them.

"The sheriff's gone, Curland," said Ison Prine, who'd stayed behind with Flake to clean up the bloody mess on the office floor, the walls, the ceiling.

"Oh my God, *no!*" Curland wailed, playing it up. He bowed at the waist a little as if stricken in the guts. Duckworth saw his hand go to his cheek— *almost womanlike?* he wondered.

"No, wait!" said Prine, correcting himself quickly. "I mean he's not *here.* They took him to the doctor's."

"You ignorant pig," Curland growled at the teamster, collecting himself quickly. "Why didn't you say so?"

Prine stared at him, ignoring the insult.

"Doc says he's done for, though," the teamster said through a red-gray beard. "No doubt about that."

"Let's have faith, gentlemen," Curland said. "Doctors have been wrong before." He pivoted back and forth, his hands spread, looking from one solemn face to the next. "I'm going straightaway to the doctor." He started to run toward the door but then stopped himself in second thought. "I realize this is a terrible time to mention it, but has anyone taken on the mantle of authority?"

The townsmen gave one another a puzzled look.

"The *law,* gentlemen," Curland said. "Who's going to wear the sheriff badge, uphold the law in Mesa Grande?"

"We haven't talked about it none," said Prine, his fingertips scratching deep into his tangled beard.

"Well, let me suggest that we most certainly *should* discuss it," said Curland, "and without delay. This town cannot go without a sheriff. We must appoint someone—"

"Without waiting until Winters is dead first?" said Sherman Geary, who stood behind the group, his short cigarette between his blood-crusted fingers.

Curland swung around toward him.

"What *say* do you think you have in this, Sherman Geary, you drunken ne'er-do-well," said Curland. "You hated the poor sheriff so bad you couldn't be around him without trying to rip his head off."

"*Poor sheriff?*" said Geary. "Stop talking like he's dead already. You said yourself, doctors are not always right—"

"That's enough out of you, swamper," said Duckworth, stepping in close, cutting Geary short. "One word from Mr. C, I'll crack your crown like a monkey's egg."

A monkey's egg?

Geary just stared at him through his thick eyeglasses, not knowing what to say to that.

Curland took a threatening step toward Sherman Geary.

"Easy, Curland," said Flake, seeing Geary drop his stub of a cigarette, grind it out under his boot and ball his fists at his sides. "It was Geary here who saved the sheriff's life. Doc said Winters would already be dead, hadn't been for this one. Geary is Mesa Grande's hero—man of the hour."

Curland stopped; his face reddened. He could have killed Geary without batting an eye. But he kept calm, steadied himself.

"Is he, then?" he said. He stared at Geary, trying to form a thin, stiff smile. Duckworth couldn't help seeing that his boss was seething with anger, an anger that seemed only heightened by the townsman's words of praise for Sherman Geary.

"He dang sure is," said Prine. "I say we owe Sherman here a hip hip hurray for what he done."

"No, please, none of that," said Geary, seeing

the teamster ready to raise a cheer. "I'm no hero. I only done what any man would do. I only wanted to beat him senseless when I was drunk—" He gave a shrug. "Which means anytime we saw each other, I reckon. Still, if ever I'm sober, I've got nothing but respect for the man."

While Geary spoke, Curland took the opportunity to compose himself some more. He gave Duckworth a nod to move back a step, causing Geary to open his fists. "Well . . ." He settled himself more. "That being the case, I must apologize. I'm afraid the sheriff's death—*shooting*, that is," he corrected, "has us all a little on edge." He held out a hand to Geary. But Geary showed him his bloody hands and forearms, and Curland withdrew his offer and wiped his hand on his swallowtailed coat.

"At any rate, you will not go unrewarded, sir," Curland said in a convincing air of nobility. "It will be a long time before you'll have to pay for a drink at my Old Senate Saloon." He looked around, his smile appearing more real now. "In fact, I'm going to invite all of you there right this minute—drinks on the house—while we discuss who will be our appointed sheriff."

"What about going to Doc's, seeing about the sheriff?" Prine asked.

"Oh, I meant after we go see about the sheriff, of course," said Curland.

Duckworth couldn't help seeing that his boss was stalling about something—he just wasn't sure what. He watched Curland step beside Geary as if they were old friends.

"But as soon as we check on our poor sheriff, it's

off to the Old Senate," he said, "and a few rounds on the house, eh?" He smiled at Geary.

"Obliged," said Geary, "but I'm staying sober for a while, just to see what it feels like."

"Certainly, I understand," said Curland. "But I want us to talk some, get to know each other. I believe we could use a good man like you. Am I right, Duck?"

"Sounds right to me," Duckworth said half-heartedly.

"But I was working for you," said Geary. "I was a swamper, remember, cleaning up, shining spittoons and that? You fired me."

"Well. What can I say?" said Curland. "It was a mistake. We want you back. Right, Duck?"

"I'll say," Duckworth said flatly, seeing that Curland was still stalling around. *Why? What's going on here?*

All heads turned toward the sound of boots hurrying across the boardwalk. They saw Denton Shenny step inside and stop and look all around.

"I heard what happened here," he said. "I want everybody here to join with me and search out whoever did this. We don't have a minute to spare."

"Don't you want to hear what happened first?" Prine asked.

"Tell me while we're searching for the shooter," Shenny said in a strong tone. "This is time to act, not talk."

"He makes good sense, gentlemen," Curland said. "I suppose he would, having been a lawman himself for so long." He looked Shenny up and down as if having seen him for the first time. "Come to think of it, this is the man we should appoint as sheriff."

"No, not me," Shenny said, playing it out. He stopped and looked around, then said, "Unless—I mean unless it's for the good of Mesa Grande . . . ?"

Duckworth just watched.

"Of course it's for the good of Mesa Grande," said Curland. "Why else?" He looked all around. "What say we all? Let's appoint Shenny as sheriff and let him get after the fiend who did this."

The townsmen looked at one another, appearing to be in agreement with Curland.

"One thing, though," said Flake, raising a long knobby finger for emphasis. "We can't make him town sheriff so long as Winters is still alive."

"He's right," said Prine. "So I say, let's make Denton Shenny town deputy until we see how this thing is going to go."

Town deputy? Son of a bitch! Curland stared for a moment with a bemused look. Finally, seeing no way around it, he nodded. "Right you are, then," he said. He turned to Shenny quickly, before anyone else could speak. "Mr. Denton Shenny. On behalf of Mesa Grande, I'm asking you to serve as our appointed town deputy."

Duckworth watched in silence. Was this why his boss was stalling? Waiting for Shenny to show up? He kept quiet. Whatever Curland was at work on here, he had no doubt there would be money involved. His boss hadn't included him in on it. But that was all right. He'd find a way to include himself. He wasn't going to allow himself to be passed over.

"I accept the appointment of sheriff's *deputy*," said Shenny, giving Curland a guarded look of displeasure over the deputy part of the title. But this was not the time to get into all that, he decided. He looked all around, then said, "I'm wasting no time. I'm getting on the trail of the shooter. Anybody riding with me, get your horse and catch up to me on the south trail."

"Wait," said Flake, stepping over from an open drawer in the sheriff's desk. "Here's a deputy badge for you."

"Obliged," said Shenny, taking the badge and sticking it onto his bib-front shirt. He passed another guarded look of displeasure to Curland. "I'll wear it with pride," he said. Turning, he walked out the door to where his horse stood ready and waiting.

Chapter 3

The Ranger had heard the single rifle shot earlier. From the powerful sound of it, the shot had come from a large-caliber—the kind of rifle he'd carried when he was a young buffalo hunter. The sound was such that both Cero Atwater and Rollo Parker perked upright in their saddles on the narrow trail in front of him.

"Damn! That sounded like a cannon, Ranger!" said Parker with a dark chuckle. "Suppose they're celebrating us coming to town?"

"That wouldn't be my first guess," Sam said, edging his horse closer to the side of the trail overlooking a stretch of flatlands a few hundred feet below them.

"It might not'a been for us, but it sure enough come from Mesa Grande," Atwater offered. "There's no two ways about that."

"Yep, it sounded like it," Sam said. He gazed ahead on the lower flatlands as far as his eyes would allow, until the swirl of the heat and the shroud of dust overcame his vision. "Could be some hunter checking out his rifle, getting ready," he added.

"I'd like to know what he's hunting," said Parker, "so's I can avoid ever running into it."

"Whatever he goes to hunt, he figures he'll kill it with one shot," Atwater added. "A man needing only one practice shot has more confidence than good sense."

"Else he's awfully short on bullets," said Parker.

Sam considered what the prisoners said. They were right. It was unusual to hear one single shot from a large-caliber rifle. It could have been a practice shot; it could have been a misfire. Whatever it was, he'd be sure to ask about it once they arrived in Mesa Grande. But meanwhile . . .

"Turn at that fork on your left," he said to the two as they rode their horses along at a careful walk on the narrow rocky trail.

"Fork?" said Parker. "Dang, Ranger, that ain't a *fork in the trail.* That ain't *nothing,* just a spot where all the edge rocks has washed away. We'll break our necks sure enough trying to ride down that coyote path." The fork led off onto a steep twisting path that led downward toward the flatlands through a maze of broken jagged rock.

"Just imagine there's a hanging posse chasing you," said the Ranger. "You'll do fine."

"That ain't funny, Ranger," said Parker. "There is such a thing as cruelty to a prisoner."

"Get moving," Sam said. "Don't forget I'll be keeping this rifle trained on your backs all the way to the flatlands."

The two men grumbled under their breaths, but when they got to the spot the Ranger had motioned toward, they turned their horses onto the narrow path and held them closely reined as the animals picked their footing carefully and started downward into a long, steep labyrinth of rock and gravel.

For an hour the three rode diagonally, following a path long traveled and worn by the sure hooves of ancient mountain elk and the padded paws of hungry predators in their pursuit. At the sharp edge of a cliff, the Ranger called for the two prisoners to stop a few feet in front of him. The two did so and sat looking back at him, seeing he had stepped down from his saddle.

"Get the leather out from under you," the Ranger said. "We're walking the rest of the way down."

Rollo Parker and Cero Atwater looked at each other, then back at the Ranger.

"You must be joking," said Rollo Parker.

"This is not my joking face," Sam said flatly.

"We best do like he says, Rollo," said Atwater.

"Huh-uh, I'm not getting off this cayuse," Parker said defiantly. "This hillside is crawling with rattlesnakes. I'd as soon take a bullet as a snakebite any day."

Atwater climbed down from his saddle quickly and raised his hands chest high, making sure the Ranger saw he was following orders.

"Suit yourself, Parker," Sam said, certain the outlaw was only testing him—he'd done so all day. He raised the rifle butt to his shoulder and took aim, at a spot high on Parker's right shoulder.

"Wait a minute, dang it!" Parker said. "I'm coming down too." He gave Atwater a scorching stare. "Since my pard here can't seem to back me up on anything." He swung down from his saddle and stood beside his horse. He looked all around on the rocky path as if fearful of rattlesnakes. "I get bit and die, it'll be your fault, Ranger."

"I can live with that, Parker," Sam replied. "We're close enough I can take you the rest of the way hung over your saddle."

"That's a hell of a thing to say," Parker replied. "I expect if you can tell the judge everything I've done or said, I can tell him the same about you?"

"You can try," Sam said, use to prisoners acting this way, but tiring of it all the same. "But I doubt if he'll listen."

"That's a hell of a note," Parker said, shaking his lowered head.

"Why don't you shut up for a while, Rollo?" said Atwater, also tiring of his partner's constant grousing. "The Ranger's told you more than once that everything you say is going to be held agin you once we get before the judge—"

"Shut up, both of you," the Ranger said in a lowered tone, looking down past them at where the narrow path disappeared down between two towering chimney stones.

The two fell silent, realizing in the Ranger's hushed tone that something more important than their bickering had come into play. They followed his eyes toward the tall chimney rocks and stared along with him.

"Apaches?" Parker whispered, seeing the Ranger had caught sight or sound of something on the descending path ahead of them.

Sam didn't reply; he held a hand toward them cautioning them to stay quiet.

The two looked at each other as the Ranger stepped in quietly and cuffed the two men's wrists together before they fully realized what he was doing.

"Holy Joseph!" whispered Parker. "You can't do this to us. If it's Injuns coming upon us, we're dead."

"All the more reason to keep your mouths shut," Sam whispered. Even as he spoke, he took out another pair of cuffs from behind his back and cuffed Parker's other wrist to his saddle stirrup.

"Ranger, don't do us like this," Parker pleaded in a hoarse whisper. His phony pleading voice had gone now. There was real fear in its place, the Ranger noted. What he didn't tell the two was that he had made out the slightest sound of metal striking stone farther down along the path. He'd watched closely, yet above the path he'd seen no rising stir of dust. He was certain there was only one rider coming toward them. But he wouldn't reveal that right now. This was a good time to leave them wondering.

"Stay right here," Sam whispered as he turned and walked away. The two watched him swing wide of the chimney rock on their right and climb up a steep path of rock and gravel to a higher level above the trail. As the Ranger climbed up and out of sight, the two outlaws stooped and rested on their haunches.

"What are the odds that it's some of our pards come to set us free?" Atwater asked in a hushed tone, staring toward the tall chimney rocks.

"The odds are slim to none, Cero," said Parker. "If we had any pals to begin with, I'd say they are long gone by now. We're going to Yuma Prison, ol' pal, 'less we find ourselves a way around it." He jiggled the cuffs clasping the saddle stirrup. "I keep griping, trying to get this lawman rattled. So far it ain't working."

Ozzie Cord climbed down from his saddle and had led his tired horse halfway through the narrow corridor between the chimney rocks when he froze in place. He faintly heard the sound of loose gravel showering down from a ledge above him. Without looking up, he eased his hand to the butt of a Colt standing shoved down into his waistband.

"Take your hand away from the gun, easy-like," the Ranger called down to him. "I'm Arizona Territory Ranger Sam Burrack."

Ozzie pulled his hand away from his gun and tilted his head enough to look up at the Ranger standing above him in the white sunlight. He saw the Winchester aimed down at him.

"A policeman, huh?" he said up into the harsh glare. "What kind of policeman aims a gun at a man for no reason?"

Sam considered it, looking the young man up and down, noting a soft cap atop his head, a single-button jacket, high trouser cuffs above a pair of scuffed brogan boots.

"I aimed it at you when you decided to grab your gun," he said. He lowered the Winchester an inch.

"All right, there," said Ozzie, raising his hands chest high, his horse's reins hanging from his right fist. "You took me by surprise, is all."

"I understand," Sam said, easing down around edges of rock on the steep gravelly hillside. Loose dirt and gravel spilled beneath his boots. He kept his eye on the young man until he stepped out onto solid ground a few feet from him.

"What brings you this way, mister?" he asked. He'd lowered the rifle, but his finger was still poised near the trigger ready for any kind of move.

"Well, the thing is . . ." The young man stopped talking as he levered his right forearm at Sam. "That's none of your business—"

Sam saw the move coming and was ready for it. As the young man slid a derringer from his jacket sleeve, Sam swiped his rifle barrel sidelong and dealt a solid blow to the young man's fingers.

Ozzie let out a painful yelp as the derringer flew from his hand and landed on the rocky ground. He grabbed his hand and squeezed it against the crushing pain running through it. He cursed as he turned his eyes to the Ranger and the blur of a rifle butt as Sam brought the rifle forward and stabbed him with a short sharp blow to his chin. Ozzie went down, his head and chin swimming in a red sea of pain.

When he began to come to, he saw the Ranger standing over him with his uncle's big double rifle in his hands. Ozzie had to work hard to get the Ranger and the rest of his surroundings to stop floating around and stay in one spot. His horse stood with its head lowered, sniffing at his chest. He tried to shove the inquisitive animal away but couldn't get his hands to do as he instructed them.

The Ranger pulled the horse away and spoke down to Ozzie.

"Is this the rifle I heard earlier?" he asked.

Ozzie garbled something that he himself didn't understand.

"All right, on your feet," Sam said, reaching down and pulling the young man up by his jacket. "It looks like you're going to have to walk it off some before I'll get any sense out of you."

Ozzie wobbled in place; the Ranger helped him keep his balance. He handed Ozzie his horse's reins and gave him a slight shove in the direction of Parker and Atwater on the narrow path. As he staggered forward, Sam noted a small dusty black scalp hanging from his saddle horn. He noted that in spite of the dust, the underside of the scalp looked uncured.

Scalp hunter? Maybe, Sam speculated. Scalp hunting was illegal here, but not across the border close to this part of the territory. He moved over beside the young man's horse. It was a bad idea having a fresh scalp hanging like a trophy in Apache country. He reached over and lifted the scalp and dropped it into the staggering young man's saddlebags. He would ask about the scalp later. He looked ahead at Parker and Atwater.

When the two prisoners saw the young man weaving toward them like a drunkard, they stood up as one. Parker shook his head and stood with his right hand holding the stirrup, keeping it from hanging heavy against his wrist.

"Looks like we've got ourselves some company, Cero," he said, relieved that what the Ranger had heard on the path wasn't a band of Apaches.

"Does he look drunk to you?" Cero asked, seeing the man walking unevenly, leading his horse along in front of the Ranger.

"Call this no more than speculation on my part, Cero," said Parker. "The man looks like he might have said hello to the Ranger's gun barrel."

"Or maybe his rifle butt?" said Cero.

Parker shrugged, watching the Ranger and the wobbling man draw closer. "That's a whole other possibility," he said.

They watched as the young man staggered and dropped to the ground, slumped in front of them. They both eyed the handsome double rifle in the Ranger's left hand, his Winchester in his right.

"My, my, Ranger," said Parker, "that might be the best-looking rifle I've ever seen."

"What is it?" Atwater asked as Sam stepped over to his horse and slid his Winchester into his saddle boot.

Sam walked back to the prisoners, double rifle in hand, and unlocked their cuffs as he spoke.

"It's a fifty-six-caliber Pryse and Redman," he said. "Custom-made. Used for killing big game on the African plains."

"Fifty-six caliber. . . ." Parker whistled under his breath. "That ought to knock a hole in a fellow big enough to read a book through. Reckon that's what we heard earlier?"

"I wouldn't be surprised," Sam said. He uncapped a canteen from Parker's horse and poured a trickle down onto the back of the young man's bare neck.

"You're awfully obliging with *my* water, Ranger," Parker protested.

"Here, hold this for me," Sam said, pitching the handsome rifle to Parker, who caught it deftly. "Careful it don't go off," Sam added.

"You mean—" Parker stopped short; he quickly

turned the metal lever below the triggers and broke the rifle open and looked into the two empty barrels.

"He's only fooling with you, Rollo," Atwater said, watching the exchange.

"Well, ha-ha, Ranger, that's real damn funny," Parker said bitterly. He looked at the Ranger pouring the trickle of water as he shut the double-barreled rifle and hefted it in his hands.

Seeing what ran through Parker's mind, Sam stopped pouring the water onto the young man's neck.

"Before you swing it, Parker," he warned, "ask yourself if you want to arrive in Mesa Grande lying over your saddle, not knowing up from down."

Parker bit his lip; he stepped back and examined the big rifle in his hands, as if swinging it at the Ranger's head had never entered his mind.

"It is a fine-looking piece, Ranger," he said. Atwater stepped in beside him and looked down at the big custom-made Pryse & Redman, its ornate side-by-side double barrels glinting in the sunlight. He pressed the tip of a finger to the end of a barrel. He examined the indentation left there, speculating the rifle's caliber, even though Sam had already declared it a fifty-six big game gun.

"Dang, looks like you could load this thing with billiard balls," he said jokingly to Parker. He held his fingertip up for Parker to see. "Look at this, Rollo."

But Rollo Parker would have none of it.

"Get that grubby finger out of my face," he growled, "or guess where I'll stick it."

Atwater shrugged and turned his indented fingertip to the Ranger. "What would a man be shooting at in Mesa Grande that would require such a caliber as this, Ranger?"

"That's what I'm going to find out," he said. He capped Parker's canteen and hooked its strap back over Parker's saddle horn. Pulling the dazed young man to his feet, he leaned him against the side of his horse.

"What's your name, mister?" he asked, wanting to see if the man was recovered enough to ride.

"Ozzie," the young man said, cocking his head slightly, trying to focus on Sam's face. "And I don't talk to policemen."

Policemen . . . ? Atwater and Parker both grinned.

"He ain't from here, Ranger," said Parker, handing the rifle to Sam.

"I didn't break no law," the dazed young man offered. "You've no right arresting me." As he spoke Sam gave him a shove upward until he managed to flop onto his saddle. He steadied himself with both hands on the saddle horn.

"Ozzie," Sam said. "Believe it or not, Arizona Territory takes a dim view of people trying to shoot a lawman."

"But I never pulled the trigger," said Ozzie.

"Tell the judge all about it," Sam said, leading Ozzie and his horse by its reins.

"To hell with the judge," Ozzie said. "I'll spit in his face."

Sam gave Parker and Atwater a look. The two chuckled under their breaths and turned to their horses.

"Ranger, maybe you ought to tell him that everything he says will be used against him when you get him before a judge."

Ozzie blinked and tried to clear his head. "What's he talking about?" he asked Sam.

"Nothing," Sam said. "If you're not going to talk to me, I'm not going to talk to you." He led the young man's horse over beside his dun and swung up into his saddle. Ozzie managed to turn in his saddle and look at Parker and Atwater.

"What's that about the judge?" he asked in a still-blurry tone.

Before either man could reply, the Ranger cut in.

"Both of you keep your mouths shut," he said. "Until Ozzie here has something to say, let's just enjoy the quiet the rest of the way to Mesa Grande."

Chapter 4

The Ranger and his three prisoners rode in silence down the narrow maze of rock until the path turned onto a more accommodating trail that circled back upward in the direction of Mesa Grande. When they stopped at a fork in the trail, Ozzie sat staring all around as if trying to recognize the place. Sam stepped down from his saddle, reached down and picked up a weathered direction board with the words MESA GRANDE carved across it above an engraved pointing arrow. A nail stuck through the board.

"Good thing you already know the way, huh, Ranger?" said Parker.

Sam nodded and carried the sign over and drove the nail into a pine with a rock he picked up from the ground. Ozzie sat looking at the sign as if in defeat.

"I'll be damned," he whispered. "I took the wrong turn."

The three looked at him. Sam pitched the rock away and stepped over beside Ozzie's horse.

"So you were coming from Mesa Grande," he said matter-of-factly, dusting his hands together. "Instead of riding away, you made the wrong turn, rode in a long circle and followed the trail we're on."

Ozzie started not to answer, but then he let out a breath and hung his head.

"Yes, that's what I did," he said. "This sign was in the dirt. I had no idea one trail would take me in a circle all day."

"You managed to get lost *leaving* where you'd been?" Sam said, a little bemused. "Usually folks get lost finding where they're headed."

"Ever thought of being a trail scout?" Parker asked with a chuckle. His humor waned when Sam gave him a stern look.

Ozzie's face reddened. He stared down in shame, avoiding the eyes on him.

"It's not my fault these rubes can't put up signs that stay in place," he said.

Parker and Atwater stifled their laughter under a flat stare from the Ranger. As they collected themselves and stopped laughing under their breaths, Sam looked back at the confused young man sitting slumped in his saddle.

"My guess is you left Mesa Grande in a hurry," he said to Ozzie Cord. "I figure the shot we heard was the reason why. Before we get to town you'd best let me know what that shot was all about. Bad as you hate talking to *policemen*, I'm advising you to level up with me here and now—" His words stopped short.

"You there, on the trail," a voice boomed from the rocky hillside above them. "Raise your hands! Don't try to make a run for it. We've got you surrounded."

The three prisoners stuck their hands high in

the air; Sam raised his hands slowly, chest-high, as he searched the hillside and saw a tall figure standing atop a rock with a rifle aimed down at him. A few yards on either side of the rifleman stood another gunman, each with a rifle raised and ready. Sam was certain there were more than these three—other gunmen up there out of sight. These three had revealed themselves as a show of force.

"I'm Arizona Territory Ranger Sam Burrack," he called out. "Who are you, and what's your business here?"

"I'm sheriff's deputy Denton Shenny," the rifleman called out. "These men are my posse. We've been following an assassin's trail out of Mesa Grande. Now show me a badge, slow-like," he said in summation.

The Ranger slowly pulled aside the lapel of his duster and revealed the five-pointed Ranger badge on his chest. He held the lapel open and watched the rifles in the men's hand lower a few inches.

"An assassin, you say?" he called out, shooting a glance sidelong at Ozzie. "Who did he kill?"

"He killed—that is, *he shot* our sheriff," Shenny called out, correcting himself. "I'm sure the sheriff's dead by now."

Sam repeated the deputy's words in his mind. He noted something peculiar there, but he wasn't sure what.

"Deputy, does this have anything to do with the sound of a big-caliber rifle shot we heard earlier?"

Sam noted to himself that the deputy's voice

sounded almost hesitant as he stepped down the rocky hillside.

"Well, yes, it does, in fact," Shenny said. He lowered his rifle and motioned his men down behind him. Three more men stood from the cover of rock lower down along the hillside. The deputy was right, Sam remarked to himself; they were surrounded. But why had they stopped here and set up on this hillside? Why were they this far behind if they were on the trail of a man who'd shot their sheriff?

"I think I might have your man here beside me, Deputy," Sam called up to Shenny. "We come upon him back along the trail." He nodded at the double rifle he'd broken apart and shoved inside his bedroll for safekeeping.

"Good for you, Ranger," said the deputy as he and the others arrived, strung out along the trail. "But I don't want us jumping to conclusions here. There's more than one big rifle in the world. I can't stop and hold a man for carrying a big-caliber rifle."

What was this? Sam asked himself, eyeing the deputy.

"You can't? Why not?" he said bluntly. "I smelled the gun chamber—I'd say it was fired . . . earlier today."

The deputy ignored his words. But Sam watched his reaction closely as he looked Ozzie up and down.

"Anybody witness the shooting?" Sam asked.

"Huh-uh," said Shenny, still eyeing the slumped young man. "The sheriff was shot from an alley across the street from his office."

Sam thought he saw the faintest look of relief on the deputy's face as he looked at Ozzie for a second longer and appeared to come to some sort of recognition. What was that about? What was going on here? he asked himself. But he put his questions aside, for now anyway.

Shenny turned from Ozzie to the Ranger.

"Yep, this is the assassin all right," he said with subtle relief in his voice.

Sam just stared at him for moment, realizing he had just gone full circle.

"How do you know?" he asked, deciding to go full circle himself and play devil's advocate. "You said yourself that nobody saw him." He stared at Shenny, deliberately wanting to put him on the spot, see how he reacted to it.

"Yes, I said that, Ranger," Shenny replied. "But clearly it was him." He gestured toward the broken-down rifle shoved in Sam's bedroll. "There's the rifle."

"That's not the only big rifle in the world," Sam said flatly, repeating the deputy's own words back to him.

One of the riflemen stepped forward from the edge of the rocky trail.

"Deputy Shenny ain't explaining a damn thing to you, Ranger," he said in a heated tone.

Seeing the man start to raise his rifle to his shoulder, Sam dropped his hand to the Winchester lying across his lap. He put his hands into position there as all the other men except one followed suit and raised their rifles toward him. The man who didn't raise his rifle stepped forward.

"Everybody hold it here!" the red-bearded man

shouted. "This man is a Ranger! He's as much authority here as anybody. Don't do something stupid here. We're all on the same side."

"Prine's right, Leon," Shenny said, raising a hand toward the rifleman who'd challenged the Ranger's questions. He glanced at the others. "Everybody stand down. The Ranger's only doing his job here. Right, Ranger?" He tried to give a stiff nervous smile.

Sam stared, not returning the deputy's gesture. Deputy Shenny hadn't acted like any deputy Sam was accustomed to. He had to wonder why. This wasn't the time to raise any more questions. This was the time to go along with the deputy and get to Mesa Grande, see what was going on. Still, he had to give himself a reason to ease the tension.

"How long have you been a deputy?" he asked with no smile, no show of relenting. "How many posses have you led before now?"

"All right, you've got me there, Ranger," Shenny said. "I started being deputy today, right after the shooting." He gave a slight shrug. "I admit I'm a little green to this. But this is not my first gun work."

I bet it's not, Sam told himself.

Parker and Atwater had been sitting still in their saddles with their hands high, frightened looks on their faces. Ozzie Cord sat with his hands still up, but they had fallen some as he slumped over with pain.

"I understand," Sam said quietly.

He gave a moment to let the situation settle. He looked from one man to next, noting that Prine, the one with the red beard, looked different and carried himself in a different demeanor than these others. These others looked, dressed and handled themselves like gunmen. Prine was no gunman, Sam deduced. He was a workingman. As he studied the man's weathered bearded face, a trace of recognition set in.

"You there," he said respectfully. "Have I seen you somewhere before?"

"That you have, Ranger Burrack," said Prine. "You seen me hauling freight anywhere and everywhere a white can go—some places where they can't." He gave a genuine grin. "Name's Ison Prine." He pointed a thick, tough finger. "And I've seen you before too. I was in Nogales when you shot the Fannin boys down."

Sam only nodded. He noted the riflemen passing one another a look among themselves.

"What brings you to Mesa Grande?" he asked Ison Prine.

"I domicile in Mesa Grande these days," said Prine. "I was there when the sheriff lay bleeding on the floor. Soon as they appointed this man deputy, me and Harold volunteered to ride posse with him." He gestured off onto the hillside. "Harold's up there holding our horses."

Sam turned his gaze from Prine back to Shenny.

"I'm taking these three into Mesa Grande," he said, nodding toward Parker, Atwater and Ozzie.

"That one's *our* prisoner," said Leon Fuller, the first rifleman who had confronted him. He pointed toward Ozzie.

"I caught him," Sam said, staring at Fuller with steel in his eyes. "He's my prisoner. When we get to Mesa Grande, we'll talk more about it."

"The Ranger's right, Leon," Shenny said, cutting

in before the rifleman could say any more on the matter. "The assassin is caught; that's the main thing here." He looked all around, then back at Sam. "Does that sound fair enough?"

"Suits me," said Sam.

"Suits me too," said Shenny. "Then let's haul up and get going. I expect you can use some time out of the saddle?"

"I can," Sam said, more affable now that some sort of understanding had been struck between them. He turned his eyes to Ison Prine. "Why don't you ride here beside me, Prine? We can talk about Nogales on our way in." He looked back at Shenny. "If there's no objection, that is."

"None at all," said Shenny. He gave Prine a look and said, "Ride with the Ranger, Prine. Sounds like you two have got some catching up to do."

Riding a few yards ahead of the Ranger and the prisoners and the other riflemen, Denton Shenny and Leon Fuller spoke back and forth in lowered voices. Fuller was a gunman from the Missouri-Kansas border country. He'd learned the gun trade and outlawry from the border guerrillas. His attitude was to kill anybody for the right price, and kill anybody he had to for free if they stood in his way.

"We should have nipped everything in its bud, right then and there," he said to Shenny.

"You mean the Ranger, his prisoners and the townsmen too?" said Shenny. "We'd be out of our mind doing something like that."

"Why?" said Fuller. "We could have killed them all and blamed it on Cord's idiot nephew back there." He grinned between the two of them. "We could have got so upset over it that we hanged him on the spot. Nobody would've cared."

"Cord would have cared," said Shenny. "He looks out for that fool. I reckon blood is thicker than water, as they say." He leveled his gaze at Fuller. "We're going to make a lot of money once we get those rigged gambling machines in place. I don't want Cord and his scalp hunters messing up our business. With these men if you kill one, you have to kill them all. Every one of them is a murdering lunatic."

"All the more reason to kill them too," said Fuller. He spat and ran a hand across his mouth. "Don't forget I started out hunting Injun scalps." His grin widened and darkened. "There's nobody more of a murdering lunatic than me. When I say I'm a crazy cold-blooded killing son of a bitch, I'm speaking from the heart." He replaced his grin with a deep sincere look and pounded a hand on the breast of his fringed rawhide shirt.

"I admire a man who knows and appreciates his own capabilities, Leon," said Shenny.

"Good," said Fuller, "then at least let me kill Burrack. I always wanted to kill me a lawman. From what I know about him, he'll be up on our backs from now on. Him and his damn *law.*"

"No," said Shenny. "Leave the Ranger alone, for now anyway. He'll deal with his prisoners and go his way. If he doesn't, then you can take him down."

"All right, then!" Fuller's grin returned to his face. Excited at the prospect of killing the Ranger, he fidgeted in his saddle.

"Settle down, though," Shenny warned. "For now we're going to go along with things the way Curland wants us to. I tried every way to stall and keep from catching up to this Ozzie idiot. I don't know how he managed to take so long getting away. But now that we've got the Ranger in the mix, I'm playing my cards close to my vest—letting Curland know that I'm taking care of my part of our plans."

As he spoke, he and Fuller both looked back over their shoulders at the Ranger and the two townsmen riding abreast farther back behind the three prisoners.

"I don't like them getting their heads together," Fuller said. "We don't know if that teamster and the Ranger are talking about Nogales or about us."

"That's right," said Shenny. "I've been to Nogales. There ain't that much to talk about."

"What do you suppose they're telling that Ranger?" said Fuller.

"I won't even guess," Shenny said. "Luckily we've played our hand well. All those two can say is that we've been chasing our *beloved* sheriff's assassin to the best of our ability." He smiled a little. "What more can the town of Mesa Grande ask of its brand-new deputy sheriff?"

Chapter 5

The sky had tinted purple and dimmed on the western sky as the Ranger, his prisoners and the posse men rode into Mesa Grande from the south. Townsfolk came forward from their houses and shops and gathered out in front of the sheriff's office. The Ranger saw the heated anger in their eyes as they glared at all three prisoners. The residents of Mesa Grande, men and women alike, stood with their fists clenched at their sides.

"Is Sheriff Winters alive?" Sam asked the throng of angry-looking townsmen.

"So far, he is," said one of the men.

"But we ain't seen any improvement yet," said a burly implement drummer named Ward Bartles. He held an ax handle in his thick hand. He eyed the three cuffed prisoners. "Which one's the assassin here?" He glared hard at the prisoners.

Sam nodded, grateful to hear that Winters was still alive. He ignored the man's question and turned to Ison Prine and Harold Flake beside him.

"Talk to them," he said sidelong to the two. "These folks are more apt to listen to you than they are me."

"If they don't?" said Flake in a nervous voice.

"Then I'll take over," Sam said.

"Don't worry, Harold," Prine said to Flake. "I'll tell everybody who's who here."

He turned to the growing crowd and called out with authority, "Listen up, folks. I'm not going to say all this but once. The Ranger caught all three of these men. Two of them had nothing to do with what happened here. We believe only one shot Sheriff Winters."

"I asked, which one is he?" the burly implement drummer repeated. He stood with his feet spread wide and the ax handle in his hand. "We all demand to know."

"And you will know," said Prine, "just as soon as we've gotten all three of them behind bars."

Sam watched and listened, liking the way the teamster handled the crowd. Shenny and his posse sat atop the horses. Shenny was also willing to let Prine deal with the townsmen.

"Like hell," said the burly drummer to Prine. He took a step forward toward Prine's horse and reached out as if to grab it by its bridle. But Prine jerked his horse's head away and threw his hand on the Colt holstered on his side.

"Make no mistake, Ward Bartles," Prine warned the drummer by name. "We'll deal with this man in a court of law, but not out here in the street. I'll start shooting toes off anybody that thinks otherwise."

Bartles backed a quick step as Prine's Colt came up from the holster. He turned and looked up at Sam, who sat watching, keeping an eye on the situation.

"Are you backing him on this, Ranger?" he asked.

"I am," Sam replied.

Shenny swung down from his saddle and pulled the prisoners' horses over to the hitch rail.

"What about you, Deputy?" said Bartles. "Are you going to tell us which one it is, or do we take them all three from you?"

With a nod from Shenny, Leon Fuller and Tom Dukes leaped down from their saddles and leveled their rifles at the drummer's chest.

"You're not taking anybody, Bartles," said Shenny. "One more word out of you and my posse men will do what they've been itching to do all day."

"I've always wanted to shoot you, Bartles," Fuller said up close to the drummer's face. "Today could be my lucky day." He wore a strange crazy grin. Dukes stood back, ready, stone-faced.

Bartles wanted no more to do with Leon Fuller. He cowered back a few more steps and kept his mouth shut. The townsmen milled and grumbled and cursed among themselves.

Atwater and Parker climbed down from their saddles, eager to get inside the jail, away from the angry crowd. Ozzie Cord climbed down with an air of calmness. Seeming to have no regard for what the townsfolk were capable of doing to him, he stared at them with contempt in his eyes—a haughtiness—as if defying them to raise their hands against him. He was wide-awake now, his chin bruised and throbbing. When one of Shenny's posse men tried to hurry him along onto the boardwalk and inside the safety of the jail, he snarled at him like an angry dog.

"Get inside, idiot," said Fuller, giving Ozzie a hard shove.

"We'll see who's the idiot here when my uncle comes to get me," Ozzie said over his shoulder.

Sam heard him, but he noted that the two posse men only ignored Ozzie's words. He held back with his Winchester in his hands. He and Ison Prine followed the last of the posse men into the office. Prine closed the door behind them and bolted it. He leaned against the door and looked at the Ranger.

"These are good folks. They'll settle down. I'm glad I didn't have to shoot a couple toes off."

Sam nodded and followed the posse men over as they ushered the three prisoners into a large cell and closed the barred door. When Shenny reached over to hang the cell key's brass ring back on a wall peg, Sam grabbed the key from his hand.

"I'll take the watch for now," he said.

Shenny and the others turned and stared at him.

"By what authority?" Shenny asked, his voice sounding a little more in control now that they were back in town, back on his terrain, Sam decided.

"Being a territory Ranger gives me the authority to act in the absence of a sheriff being able to fulfill his duties of office," Sam said. "You'll find it written in the territory book of law and procedure," he added.

"Wait a minute," said Shenny, getting testy. "I'm the appointed deputy here."

"That you are," Sam said, "and until Sheriff Winters is either on his feet or in the ground, you'll be working as town deputy under me."

"The hell I will," said Shenny. He looked around

at the other posse men. "You can't come in here and take the town over."

"You're wrong," said Prine. "He can. I've read it in the territory laws, and I've seen it done before."

"What the hell do you know about it, Prine?" Leon Fuller said in a nasty tone. "You're nothing but a damn teamster."

But Prine gave him a cool, calm look in spite of Fuller's reputation for being a hotheaded gunman.

"I just told you what I know about it," he said evenly, staring Fuller in the eye. "Read it for yourself, if you *can*."

"Why, you. . . ." Fuller started to come at him; so did Dukes. Prine didn't budge a step. He clasped his thick hand around his holstered gun butt.

"Come on, then, *gun dog*," he said, letting Fuller know he wouldn't be intimidated.

"Gun dog . . . ?" Enraged, Fuller grabbed his gun butt too.

"Hold it, damn it," Shenny said, half stepping between the three parties. "We've got some sorting out to do here. Everybody keep their hands empty while we get it done."

Sam watched. This was the time to see where Deputy Shenny and everybody else stood in Mesa Grande. Something was afoul in this town.

Time to go to work and find out what it is, he told himself.

He'd watched quietly the whole ride in. He'd heard about how the sheriff had been shot from an alley; he'd also heard that Sheriff Winters had been opposed to new gambling laws put into effect only two days ago. Did this have anything to do with the sheriff being shot down? He didn't know, but it was worth checking on now that he'd gotten the prisoners to town without incident.

Here goes, he told himself.

"I don't see us having a whole lot to sort out, Deputy Shenny," he said calmly, knowing that he was about to jam a stick in a hornet's nest. "I represent the law for the entire territory. I'm taking over this jail and these prisoners, until such time as I say otherwise."

Shenny just stared at him; so did the others.

"I'll pass that authority back to you once I see the sheriff and get an idea whether or not he's going to live through this."

"Ranger," Leon Fuller cut in, "there is no way we're going to let you come in here start bulldogging our town—"

In one motion, the Ranger's Winchester swung up, levered and cocked, with the tip of its barrel against Fuller's chest. Dukes jumped back.

"You're not going to *let me* do anything, Fuller," he said, giving an extra poke with the rifle barrel. "I'm doing it. Save yourself some teeth and bone by keeping your mouth shut unless I'm speaking to you."

Fuller stood frozen but gave Dukes and Shenny a sidelong glance.

"Unless there's somebody else wanting their head creased by a rifle barrel," the Ranger said, "I'll be going to the doctor's to see how the sheriff's doing." He turned his gaze to Shenny. "Are you coming along?"

"Yes, sure thing," Shenny said. He started to turn to Fuller and the others and give them orders to watch the prisoners, but he caught himself and looked to the Ranger.

Sam looked at Ison Prine and Harold Flake.

"You two are still posse men until I get back," he said.

"I—I have a business to get to, Ranger," Flake stammered, nervously eyeing the gunmen standing around.

"What about you, Prine?" Sam asked.

"I'm good, Ranger," Prine said, staring narrowly at Shenny's gunmen. "Good for as long as you need me."

Sam nodded and looked from man to man, then at the prisoners. Atwater and Parker stood staring out through the bars.

"Let's go, Deputy," he said to Shenny, the two turning toward the door.

At the doctor's office, Bob Duckworth turned from the window where he'd stood watching the posse men and the Ranger ride in from the trail and make their way into the sheriff's office. He could not see over the heads of the crowd well enough to see Ozzie Cord or the other two prisoners. Behind him, in a chair in the waiting room, Joseph Curland sat smoking a cigar, holding a newspaper spread in front of him. Through a narrowly opened oak door, Duckworth saw the doctor move across the surgery room where the sheriff lay unconscious on a wooden surgical table.

"Your boy is back, boss," Duckworth said quietly to Curland. Curland smiled slightly as he stood up and laid the paper aside and straightened his vest and suit coat.

"Please, Duck," Curland said, holding his cigar in the fork of his fingers, "you must refrain from calling him 'my boy.' It doesn't play well with what we want the town to think of us."

"Sorry, boss," said Duckworth. "Anyway, you said to tell you when I see them coming. Here they come."

"Yes, thank you," Curland said in a calm, confident tone. "And who might you mean by 'they'?"

"Well, there's Shenny . . . ," he said. He watched as the Ranger and the deputy walked side by side into sight from within the crowd outside the sheriff's office. "And it looks like a . . . " He paused, then said, "Damn, it's that Ranger that comes riding through here every once in a blue moon."

"A what? A *Ranger*?" Curland said, his demeanor changing quickly. "Which Ranger?" He hurried over to the window and looked out beside Duckworth. Recognizing the Ranger, he let out a breath and cursed as he answered himself. "Samuel *by God* Burrack. . . ."

"Yep, that's him," said Duckworth. He studied the Ranger, sizing him up and down, having never been able to do so before, not without the Ranger also seeing him.

"Jesus, that's all I need," Curland murmured under his breath.

Duckworth watched as the Ranger's long duster swayed back and forth, revealing the big Colt holstered low on his hip.

He ain't so much, he told himself. A second shorter Colt stood higher up under the Ranger's left arm, butt-forward in a cross-draw shoulder rig. The Ranger's Winchester hung in his hand, its barrel tipped down at the ground, as if sniffing out the trail ahead of him.

"I can take him," Duckworth said, not realizing he was talking out loud until he heard Curland's reply.

"Don't get full of yourself, Duck," he said. He stepped back away from the window.

Now that Duckworth had spoken his thoughts aloud, he felt he had to back them up.

"I'm not full of myself, boss," he said. "All I see are a couple of big holstered guns and a rifle swinging. I can't say nothing for the man behind them." He shrugged. "I've heard talk, but talk's all it is, far as I'm concerned."

"What about all the men he's killed?" said Curland, appearing to taking an interest.

"What about them?" said Duckworth. "I didn't see it. For all I know it's all made up. I don't believe nothing that I ain't seen before my own eyes."

"Interesting," said Curland, puffing his cigar, watching the Ranger and Shenny draw closer to the doctor's big, white clapboard house. "Have you ever seen Paris, France?"

"No," said Duckworth.

"Do you believe such a place as Paris exists?" asked Curland.

Duckworth's face reddened.

"You know what I mean, boss," he said. "Rumors get started about a man's gun-handling. Most times it ain't worth the spit it took to tell about it."

Curland just stared at him for a moment as boots walked across the wooden porch to the front door.

"So you think you can take the Ranger?" he said finally.

"I can take him or leave him," Duckworth said. "All's I'm saying is he don't show me much." He paused as if considering the matter closer. Then he cocked his head a little and said, "Yeah, hell yes, I can take him." His confidence rose as he thought about it. "I'm faster than a rattlesnake when it comes to raising this smoker." He patted the gun on his hip. "Killing doesn't bother me, like it does some people."

"That's good to hear, Duck," said Curland as the Ranger and Shenny started up the stone walkway to the house. "I may well be calling you to task, should this Ranger try to get in my way."

"Yeah? What about your new 'deputy' there? Are you thinking maybe he can't handle killing the Ranger on his own?"

Curland backed to his chair and sat down, his open newspaper in hand.

"What I'm thinking, Duck," he said with a flat stare, "is that there may be plenty of *killing* for every man here, if folks start getting in my way."

They two stared at each other for a moment longer until the front door opened and Denton Shenny and the Ranger walked in.

Chapter 6

"Well, well," said Curland, "who have we here, Deputy Shenny?" He lowered his newspaper as the Ranger stood before him and Shenny closed the door behind them. He offered a practiced businesslike smile, his head tilted slightly aside.

"This is Arizona Territory Ranger Sam Burrack," said Shenny, stepping forward beside the Ranger. "Ranger Burrack, this is Mr. Joseph Curland, one of Mesa Grande's leading businessmen."

"You flatter me, Deputy," Curland said, still seated, appraising the Ranger from behind a smug businessman's smile. He noted that the Ranger took off his wide-brimmed gray sombrero. "To what do I owe the honor of this meeting?"

Sam studied his eyes for only a moment, then delivered what he considered would be a double punch to Curland's pride and authority.

"You don't," Sam said flatly in just the tone he'd intended to use. "I'm not here to meet you. I'm here to check on my friend Sheriff Winters."

"Oh yes, of course. I understand," said Curland. He'd been disarmed by the way the Ranger removed his sombrero and stood before him as if supplicating himself to Curland's importance. But then the

Ranger had swept that impression aside and deflated Curland casually. "You must excuse me, Ranger Burrack. We have all been dealt a terrible blow, everything that has happened—"

"Can you think of anyone who would want to kill the sheriff?" Sam asked, cutting Curland off, already sensing that this was not a man used to being cut short in any way. Sam sounded rude, inpatient, pushy, exactly how he'd meant to sound. Whatever polished veneer Curland partitioned between himself and the rest of the world, Sam wanted it out of the way. He wanted gut responses.

"No, Ranger Burrack," Curland said, regaining his dominant nature almost as quickly as he'd just had it taken away. "I'll admit that not everyone got along with the sheriff. Why, he and I myself even had differences on issues regarding town ordinances—"

"Really? Did you shoot him, then?" Sam cut in with no show of difference for the man or his prominence.

"Ranger, you're out of line," Shenny said gruffly. Sam noted the difference in the deputy's tone and demeanor now that they were in front of Joseph Curland. Was this because Curland was one of the town leaders, or was it something more than that?

Keep it moving, he told himself. *Keep churning the waters.*

"I'm sorry, Curland," he said, without looking around at either Shenny or Duckworth, who stood off to the side. "Let me put it to you another way. Did you *have* Sheriff Winters shot?" He cut his eyes to Duckworth with intentional suspicion in them. "Is that the way it's done here?"

"Why, you—!" Shenny stepped toward him; so did Duckworth.

"Whoa, easy, now," said Curland, the only one in control of himself. He rose from his chair and held a hand out toward each of them, deputy and gunman alike. "You're upset, Ranger. That's understandable. But that's no excuse for you flying off at me or either of these men."

Sam raised his hands a little, showing Curland he was calming himself. That was as far as he could take it for now. Joseph Curland was no fool. If he pushed any further right now, Curland would see through his ill-mannered lawman ruse.

Sam gave a repentant nod. Then he looked between Duckworth and Deputy Shenny.

"Who appointed this man deputy? You?" he asked Curland, as if Shenny hadn't already told him on the trail.

"No, I did not," said Curland. "Our town selectmen appointed him. Our town leaders, I should say. Although I did say I thought he was the best man for the job."

"Town leaders?" Sam said.

"Yes," said Curland. "You see, rather than an elected town council, we have selectmen who have their lives and fortunes at stake in Mesa Grande. We rely on their decisions, rather than on politicians who will make decisions based on whose vote they can snag for themselves." He offered a thin smile. "It seems to work for us."

"I'm familiar with the process," Sam said. "I take it you are one of these selectmen?"

"Me? No, no," said Curland, shaking his head. "I run my business and avoid town matters—

admittedly, I do spin an opinion time to time, on issues that pertain to my mining interests, my saloon, my realty interests."

"That's all for now," Sam said, cutting him short again. "I'll have some questions later. I want to see the doctor now, see how Sheriff Winters is doing."

Curland stood looking at him, at a loss for words right then. He looked at Shenny, then at Duckworth, the two also looking puzzled by the Ranger's words.

"Ranger Burrack," Curland finally said, "am I a suspect in the attempt on the sheriff's life?"

"Why would you think that?" Sam said.

"Because you're acting as if I'm being questioned on the incident," said Curland.

"Oh . . . ," Sam said. He let his words hang unfinished, hearing the sound of the doctor walk to door.

"Well, *am I*?" Curland asked impatiently.

The Ranger acted as if he was going to answer, but then he stopped short as the doctor opened the door, looked out and saw the badge on his chest.

"I heard you were in town, Ranger," the doctor said. "I suppose you want to talk to the sheriff right away."

"The sooner the better, Doctor," the Ranger said. "If he's able, that is."

"I understand," said the doctor.

"How is he, Doctor?" Sam asked.

The doctor stepped aside in the doorway and turned a hand toward the room.

"Come in—see for yourself," he said. "I'm going

to let you talk to him, but keep it short. He's awfully weak."

"Much obliged, Doctor," Sam said. He stopped before walking into the surgery room; he looked Curland up and down, as if reappraising him.

"I'll get back to you, Curland," he said coolly. "Have a seat. Wait for me out here."

Curland, Duckworth and Shenny stood staring at the door as it closed behind the Ranger.

"Like hell *I'll have a seat and wait here* for him," Curland said. "The nerve of this lawman."

Shenny lowered his voice to a whisper.

"He kept me sitting on prickly pear all the way here," he said. "Strikes me he knows something but won't let it out."

"That's just the way a damn lawman does it," said Curland. "Don't let him rattle you. It's all a part of his game. He's fishing around, seeing what he can stir up."

"I saw how he does it," said Shenny. "He caught that idiot Ozzie carrying Cord's big rifle—"

"Shut up, damn it," said Curland, cutting Shenny off. He looked at Duckworth. "Duck, stay here— keep your eyes and ears open." He nodded toward the street and spoke to Shenny. "You come with me. Tell me everything on our way to the saloon." He turned on his heel and walked out the front door.

Shenny and Duckworth gave each other a look. Shenny turned and hurried through the door behind Curland.

"Where's Fuller and Dukes?" Curland asked.

"I've got them cooling for now," said Shenny. "But they're ready for any move I want them to make."

"Good," said Curland, walking on briskly. "Now, what the hell happened out there on the trail, *Deputy*? Is this job going to be more than you can handle?" he added with sarcasm.

"I am handling it," Shenny replied sharply. "It went just like we planned. We let Cord and his nephew stay well ahead of us but still made it look like we were hot on their trail. It was working out fine until Ozzie managed to get himself caught by the Ranger. The damn fool even tried to shoot him. Burrack knocked him cockeyed."

"Damn it all," said Curland, the two of them walking along briskly. "Why did Cord have to bring that grinning idiot along with him?" He looked at Shenny.

"I don't know . . . because they're kin, I reckon," said Shenny. "As soon as I saw the Ranger had Ozzie and not Cord himself, I figured the best thing to do was go along with things, bring Ozzie in, figure a way to slip him out of town later and call it a jailbreak."

"You were right in doing that," Curland said, letting out a breath. "But we can't let anything happen to him. We'd have Cord's scalp hunters all over us."

"How far will those scalp hunters go, following Cord's orders?" Shenny asked.

"They rode with him in the war. They still call him Captain Cord," said Curland, looking closely at him. "Does that tell you anything?"

"Yes, it tells me a lot," said Shenny. "Those damn old rebels."

"That's just the kind of crazy sons a' bitches they are," said Curland, walking on.

"Then what are we going to do?" Shenny asked. "I'm willing to do whatever it takes."

"We're going to let things simmer for a while, Deputy," said Curland. "The Ranger doesn't want to be here any longer than he has to. Once he's gone, Mesa Grande will go back to what we want it to be—a peaceful town where we all take care of our own."

"What about our new gambling devices?" Shenny asked. "Are we going to wait until Burrack leaves before we set them up?"

"No," said Curland, "it would look too suspicious. We set them up just like we've planned."

"Even the French Wheel?" Shenny asked.

"Especially the French Wheel," said Curland. "We'll keep our foot off the brake pedal until everybody gets used to playing it, maybe even let them win some." He smiled. "Roulette is a fine game of chance. The miners will love it. They're starving for more gambling. It'll be our biggest moneymaker." Talking about money made him want a cigar. He fished a silver case from inside his lapel, took one out, bit the tip off it and spat it away.

"Even while the Ranger's still here?" asked Shenny.

"To hell with him," said Curland. "He has no say over how we gamble here in Mesa Grande. We just can't let him connect it to Winters getting shot." He eyed Shenny. "Got it?"

Shenny let out a breath, taking it all in. "Yeah, I got it. What about Geary? We ought to kill him for saving Winters' life."

"Oh yes, to be sure we will," said Curland. "Right now I'm showing him a hero's reward. But as soon as everything settles down, he'll be a *dead* hero, for all the troubles he caused."

"I hate a damn do-gooder like Geary," said Shenny. "When the time comes just say the word. I'll take care of him."

Curland gave Shenny a critical look.

"Damn right you will," he said. Just make sure that you take care of everything and everybody when the time comes. I can't help feeling like you let this situation get away from you. Now we've got to backtrack and clean up your mess—"

"My mess?" Shenny protested. "None of this would have happened if you hadn't told me to take those two townsmen along on the posse."

Curland saw he was pushing the man too far.

"All right, *our* mess," he said, giving in a little. "Either way we have to clean up this mess and put the whole plan back on track. We're going to need to show a united front here."

"I agree with you there," said Shenny. "Some things haven't gone exactly as we would have liked, but now we've all got to work together."

"Yes," said Curland, "my thoughts exactly. I'm glad we *agree*." He managed to hide the scowl on his face by looking away across the dirt street.

The Ranger stood beside the bed and looked into Sheriff Winters' pale drawn face. In spite of his wound and heavy loss of blood, he opened his eyes a little as the doctor led the Ranger to his bed and spoke to him as he checked his pulse.

"I have a fellow lawman here to see you, Sheriff," he said, watching the sheriff's eyes, gauging his response.

Sheriff Winters' eyes moved slightly.

"Bring . . . him in," he whispered, as if unaware that Sam was standing bedside.

The doctor and the Ranger gave each other a dubious look.

"You do most of the talking, Ranger Burrack," the doctor said quietly. "And keep it short."

Sam only nodded and leaned in as the doctor moved away from the bed. When the doctor was out of sight, he leaned in even closer and kept his voice low and even.

"Bronco Dave, it's me, Sam Burrack." He waited until he saw the sheriff's eyes find him and register recognition.

"Sam . . . ," the sheriff managed to whisper. "You . . . got here . . . quick."

"Don't talk, Sheriff. Let me talk," Sam said. "I was headed here with a couple of prisoners and heard a shot from the direction of town. Later I ran into a fellow carrying a large-caliber English rifle. I brought him in."

"You . . . caught . . . him?" the sheriff asked haltingly.

"Shhh, just listen, Bronco," Sam said, seeing the sheriff try too hard to talk. "I brought in the man, and I brought in the rifle. It had been fired."

The sheriff only gave a slight nod of appreciation.

"But I get the feeling things aren't right here in Mesa Grande, Bronco," Sam said. "I have the man, and I have the gun. But I don't think this is the man who shot you. His name is Ozzie Cord—"

Before Sam finished his words, the sheriff shook his head weakly, rejecting the idea.

"Idiot . . . ," he managed to whisper.

"Good," said Sam, "I didn't figure him for an assassin." He started to reach out and pat a hand on the sheriff's shoulder. But he caught himself and stopped, realizing the sheriff's critical condition. "The trouble is, if it wasn't him acting alone, that means there's still somebody out there wanting you dead." He paused to make sure the sheriff understood him.

The sheriff raised his eyes to the Ranger's and managed another slight nod.

"I'm going to take your town over, Sheriff," Sam said. "We both know I have the legal right to do it. But I'd feel better knowing you approved of it."

The sheriff gave another nod, this one weaker. Sam saw that this visit was wearing the man out.

"You rest up, Bronco. I'll be back when you can tell me more," he said. He paused, then said, "I'm going to be rousting your town some. Whoever wants you dead, I need to draw their attention away from you and onto me. I hope you understand. . . ."

Sam trailed off, seeing the sheriff had drifted back off to sleep. He backed away from the bed as the doctor came back in from another room.

"I'm afraid that's all for today, Ranger," the doctor said, looking around at him from beside the wounded sheriff. "You need to leave now, and let the sheriff get some rest."

"Just a few minutes longer, Doc," Sam said. He gestured toward a large clock on the wall. "Let me sit with my friend here?"

The doctor looked at him and nodded. Yet he

saw there was more to it than the Ranger wanting to sit near the wounded sheriff.

"No harm in that," said the doctor. "Why don't I have Rita bring you some cool water while you wait?"

"Obliged," Sam said. "Some cool water would be nice." He watched the doctor turn and leave the room. Only a moment passed before a Mexican woman came into the room carrying a pitcher of water and a tall wooden cup on a tray. Sam thanked her and watched her turn and leave. When he'd drunk the cup of water she poured for him, he looked up at the clock and walked out of the room.

"How is he, Ranger?" Duckworth asked before Sam had even closed the door behind himself.

Sam put on a blank face and looked Duckworth up and down.

"Better than I expected," he said. "He was able to talk, if that's what you'd like to know."

"Ranger, I'm just a *concerned* townsman," Duckworth said in defense.

"I bet you are," Sam said. He looked the man up and down again, giving the look a suspicious tone.

Duckworth paused, but only for a moment. Then he grew anxious under the Ranger's gaze.

"Able to talk about what?" he asked, unable to keep himself in check any longer.

"Everything . . . ," said the Ranger. "I hope you weren't fixin' to leave town anytime soon."

"Leave town . . . ?" Duckworth took on a strange look. "Well, I—no, I hadn't planned to. Why?" he asked.

"Because there are some things we need to talk about. About how you and the sheriff got along."

"How we got along?" said Duckworth. "Hell, we got along fine. Just *fine*, him and me!" he said, raising his voice, seeing the Ranger already headed to the front door.

"That's good," Sam said as he pulled the door open and placed his sombrero atop his head. "You'd best hope you're able to prove that when it comes to a court of law."

"Whoa, hold on, Ranger," Duckworth said, stepping over closer to the door. "What did he say? Did he say different?"

"Never mind what he said *for now*," Sam replied, with a hard stare. "Whether he lives or dies, *somebody's* going to pay for shooting him." He made it a point to look the worried man up and down one more time with a knowing look in his eyes. "Ask yourself if you want to be that *somebody*."

"But, Ranger, I ain't done nothing," said Duckworth.

"Then you'd best have your story straight. You can bet everybody else will." He walked out, left Duckworth staring in the open doorway.

PART 2

Chapter 7

The first thing Erskine Cord realized when he spotted his men up among the rocks in Pine Canyon was that the camp had moved a full seven miles closer to the main desert trail leading to Mesa Grande.

He stopped his horse and waited. When the men recognized their leader, they began to climb down and gather around him. A sturdy-built man dressed in rawhides and knee-high vaquero boots led the others down and stopped within ten feet, when he saw the look of displeasure on Cord's face.

"This is not Hanging Pine, Sterling," Cord said down to the man in a harsh tone.

"I know that, Cap," said Sterling Childs. His voice also carried a firm tone. "We had no choice. We got pressed by a damn band of Apache—look like Quetos and his Wolf Hearts. We couldn't hold out at Hanging Pine. Figured you had to come this way, so we moved forward, hoping to shake them off our tails."

Cord gazed farther back along the canyon,

past his gathering band of ragged, skin- and fur-clad men.

"And did you *shake them off*, Sterling?" he asked drily.

"It's too soon to tell, Cap," said Childs. "If I was to guess, I'd have to say no, we didn't." He gestured a rugged hand back toward men leading their wounded forward.

"You can see how they've been nipping away at us all the day and night, Cap," said Childs.

Four men leaned on their comrades for support. One's head was wrapped in dirty blood-soaked bandages. Another limped along using his rifle as a walking stick. Two men helped each other along, both with bandages showing behind their open shirts.

"Jesus. . . ." Cord spat and ran a hand over his parched lips. "I can't go do something as simple as kill a son of a bitch without coming back to a bucket full of trouble." He stared at Childs.

"So it appears, Cap," said Childs. "These Wolf Hearts have been all over us ever since we skint out their womenfolk and their nits. I didn't expect they'd stop while you went off to take care of some killing—did you?"

"No, I didn't," Cord said, knowing Childs was right. He managed a slim, parched grin and reached down as a man walked up and held up a water bladder. "They get testy as hell, you skin out their kin. Can't really blame them, I expect." He paused as he raised the water bladder for a drink. "But a man has got to make a living, eh, Childs?" He tilted the bladder and squeezed a long squirt of water into his mouth, all over his face, then handed it back down. *"Gracias,* Eldo," he said to Eldo Berne, the water bearer. Berne wore a black scarf drawn low across his forehead, partially hiding the initials CV that had been carved deep to the bone. CV stood for *Cheval Voleur*—French for *horse thief.*

The short, barrel-chested Frenchman stepped back, closing the bladder spout.

Cord looked all around again at the dusty baked faces of his gathering scalp hunters.

"Speaking of *kin,* where's my nephew?" he asked.

Childs shook his head slowly.

"He never showed, Cap," he said.

"Never *showed*?" said Cord, his eyes and nostrils flaring a little.

Childs raised a consolatory hand.

"Now, hold on, Cap, I know that you're thinking," he said. "But the fact is we waited long as we could. If he was coming to Hanging Pine, he'd've been there already."

Cord took a deep breath, staring off along the high distant edges of the canyon walls.

"You figure the Wolf Hearts got him?" he asked.

"If they didn't, something else must've," said Childs. "He flat didn't make it."

"Damn it," said Cord.

"If he showed up late at Hanging Pine, he'd be dead by now anyway," said Childs, keeping a respectful tone. "Quetos has a mad-on stiffer than a hickory plank. I hate to say it, but we need some cavalry to ride out here—settle these desert *los* down some before we get back to any serious scalping."

"Blast it all!" Cord said. He gazed off and sucked a slice of air through his side teeth.

"I'm just saying," Childs continued, "the Mex could lift their hair bounty any day. We need to be slicing and curing right now, not being stuck with arrows every time we walk out to squat."

"Damn it," Cord repeated. He lowered his head and shook it slowly.

"I'm just reporting what I think, Cap, same as always," said Childs. "I don't mean to raise a roil over it—"

"He's got my rifle," said Cord, cutting him off. "I let him carry it back for me."

Childs gave him a look.

"You *did*?" he said, almost in disbelief.

"Damn it, Sterling, what was I supposed to do?" said Cord. "He's my nephew—my oldest brother Grayson's son, for God sakes."

Childs stared at him.

"I gave Grayson my word I'd look after Ozzie, teach him the trade. Taking Ozzie in settled a little falling-out between us." He paused, then said, "I'll tell you all about it sometime, when there's a bottle of whiskey in my hand."

"I hope you will," said Childs, "because it's easy to see you hold the boy special—"

Before his words ended an arrow sliced through the air between them and turned to long splinters against a tall rock.

"Here they come!" shouted one of the men.

"Take to cover!" shouted Cord, leaping down from his saddle and swinging his horse around between himself and the high rock walls.

Arrows whistled in from both sides of the canyon. The men quickly ducked into the rocks and returned fire with their rifles and sidearms. Cord followed Childs on foot, leading his spooked horse by its reins. When they had pulled the unsettled horse behind the cover of a large boulder, Cord drew his Winchester from his saddle boot and levered a round into its chamber.

"Are the other horses safe?" he asked, hugging against the boulder, watching arrows whiz past.

"I put three men guarding them up on the hillside," said Childs. "No Apache is going to get near them." He peered around the boulder, then ducked back. "Besides, these warriors haven't shown any interest in horses or nothing else . . . except to kill us."

"Apache are always after horses," said Cord. "It's their nature." He paused as if concentrating his listening toward the Indians on the higher walls of the canyon. "Hold it—listen to this."

"Listen to what?" said Childs, hearing the return gunfire from their own men. He also heard gunfire erupt from the direction of the horses.

"All they're shooting at us is arrows," said Cord. "Why do you suppose? They've got guns. We know that. Every one of them we've killed has been armed."

"I don't know," said Childs. "I tell you, this bunch doesn't act like any Apache warriors I've ever seen. They're madder than hornets and as unpredictable as my drunken aunt Bess. I can't figure it."

"They are going for the horses," Cord said.

"Come on. We're getting out of here. I don't like the way they're acting. We've had these Mescaleros outnumbered all winter. But they could have Chiricahuas and White Mountain warriors straggling in without us seeing it happen."

The two reached their guns out around the boulder, fired a few shots up at the hillside, then ducked back as arrows streaked past them.

"Which way we headed?" Childs asked, glad Cord was back, taking some of the responsibility off him.

"Toward Mesa Grande," Cord said. "I had to go back there soon and get the rest of my money anyway. We might as well do it now. They won't follow us much closer to town."

"Ordinarily they wouldn't," said Childs. "Quetos and these crazy bastards, it's hard to say what they'll do."

"If they do follow us in closer, we'll tell the people we've got Apaches storming us, and let them figure how to handle them."

"Whatever you say, Cap," said Childs, as an arrow pinged down off the boulder and skipped away across the dirt. "Anytime you're ready, let's get our horses and hightail it out of here."

"I'm ready right now," said Cord, standing out from behind the boulder, firing round after round into the hail of arrows coming from the rocky canyon hillsides. He shouted out to his men who'd taken cover among the rock, "Follow me, men. Make for the horses."

The two turned and ran, Cord leading his frightened horse as the sound of war cries rained down with the arrows. Rifle and pistol fire answered the war cries. When the two stopped and looked down at the small clearing where the horses were stashed, they saw only one of the guards left alive, fighting back a wave of young Apache braves.

"Half our horses are gone already!" shouted Childs, seeing two braves leading horses away into the rocks.

"I see that," Cord shouted in reply. "Let's see what we can do about the rest of them!" He leveled his big Colt and shot one of the braves in the back, sending the horses he led running off wildly.

A few yards below Cord and Childs, the remaining horse guard fought hard, but he couldn't hold back the Apaches much longer.

"We're here, Bud!" shouted Childs, his rifle bucking at his shoulder, sending another brave flying away from the horses.

"Much obliged!" shouted Bud Shank, levering and firing shot after shot as arrows whizzed past him. "Come on down here and get some." In the dirt at his side lay two dead Apaches that he'd dragged over to him as soon as he'd shot them down. Their scalps had been sliced off and lay in the dirt. His scalping knife stood stabbed into the rocky ground beside him, ready for use.

"Ol' Bud," said Cord with a dark chuckle, "always with an eye on the business end." With his empty Winchester under his arm, he closed the firing gate on his smoking reloaded Colt and stalked toward the braves in the rocks, firing round after round, pushing them back as he and Childs closed in.

———

Evening shadows had started to gather and spread long beneath the hill line west of Mesa Grande beyond the rocky desert flatlands. In his office above the Old Senate Saloon, Joseph Curland stared out at the hill line, cigar in hand, and tried to keep his thoughts collected. He had wanted everything to go smoothly, simply. Yet, in spite of all his planning and efforts, that had not been the case. Behind him Bob Duckworth continued speaking, talking about what the Ranger had said earlier in the doctor's office.

Curland blew a long stream of smoke out the open window and turned and sat down behind his large desk. He folded his hands with his cigar between his fingers and nodded slightly as if hanging on every word Duckworth had said.

Beside the desk stood Deputy Denton Shenny.

"The only thing that bothers me about it," said Shenny, "is that what the Ranger told Duck here could be right—"

"Hold it right there," said Duckworth, cutting him off. "You being French-Canadian, it might take you longer to get this than it would some folks, but I've told you before, nobody calls me 'Duck' except my best pards."

"Right you are, my mistake," said Shenny with a cold stare. He corrected himself. "What the Ranger told *Bob* here could be right. If he starts pressing everybody, somebody might tell him about the sheriff's shooting just to keep themselves clear of it."

"Oh . . . ?" said Curland. He puffed his cigar. "Listen to you. You both sound as if everyone in town knows all about this." He eyed both men critically. "Should I be concerned about you two?"

"Not me, by God," said Duckworth. "I'm American born and bred. I know how to keep my mouth shut no matter how hot the water gets." He turned a hard stare toward Shenny. "I'm only able to vouch for myself, though."

Curland ignored the remark; so did Shenny.

"Let's take stock," Curland said. He drew and blew. Smoke roiled and drifted overhead. "Only we three know about it. Us, and of course Erskine Cord, . . ."

"And maybe he told his idiot nephew, Ozzie," Shenny offered.

"Kill Ozzie, first thing, to make sure," Duckworth threw in, stepping forward hastily with his knee-jerk idea.

The two just looked at him; he withdrew.

Curland considered everything for a moment while the two watched him negotiate and adjust the cigar between puffs. Finally, he blew out a long gray stream toward the ceiling and gave a clean, smug grin.

"The Ranger is bluffing, of course," he said. "What could the sheriff have possibly told him?"

Shenny and Duckworth stared at each other. Curland studied them for a moment, then saw they appeared to be stuck for a reply.

"Nothing, that's what," he said. "He could have told him he didn't agree with allowing me to bring in gambling devices. So what? I practically told the Ranger that myself—I said we'd had our differences."

The two men settled a little, mulling things over for themselves.

"Yes, that's it!" said Curland, giving a little laugh. "The Ranger is bluffing. He doesn't have anything to go on, and it's eating him up."

Shenny and Duckworth looked relieved. Duckworth smiled. "That bluffing dog," he said. "He almost had me." He looked back and forth between Curland and Shenny. "The only one we might have to worry about is Erskine Cord, and hell, he's not going to say anything."

"Quite right, Duck," said Curland, tipping his cigar toward his right-hand man. "He'll drift through here long enough to pick up the rest of his pay, then move on. Assassins can't afford to stay around *anywhere* long. Besides, he got a scalping contract with the Mexicans. Pays well, I understand." He grinned and settled back in his soft chair. "All we're going to do is sit still and let the Ranger chase his own tail. *Business as usual*," he added, lifting a boot and resting it on his desktop. "Deputy, tell Fuller and Dukes to stand down, even get cooperative with the Ranger."

"Right away," said Shenny, turning to the door.

Curland looked at Duckworth as the door closed behind the deputy.

"Duck, have the French Wheel and other devices set up and running by first thing tomorrow morning. Miners are getting paid this week," he said.

"With the brake pedal hooked up, ready to work?" Duckworth asked, already turning toward the door himself.

"Oh yes," Duck," Curland said. He raised his finger for emphasis. "And don't forget to break out those marked card decks from St. Louis." He grinned. "From now on we offer no games of chance unless we can control them."

Chapter 8

At daylight a boy from the town's restaurant left the sheriff's office carrying a tray loaded with empty dishes and coffee cups. When he left, the Ranger and Ison Prine had escorted the prisoners to the double privy that served both the jail and the general public. Afterward, the Ranger stood rifle in hand while Prine unlocked the long shackle chain from the prisoners' ankles and closed and locked their cell doors. Ozzie Cord sat in a cell by himself; Rollo Parker and Cero Atwater shared the only other cell in the two-cell jail.

"I'm picking up a load over at the freight station in Dorsey today, Ranger," Prine said, hanging both the cell and shackle keys on a wall peg. "I always allow a day there and a day back. Wish I could stay here and help out more."

Sam nodded.

"I understand," he said. "I'm obliged for all you've done so far. It helps having a townsman keeping peace at a time like this."

Prine nodded. "People get awfully riled when their sheriff gets shot in such an underhanded way," he said. "I'll help some more, soon as I get back. I'm hauling in a piano and some more gaming equipment for the Old Senate Saloon." He'd already mentioned that he'd hauled a lot of gaming devices for the saloon lately. Sam had duly weighed and considered the information closely, knowing that the saloon belonged to Joseph Curland, as did a lot of other thriving enterprises in and around Mesa Grande.

"Curland must be doing well in Mesa Grande," Sam commented.

"He ought to be," said Prine, "he's a greedy man, manages to keep his hands in a lot of pots." He studied the Ranger's face, then said in a lowered tone, "I get the feeling you think he had a hand in the sheriff getting shot."

Sam returned his gaze with a poker face. "At this point nothing would surprise me," he said. "A man as ambitious as Curland has to either buy off the law in town or know how to weave his way around it. I've never known Bronco Dave Winters to sell out his badge."

"You're right about that," said Prine. He turned toward the door. "Anyway, I'll take my leave now. See you tomorrow evening, all things going as planned."

Sam walked to the door and stood looking back and forth along the waking street as Prine walked out of sight toward the freight office around the corner. In a moment he gave a short wave and watched Prine's four-mule wagon roll onto the street and head out of town on its thirty-eight-mile trip to the freight station in Dorset.

As the wagon ambled along, Prine gave a

whistle and a big red-and-black-spotted hound loped out of nowhere and shot up onto the driver's seat beside him. Sam smiled to himself and walked back inside.

"Any chance we can get out of this town today, Ranger?" Rollo Parker asked, his thick hands gripping the bars on the cell. "I can't help feeling like Cero and I are going to end up stretching rope for something we played no part in. Gives me the willies, that ol' desert teamster having to stick around here just to keep the townsfolk from going hang-crazy."

"Stop worrying so much, Parker," said Sam. "Things have settled down here thanks to that *ol' desert teamster* showing he's on the side of the law. I'd say that man is well-respected here."

"Respected, ha!" said Parker. "All he's done is spent his life staring up a mule's back end. I don't know why that gets him any respect." He looked at Atwater for support. The two nodded. Ozzie sat brooding in his cell, his head lowered.

"If you don't know why, there's no point in me trying to explain it," Sam said. "Whether you respect him or not, he might be the reason this town hasn't gotten out of hand and strung the three of you from a porch rafter." He looked toward Ozzie as he spoke and saw the young man raise his head.

"My uncle hears about this," he said broodingly, "you might be the one strung from a rafter."

"Whoa, look here, Cero," said Parker, "it can talk some after all." The two chuckled between themselves.

"Not much," Atwater replied, "but a little."

"Maybe it knows that whatever it says the Ranger will go tell the judge when it's court time." They cackled aloud.

Sam only watched.

Ozzie looked at the two other prisoners with a sour expression. He'd said almost nothing since the Ranger took him into custody. Part of his silence had been due to the Ranger's rifle butt jabbing into the face. But even as he recovered he'd said very little to Atwater or Parker.

"When my uncle comes, gets me out of here, I'll have him carve out both your tongues and nail them to a board."

"All right, that's enough," Sam said quietly, seeing the conversation turning ugly.

Parker's and Atwater's laughter waned, then stopped. With no regard to the Ranger's order, Parker moved closer to the wall of bars separating the two cells. Sam laid his Winchester across the desk.

"Will you, then?" Parker said to Ozzie, all humor gone. "What if my uncle gets here first? Maybe I'll just have him do the same to you."

Atwater moved alongside Parker; the two stopped a foot back from the bars. Even with the cells separating them, Ozzie stood up and faced them in defense, as if the two might come through the bars for him.

"I said, that's enough," Sam demanded, stepping forward himself, picking up a wooden bucket of drinking water on his way. He took the dipper from the bucket, pitched it over onto the desk and drew the bucket back, ready to throw water on the three, a method that worked on growling dogs.

Atwater and Parker backed away from the separating bars; so did Ozzie.

"Ozzie," Parker said in a calmer tone, "you sure have a peculiar way of making friends. I'll say that." As soon as his words were spoken, he raised a hand toward the Ranger, letting him know that was the end of it. "I had to say that, let this boy know he's not messing with greenhorns here. He could get himself killed talking like that to our bunch."

Sam just looked at him. He knew these two weren't hardened gunmen, not yet anyway. They had been hired to furnish fresh horses and a hideout for the Clyde Feral Gang out of New Mexico. They'd both admitted they hadn't been in prison— never been *caught* before. Was this all tough talk? He believed it was. But that made them no less dangerous, he reminded himself. They could have broken a lot of laws, yet never really made a name for themselves.

Outlaws still in the making? he asked himself. *Maybe.*

Before he could give the subject any more thought, he spun toward the sound of running footsteps along the boardwalk. His right hand went to the butt of his holstered Colt as the door flew open and Harold Flake ran inside, red-faced and wide-eyed. He glanced at the water bucket in the Ranger's left hand.

"Ranger, you'd best come quick," he said, breathing rapidly. "You ain't going to believe what's riding into town!"

As Flake spoke, Sam heard and felt the hoof-
beats of running horses coming up onto the hard-
packed dirt street from the south of Mesa Grande.
Setting the water bucket down, Sam picked up his
Winchester from the desktop. He happened to pass
a glance toward Ozzie Cord and saw a faint strange
smile on his face.

"Let's go," Sam said to Flake, passing the alarmed
townsman on the way out the front door. He hurried across the boardwalk, onto the street, arriving
just in time to see six horsemen thunder into sight,
raising a thick cloud of dust.

Standing firm, Sam watched as the horses slid
down to a halt and the riders spilled from their
saddles out in front of the Old Senate Saloon. Sam
started to move forward, but then he decided to
wait as he saw one of the men go around the side
of the building while the other five spun their
horses' reins around a hitch rail and went straight
into the saloon through the front door. Townsfolk
gathered at the sight of the ragged, fur- and leather-
clad desert plainsmen.

"Flake," he said over his shoulder as the nervous townsman sidled up to him, "I'd be obliged
if you'd stay here and watch about the prisoners."

"What—what is it, Ranger?" Harold Flake asked
tentatively, eyeing the riders and their lathered,
wild-eyed horses. "Who are these men?"

"I don't know," Sam said, "but from the looks
of them I'd say they're scalp hunters." As he spoke
he thought about the single small scalp that had
been hanging from Ozzie Cord's saddle horn
when he took him into custody.

Flake cupped a hand to his cheek. "We don't

need their kind around here. We're almost at peace with our red brethren."

Sam only looked at him for a moment. "Go on inside, Harold. I'll be back as soon as I can."

"But—but what are you going to do?" Flake asked, his hand still against his cheek as if in distress.

Sam just stared.

"All right, Ranger, I understand," Flake said as he backed away, turning toward the sheriff's office.

As dust settled along the street, onlookers gathered to peer into the saloon through the large wavy front windows. Others had drawn around the scalp hunters' horses and eyed the strips of human hair and finger bones entwined in leather and sinew hanging from their saddles. The tired, lathered desert horses snapped at the curious townsfolk like angry dogs. An arrow stub stood embedded in one of the horse's saddle cantle. Another horse carried a long bloody cut along its rump.

Seeing the Ranger approach, the onlookers at the door and windows made room for him to walk into the Old Senate.

"This blasted animal tried to bite me!" a man cried out as Sam entered the saloon and stopped and looked the five men, two of whom had fallen onto chairs at a card table. The other three had sprawled along the bar, shoving other drinkers aside and commandeering the mugs of beer and shots of whiskey they left abandoned.

"Who's the leader here?" Sam asked. He saw the bloody stub of another broken-off arrow sticking from the shoulder of one of the men seated at the table. The hunters turned their tired dust-coated faces toward him.

"That would be me, Sterling Childs. I'm the *segundo* of this bunch," said Childs. He straightened a little as a bartender poured him a fresh shot of rye. "What can I do for you, Marshal?"

"It's Ranger," Sam corrected, knowing that Territory Ranger was clearly lettered around the center of his five-point badge. "Where's the main leader?"

"He's busy right this minute," said Childs, "not taking any visitors." He turned more toward Sam with his shot glass in his left hand. "Can't talk to the number two in charge, huh, *Marshal*?"

Sam saw that calling him *Marshal* was this man's way of goading him a little. He let it go for now. He nodded at the man with the arrow stub in his shoulder.

"Looks like you've had some trouble with Apache," he said to Childs.

"We sure enough have," Childs said. "A band of wild Mescalero called the Wolf Hearts has been up our shirts the past week. Led by a school-learned fellow named Quetos. Nothing worse than an educated Injun—finally got up the nerve to hit us earlier today. Strictly bows and arrows. But out of twenty-four men, we've lost all but what you see here."

"You saw all the others die?" Sam asked.

"Most," said Childs. "There might be some

come straggling in. But I won't hold high hopes
for it."

"How close did the Apache follow you to town?"
he asked, looked all around at the five men.

"For all I know they might still be following
us," said Childs. "These Wolf Hearts are a bad
bunch. They seem to hate giving up their hair."
He gave an oily grin.

"So you're scalp hunters, then?" Sam asked flatly.

"We are that," said Childs. "But we're legal as
the day is long. We're contracted with the Mexican
government for all the scalps we can bring in."

"That's Mexico," Sam said. "I don't want to
think they're after you for killing Apache in the
territory and taking their scalps into Mexico for
bounty." He stared at Childs. Again the small,
fresh scalp hanging from Ozzie's saddle horn
crossed his mind.

"Why, we wouldn't do a thing like that, *Marshal*," said Childs feigning naive innocence. "That's
against the law." He gave the tired men a look;
they managed to grin among themselves.

Sam wasn't going to correct him again on calling him *Marshal*, seeing it to be the man's idea of
goading him. He'd wait for a better time—make
sure next time that he got the point across, even if
it took the end of his rifle butt to do it.

"What we ought to be talking about, *Marshal*,"
said Childs, "is that a band of heathens are coming this way, and just because they was shooting
arrows doesn't mean they don't have guns. It
might just mean they're saving bullets until they
get Mesa Grande in their gun sights."

Sam just looked at him, knowing he was right. But relations with the Apache, while always unpredictable, had grown less so over the past year. Local mining companies were armed, local settlers and their communities were dug in and ready. Reservation Apaches had settled down a lot. The wild roaming Apache bands had taken to the recluse hill country of Old Mexico. These scalp hunters had them stirred up, he was certain of it.

"The reason he's calling you *Marshal* is the sumbitch can't read nothing, Ranger," said the voice of Leon Fuller, who'd just stepped inside the saloon, Tom Dukes beside him.

Rage flashed across Childs' face. But Sam saw it dissipate as recognition set in. His rage turned into a slight grin.

"Well, well, look at what the pigs spit out," he said to his men, who were ready and waiting to draw iron.

What was this?

Sam stood firm and waited. On either side of him, Fuller and Dukes stepped into sight, each of them holding a sawed-off shotgun cocked and poised.

"Howdy, Leon," said Childs. He looked Fuller up and down. "My goodness, man, you've got a store-bought shirt and everything. Even got a badge pinned on it?"

"Yes, I do," said Fuller, wearing a wide grin. "This one says Deputy on it. See? Follow me." He raised a finger to the tin badge and said, "D-E-P-U—"

"A deputy, boys!" Childs said to his men. "Can

you believe this?" He cocked his head a little at Fuller. "So, you're no longer in the hair trade?"

"I left long ago," said Fuller. "My hands don't even smell like sour meat no more."

"Really?" said Childs. "Well, I'm sorry to hear that, Leon. If you want back in, we've always got a spot for you." As Childs spoke, Bud Shank, seated at the table, raised his fingers beneath his nose and gave a sniff.

"Obliged," said Fuller. "But I lost my taste for mule meat and buffalo chip tea." He paused and then said, "Anyway, I was just complaining to my pal Dukes here that it's been over a week since I shot somebody, and damn, here you come riding in."

"My, my, but look at the two of yas," said Childs, still grinning. "Clean shirts, shotguns cocked and pointed. All set to back this lawman, in *his* town."

Sam noticed the *Marshal* goad was gone. He watched and listened, not knowing what to make of Fuller and Dukes showing up on his side.

"Make no mistake, Sterling Childs, this is not *his* town," said Fuller. "Leastwise not for long. The sheriff here got shot and the Ranger is seeing to it we make a peaceful change of authority here. Sooner he's gone, the better, far as I'm concerned." He gave Sam a sidelong glance. "But while he's here, we decided we're still deputies. Right, Dukes?"

"Right as rain," said Dukes.

Sam hadn't been expecting this, but now that it had happened, he moved quick on it.

"Everybody, stay real peaceable here," he said to all parties. He stepped toward the side door leading upstairs. But once out of the saloon, instead of going straight up the stairs, he went outside to the alleyway and hurried back toward the sheriff's office.

Chapter 9

Both Shenny and Duckworth had just returned from carrying out the orders they'd been given by Curland when the office door burst open and Erskine Cord stepped inside. With his arrival the odor of woodsmoke and burnt grease from countless campfires filled the room. Dust rose from the shoulders of his buckskin shirt and spilled from his battered hat brim when he tipped it forward. He reached a fur-topped boot back and kicked the door shut.

"Gentlemen, don't get up," he said, even though the only one seated was Curland. The other two men stood at either end of his desk. Seeing the scalp hunter's hand resting on the butt of a long Colt holstered across his belly, Curland realized Cord's words were not a courteous gesture but rather an order. He made no effort to rise from his chair.

"I'm here for the rest of my money, Curland," Cord said, "and make it quick. I've got Apache riding up my shirt this minute."

Curland gave a move of his eyes and both Shenny and Duckworth rested their hands on their holstered Colts.

Seeing their move, Cord narrowed his eyes. His hand wrapped tight around his gun handle and cocked the hammer. But before he could make another move, Curland's right hand caught a hideout derringer by its handle, cocking it as it streaked out of the sleeve of his black linen suit coat.

"Let's talk about the *rest of your money*, Cord," Curland said, a hint of anger coming into his voice. "Have a seat." His words were not a gesture of courteousness either. Duckworth and Shenny drew their guns as he spoke.

Cord froze for a moment, weighing his chances— three guns to one—there in a small room. Finally he let out a breath, stepped sideways to a chair and sat down. Duckworth and Shenny stepped closer, flanking him. Duckworth leaned slightly, brushed Cord's hand aside and lifted the Colt from the belly holster.

"Careful with that shooting iron, son. She's a special hair trigger," said Cord.

With the gun aimed at Cord, Duckworth pulled the trigger but caught the hammer with his thumb and lowered it with a sharp smile.

"She sure does," he said as if in surprise. He let the gun hang in his free hand.

Curland lowered the derringer and stared coldly at the scalp hunter.

"There is no rest of your money, you turd," he said. "The sheriff's still alive. You can't imagine the consternation you've created here—you and your bungling *idiot nephew*."

"What, still *alive*?" said Cord. "How the hell can that be? I saw the bullet hit him dead center."

"Yes, it did," said Curland, "but it didn't kill him.

He's alive, in the doctor's house right this minute. The last I heard from the doctor, he's expected to *live.*"

"I don't believe it," said Cord. "I've seen what that rifle does to man or beast. He can't live with a hole in him big enough to throw an anvil through." He paused and looked at the three grim faces staring at him. "That's a little joke, boys, to lighten things up."

But the expressions didn't change.

"All right," said Cord, "here's the deal, then. Give me my money and I'll walk into his room at the doctor's house and put one through his head." He shrugged as if it were no big task.

"Your idiot nephew is in jail," said Curland, ignoring his offer. "Seems he got lost."

"He is here?" said Cord. It took a second for it to sink in. Then he said, "Well, I'm glad to hear it—"

"You shouldn't be," Curland said, cutting him off. "Ranger Sam Burrack is here, taking things over for the time being. If your nephew lets it out what the two of you did, it's not only your hides, it's mine too."

"He won't say anything," said Cord. "He knows if he did, I'd kill him, nephew or not." He paused, then said, "If this Ranger Burrack is the whole problem, I'll just kill him too on my way out of here and we'll be done with it."

"Sounds easy enough," said Curland. He gave Duckworth and Shenny a look. "Except that I'm not giving you another dollar until I've gotten what I paid for. And since you and Ozzie brought this Ranger into the game, you've got to kill him too."

Cord just stared at Curland, not liking to be told what he *had* to do.

"Let me tell you something, Curland," he said. He started to rise, but a hand on his shoulder shoved him down.

"No, let *me* tell you—" said Curland, but he stopped short as the door swung open again. This time, the Ranger stepped inside, a rolled-up blanket clamped under his left arm.

"Easy, everybody," he said. "I didn't come here looking for a fight." Yet, upon seeing guns already drawn and now pointed toward him, he stepped slowly over to Curland's desk and laid the rolled blanket down on it. "I'm here on law business."

Shenny and Duckworth both lowered their guns a little, taking the Ranger at his word. Yet as Sam stepped back from Curland's desk, they saw him raise his Colt calmly and easily from its holster. He cocked it and let it point toward them before either of them realized he'd just taken charge.

The two men looked at each other accusingly when it dawned on them that Sam had the drop on them.

"Why don't you both drop the bullets out of those shooters and ease them back down in your holsters?" Sam said in a quiet tone. "See if it doesn't help you live longer."

The two looked at each other again, but Curland let out a sigh and lowered his derringer to his desktop in submission.

"All right, men, do like he told you," he said. He shook his head slightly.

The two tipped their gun barrels to the ceiling, let the bullets fall to their feet and lowered their guns into their holsters.

"Now you," Sam said to Curland.

Curland sighed, broke his derringer open and let the two bullets fall onto his desk. Duckworth looked at Cord's gun in his hand as if not certain what to do with it.

"Empty it too," Sam said in the same quiet tone.

Duckworth opened the Colt's loading gate and let bullet after bullet fall to the floor. Then he laid the empty gun on Erskine Cord's dusty knee.

The Ranger stepped back over to the desk, unfolded the blanket and let Cord see both pieces of the big-bore English rifle lying there side by side.

"Put it together, Curland," he said. "Hand it to me."

He watched Curland snap the two pieces together and hold the rifle up to him, ready to load.

"Recognize this?" he asked Cord, taking the rifle, hanging it over his forearm. He'd figured out that this was Ozzie's uncle and the rifle belonged to him. The odds were long against a young fool like Ozzie owning such a fine firearm.

But to the Ranger's surprise, Cord let out a breath and gave a thin smile.

"I do sure enough, Ranger," he said. "It's my rifle—a rare one at that."

Sam just looked at him; so did the other three men.

"I thought I'd never see that beautiful gal again,"

said Cord. He started to rise from his chair toward the desk, but a look from the Ranger advised against it. "Truth is, a no-good thieving nephew of mine stole this rifle from me not long ago. I don't know how to thank you for bringing it back."

"You can thank me by accompanying me to jail," Sam said. As he spoke, his free hand went behind his back, brought a pair of handcuffs out and pitched them to Shenny.

"Cuff him, *Deputy*," he said.

In reflex, Shenny caught the cuffs. But then he gave Curland a curious look and froze for a moment. Duckworth, Curland and Cord all stared as if in disbelief. A tense silence set in until finally Curland broke it.

"Well, Deputy, what are you waiting for?" Curland said. "You heard the Ranger."

"Now, wait just a *damn minute*!" Cord protested, even as Shenny reached over and snapped the cuffs around both his wrists. He gave the Ranger a hard, vicious stare. "You are not taking me to jail, Ranger! I can't allow it to happen."

Listening, Sam took out two high-powered cartridges and shoved them into the double-barreled rifle and snapped it shut.

"Sure you can, scalp hunter," Sam said quietly, leveling the big rifle at Cord's chest. He nodded at Cord's cuffed wrists, the empty Colt on his lap. "We're halfway there already."

In the saloon, Fuller, Dukes and the five scalp hunters did not hear the footsteps of their leader, or the Ranger right behind him, both of them moving quietly down the stairs inside the enclosed stairwell. Sam kept his left hand gripping Cord's buckskin collar. In his right hand he carried the double rifle cocked and leveled, pressed against Cord's back just firm enough to let him know that one squeeze of the trigger would send him crashing through the plank enclosure wall.

At the top of the stairwell, Curland, Duckworth and Shenny stood staring down into the shadowy enclosure, watching both the Ranger and the scalp hunter stop at the lower landing and turn right, toward the rear of the building. At the bottom, a door opened into a long alleyway the length of the main street. The three waited and watched intently.

"Follow them," Curland said the second they saw daylight rise and fall with the open and close of the door.

"He warned us not to," Shenny reminded him.

"Follow them, *gawdamn* it," Curland growled. "Just stay out of sight. Help me keep a lid on this thing before we all get ourselves hanged!"

Duckworth and Shenny looked at each other grudgingly, neither man liking the idea of working together. But Duckworth saw no choice other than to follow orders, and neither did Shenny. Without a word more on the situation, they started down into the dark shadowy stairwell, keeping quiet themselves.

Moving along the alleyway toward the jail, the two kept to the side under the cover of crates, garbage barrels and public privies. They kept the

Ranger and Cord in sight, but kept out of sight themselves.

"I don't like how things are going," Shenny offered as they watched the Ranger and his prisoner turn the alley corner toward the side door of the sheriff's office.

Duckworth looked at him with suspicion, a man afraid to take the chance on speaking his mind. "The boss will get it straightened out," he said, again grudgingly. "Best thing we can do is keep our mouths shut and do our job. You're letting the Ranger get you overwrought. You can't take the pressure like some of us can."

"I can handle pressure as well as the next man," Shenny insisted.

Duckworth ignored his reply. "The Ranger can't stay here forever," he said. "He's got the whole territory to attend to. You would not want Joseph Curland to get wind of you talking this way." He eyed Shenny closely. "Come on, let's keep moving, 'less you're afraid of the Ranger."

Shenny eyed him right back. He saw he might have made a mistake thinking he could say something to a puppet like Duckworth and not have it reach Curland. But he moved right alongside with Duckworth. When they passed a pile of scrap iron behind the Mesa Grande Blacksmith Shop, he picked up a heavy two-foot-long iron billet bar and hefted it in his hand.

"I wasn't complaining, *Duck*," Shenny said, deliberately calling him the nickname Duckworth had warned him against using. "So you needn't twist a gut running to Curland with it." He held the iron bar back, tapping it idly against the back of his leg. In both directions the alley lay silent and empty.

"Call me *Duck* again, see if I don't do what your pa should have done the day you peeped out of the hole."

"Oh, and what would that be, *Bob*?" Shenny said calmly. He held a cold stare on Duckworth's eyes.

"I'll mash your damn head in and act as if you was never born," said Duckworth. His eyes flared angrily. "Now come on, *Deputy*," he said with a sneer, turning away from Shenny. "Let's follow them to the jail, hang around close and keep watch on—"

The first blow of the iron bar stopped Duckworth short. He crumbled down onto his knees, and tried to turn around toward Shenny. But the second blow of the bar came in on a sidelong swing and knocked him onto his side in the empty alley.

"There, *Duck*, how's that fit your style?" Shenny hissed, drawing the bar back for another vicious swing. "Oh, did I call you *Duck*?" He hit him again. "My mistake. I meant you *son of a bitch*."

Duckworth groped in the terrible darkness, barely conscious. His eyes fluttered for a last time and he tried to look up at Shenny. The deputy stood over him wielding the heavy bar like some baseball player at bat. Duck's mouth gaped open. Blood ran from his lips. He tried to utter something but couldn't form the words or get them spoken.

"What's that, *Duck*?" Shenny said. "Speak up."

He swung the bar and struck him a blow across his face. Duckworth's body went slack. The deputy drew the bar back up over his head and slammed it down hard atop Duckworth's head. "I can't hear you! Maybe you're . . . *overwrought* . . . under . . . too . . . much *pressure.*" He emphasized each word with another hard blow of the iron bar against Duckworth's skull.

He stopped swinging and staggered to the side, seeing Duckworth's crushed hat still atop his head, its crown turned red with blood spreading inside it.

"Pressure, *huh*?" He staggered, his breath heaving in his chest from the exertion of pounding Bob Duckworth's head into the ground. "Naw, Bob, no pressure here . . . not now anyway." He pitched the iron billet aside and looked down at the long strings and splatters of blood on his shirt, his hands and his boots. Well, he'd have to clean himself some, he told himself, no question about it.

He looked down again at Duckworth's battered head and wiped his bloody hands on his trousers. When he heard a hinge creak he looked up and saw a townsman standing at the open door of a privy twenty yards away. The man stood staring in horror, wide-eyed and stunned, one suspender up over his shoulder, the other still hanging at his side.

"Freeze! Stay where you are!" Shenny shouted. "Get your hands up. This is law business going on here." As he shouted he ran forward, his hand jerking his pistol from its holster and leveling it at the man.

Seeing the gun pointing at him, the man turned and darted away into a field full of waist-high wild grass.

"Stop, damn it! I'm the deputy!" shouted Shenny, running faster now, his Colt out at arm's length.

But upon hearing the click of an unloaded gun and a string of curses being shouted behind him, the man, Albert Atz, only ran faster. He bounded over rock and debris. Broken glass crunched under his boots.

"Good God!" he shouted aloud to a blue peaceful sky.

He whipped through the tall grass until he was past the town dump and stood winded and panting at the edge of the surrounding desert.

"*Good . . . God!*" he shouted again. He wheezed, squatting, palms on his knees, looking back, trying to catch his breath. He saw the deputy struggling, running, reloading his Colt as he negotiated stone, grass and broken whiskey bottles on his way. "Oh no!" He turned and tried to push himself into another run. But before he got started, he caught a glimpse of an Apache warrior rise from the grass and wrap himself around the running deputy and disappear as if into the earth with him. Not a sound from the deputy.

"Oh no! *Oh no! Oh no!*" Atz repeated mindlessly as he ran away even faster, a man who'd awakened into a living nightmare, driven by terror, by glimpses of what the Apaches would do if he fell into their hands.

He chanted and babbled and ran. Yet none of his efforts served to save him. As he reached a stretch of bare dusty ground, arrows streaked up out of the tall grass behind him. The wooden shafts stabbed into his back like the retaliation of an angered porcupine and stuck out of his chest as the last things he'd see as he fell to the ground.

Chapter 10

Atwater and Parker watched as the Ranger guided Erskine Cord into the jail cell with his nephew and locked the cell door behind him. Following the Ranger's order, Flake dropped a heavy bolt into place on the front door. Then he hurried around behind the desk and stood there looking awkward and out of place.

"The more the merrier, I always say." Parker chuckled, his hand gripping the iron bars loosely. Atwater stood beside him in the same position. They watched and listened to the heavy clink of the cell door next to them.

With the door locked, Sam raised the big double rifle up under his arm and kept guarded watch on Ozzie's reaction while he had Cord stick his wrists up close to the bars. Ozzie looked puzzled, yet strangely expectant, as if waiting to see what his uncle would require of him at any second.

"I told the Ranger here what you did, Ozzie, how you stole my sporting rifle and run off with it," Cord said without looking over his shoulder at Ozzie. He stared at the Ranger through the bars and rubbed his wrists as Sam withdrew the cuffs.

"But that's all forgiven, nephew. Name me one family that doesn't steal from one another a little. It's only natural." He gave a sly grin.

"Obliged, uncle," said Ozzie, getting into the spirit of things.

Sam shook his head a little, realizing that Ozzie was too dumb to see that going along with his uncle Erskine's ruse made him the one responsible for shooting the sheriff.

"Nothing like family, is there, Ranger?" Cord said, still wearing the sly grin.

"So I've heard," Sam replied.

With a word Sam knew he could have stopped the two from getting their story worked out between them, but he saw no point. The more they talked the better he would understand what had really happened. He'd already seen clearly that this man, Erskine Cord, would have been the one who pulled the trigger. There was no way he would have trusted Ozzie to do any shooting. From what he'd seen of Ozzie Cord, the bungling young man would have blown his own foot off.

"How long do you figure you'll be able to hold me in this iron box, Ranger?" Cord asked. He took the bars in his hands and shook them a little as if testing them.

"Until the judge makes it here," Sam said, taking a step back. Instead of hanging the keys on the wall peg he stuck them into his hip pocket for safekeeping. He lowered the big rifle from under his arm and looked at it, turning it back and forth in his hands. "I'm sure this is the rifle that did the shooting. The judge and a jury will decide who pulled the trigger."

"You misunderstood my question, Ranger," said Cord. "I meant how long do you figure before my men come and level this jail and get me out?"

"Obliged for the warning, Cord," Sam said.

Listening, Flake stepped around from behind the desk and walked over beside the Ranger. He stared back and forth between Ozzie and Erskine Cord as if in awe.

"Ranger, you mean these two men are the assassins—I mean the *attempted* assassins?"

"That's how it looks to me, Flake," Sam said. "It'll be up to the judge and jury now." He gave Flake a sidelong glance. "I need you to stay quiet about it, at least until the town has settled on letting the law handle the particulars."

"Ha, *the law* . . . ," Cord said, sneering. He turned away from the bars.

"Oh, I will keep quiet, to be sure, Ranger," said Flake. He took a breath and smoothed down the front of his suit vest. "May I go now?"

"Yes, you can go," Sam said. "Obliged for all your help. Mesa Grande should thank you and Ison Prine for all your service."

Flake's face reddened.

"We've both just done what any good citizens should do, Ranger Burrack," he said. He leveled his shoulders proudly. "Are you sure you won't need me to stay longer? I have nothing else planned for the rest of the day—"

Behind him a loud pounding on the bolted front door sent him almost leaping into the Ranger's arms.

"Easy, Flake," Sam cautioned. He caught him by his forearms and steadied him.

"Oh my goodness, I'm sorry," Flake said nervously. "This whole town is strung tighter than an Alabama banjo." He collected himself quickly, followed the Ranger to the front door. "I don't know how you've stayed so calm and unshaken by everything."

"Part of the job," Sam said over his shoulder as he reached for the door bolt, the double rifle still in hand.

Seeing the bolt lifted, Flake took the opportunity to make his exit.

"Well, then," he said, "perhaps I will just mosey on, as they say." He offered a tight, still shaky smile and touched the brim of his derby hat.

"Hold on, Flake," Sam said, taking a peep through a crack between the thick door boards. "I might just be needing you after all." He opened the door wide enough to see Fuller and Dukes staring at him.

Seeing the two half-angry faces, Flake paled, sorry he hadn't kept his mouth shut about offering to stay.

"Oh dear," he murmured to himself.

Seeing the double rifle pointed at their bellies, Dukes took a fast sidestep.

"Whoa!" he said.

But Fuller stood firm, seeing the rifle wasn't cocked. He and Dukes still carried the shotguns in their hands.

"Burrack, what the hell?" he said, barely keeping his temper under control. "You left us standing there like fools waiting for you to come back down."

"Things took a turn," said Sam. He nodded

back over his shoulder. "I've got Erskine Cord in a cell."

"We know you do," said Fuller. "Curland finally came down and told everybody what you did." As he spoke he looked over Sam's shoulder toward the cells. While he looked in at the cells, the Ranger looked along the street toward the Old Senate Saloon.

"Don't worry," Fuller said, "the scalpers will be coming soon enough. Curland's getting them worked up. They're loading their guns and their gullets right now."

"Where do you two stand?" Sam asked.

"We stand wherever Denton Shenny tells us to stand," Fuller said.

"And if Curland tells you otherwise?" Sam asked, staying in the narrowly opened doorway.

The two gunmen turned deputies looked at each other, then back at the Ranger.

"We came here working with Denton Shenny. We don't take orders from Curland unless they come to us from Shenny." He paused, then looked around inside over Sam's shoulder. "Where is he anyway?"

"Beats me," said Sam. He glanced again toward the Old Senate. Flake stood nervously behind him.

"Are you going to let us in, or what?" Fuller asked.

"I'm not letting anybody in just yet," Sam said. "But I want everybody in Mesa Grande to understand—"

"Jesus, Ranger, we're *deputies*!" Dukes cut in. He thumbed the tin star on his chest. "Denton Shenny said so."

"Hush up, Dukes," said Fuller. "He knows we're deputies in name only." He gave Sam a stare. "No more need to pretend, is there, Ranger?"

The Ranger didn't reply. Instead he continued on as if he hadn't been interrupted.

"I want *everybody* to understand," he said. "I've got Erskine Cord and his nephew in a cell, and they're not coming out until trial time. Anybody tries taking them out of here for any reason . . . " He hefted the double rifle. ". . . I'll give them both barrels."

Fuller started to speak, but stopped at the sound of a woman's voice as she raced up the middle of the dirt street.

"Oh my God!" shouted Flake, trying to push his way past the Ranger to make a run for it.

Sam gave him a shove back inside.

"Stay here, Flake. It's safer," he said. "Bolt this door behind me."

As the woman neared the sheriff's office, two townsmen sprang forward and grabbed her to pull her out of the street—a street that was emptying quickly. Sam stepped out between Fuller and Dukes and looked west along the dusty thoroughfare where seven Apache warriors sat atop the horses, rifles standing in their laps. There were others behind them, uncountable in the stir of dust. The one in the middle of the front line had a dirty piece of white thin-striped cloth tied to the end of his rifle barrel.

"Damn it, what now?" said Fuller as if personally offended by the presence of the Indians.

"They're here under a white flag," said Sam, staring at the Indians. "They've come to palaver."

"I'll *palaver* them," Fuller said menacingly, the shotgun he'd carried to the saloon still in his hands.

"What are we going to do, Ranger?" a townsman shouted at the Ranger from the doorway of the town barbershop.

The Ranger looked back and forth between Fuller and Dukes. Both men stood firm, staring coldly back at the Apache warriors.

"Get yourselves armed," Sam called back to the townsman. He walked across the boardwalk, onto the street, Fuller and Dukes flanking him. The two were on his side now, he noted, now that it came down to life or death at the hands of these merciless desert fighters.

The Apache horsemen sat stonelike, watching the Ranger and the two would-be deputies walk toward them and stop fifteen feet away from the leader. The street behind the three had emptied quickly, a ghost town now save for the faces staring out through dusty window glass, around edges of buildings and along the rooflines. The first thing the Ranger took note of among the Apaches was the shiny newer-looking repeating rifles that stood propped up in each warrior's fist. Bandoleers of ammunition crisscrossed their chests.

A show of strength, Sam told himself.

The leader looked at the big rifle in the Ranger's hands and at the shotguns in the hands of the men on either side of him.

"I am Quetos, chosen leader of the Wolf Hearts,"

the leader said in strong, confident English. "We bear the white man's sign of peace." He let the Ranger see him eye the shotguns and the big double rifle. Sam let him look for a second; then he nodded for the two deputies to lower the shotguns, as he did likewise with the rifle.

Quetos kept his eyes on the Ranger as he waved a rider forward out of the band. The rider rode forward, leading a horse carrying two bodies across its back. Sam and the two watched as the rider stopped and dragged the bodies from the horse's back and let them flop to the ground. One was Denton Shenny, a sleeve of his thin-striped shirt missing. The other man was townsman Albert Atz, an engineer for a French-Mexican mining exploration company. Fuller and Dukes both stiffened at the sight of Shenny lying dead in the dirt. Atop the bodies, the warrior flung down a coiled length of telegraph line. Then he turned his horse and heeled its sides and rode back into the ranks.

"We attacked a band of scalp hunters in the hills, and they ran from us," said Quetos. "The leader and some of his men ran here to hide." He gestured at the length of telegraph line. "We have cut the talking wires." He turned his gaze to the dead lying on the ground. "This is what will happen to anyone who comes or goes from Bloody Night unless you give us those men who killed our women and children and took their hair." He looked all around the storefronts, houses and tents, knowing the townsfolk were armed and nervous. "We chased them here with arrows. Now we come here with rifles and bullets."

Bloody Night? The Ranger realized the Apache had different names for most places, names that had been used long before any white man had even stepped foot on this harsh arid land. But he'd never heard Mesa Grande called Bloody Night. He stared at Quetos, knowing the educated man had used the name intentionally, showing defiance of the white man's rule.

"The men you're talking about are here," Sam said, realizing this man's warriors had done their job reconnoitering the town. "But their lives are not mine to give you."

"You wear the badge of law on your chest. You can give them to me."

"I wear a badge, but it doesn't give me the right or the power to forfeit men's lives."

"I have lived with your white men and gone to your schools and seen how things are," said Quetos. "I have seen lawmen like you lead men like these to the gallows for killing their own kind. I will do that to these men for killing my kind—for killing Apache and selling their hair to the Mexicans."

"I can see how standing here talking all day won't reconcile what governments do or why they do it," Sam said. "I'm here to keep the peace. That's what I'll do." He stood firm. "That's all the power of the law allows me to do."

Fuller sidled a step closer to Sam and whispered sidelong to him as the Apache leader and his warriors watched, the ragged white-striped cloth swaying on a slow, hot breeze.

"Shoot him now, Ranger!" Fuller whispered. "While you've got the chance."

"He's carrying a flag of truce, Fuller," Sam whispered back, shooting the deputy a harsh warning glare.

"Yeah, and it's made out of Shenny's shirt-sleeve," Fuller hissed. "Kill this son of a—!"

"Shut up," Sam said, cutting him off. He looked back at Quetos, not sure how long he'd be able to hold Fuller, Dukes and the rest of the town back. He knew that by now there would be rifles at every window, along every roofline. "If that's all you came to palaver about, I think we're done," he said. "Leave *Mesa Grande*." He wasn't going to warn him, mention that the town and the two deputies were ready to explode into a hail of gunfire. He didn't have to; Quetos was no fool, he already knew it.

But Quetos only stared at him. *A poker player those years living in white society?* Sam wondered.

"This place was called *Bloody Night* before white people came, and it will be Bloody Night once again. When I leave, all of you here will die. This is the vow of a Wolf Heart," Quetos said, speaking loud enough for the townsfolk to hear him. "When we come back we will kill those who killed our people and those who protected them. That is my vow."

Quetos had misread these people. They wouldn't turn the scalp hunters over to him, not when they had him in their rifle sights.

But Quetos didn't make any move toward leaving. Instead he stared at Sam and said, "I rode

here under a white flag because my warrior Bad
Eyes said the lawman who killed the half-breed
Wilson Orez with his own knife is here. That he is
a man to respect, whose word is good."

Sam didn't reply; he only stared. Quetos knew
he was that lawman. And yes, he did kill Wilson
Orez in a knife fight. But not with his own knife.
In fact, to keep Orez from killing him graveyard
dead, he'd had to resort to taking up his Colt and
shooting the man. But from there the rumor had
grown.

"I told Bad Eyes that I must come see this lawman for myself, because, well, as you can see . . . "
He sighed and tipped his rifle barrel a little
toward an older warrior seated on his horse three
horses to his right. The warrior wore a large dusty
monocle, held to his left eye by a strip of rawhide
around his forehead. His left eye looked huge
behind the thick reading glass; his right eye looked
small and beady by comparison.

"I understand," Sam said. "It's true I am that
lawman. My word is good. That's why when I tell
you I'm not giving anybody up here whether I
agree with what they did or not, you can trust my
words."

Quetos' face hardened.

"Then we *are* through talking, lawman," he said.
He stared at Sam as his hand grabbed the cloth on
the end of his rifle barrel.

Seeing what he was about to do, Sam tensed.

"No, wait," he shouted, hoping to stop the
Apache leader. But it did no good. Quetos yanked
the cloth from his rifle barrel and slung it to the

ground. Both he and his warriors started to turn their horses almost before the cloth touched the earth. In a split second, the dirty white-striped shirt sleeve dropped to the ground and gunfire erupted from every direction.

Chapter 11

The Ranger heard the shotguns in the deputy's hands fire into the turning Indians as one. Rifle and gunfire from the storefronts and rooflines roared. Sam had to run out of the middle of the street or risk getting shot himself by the townsfolk. The Apaches had turned, trying to ride out of town on the main street, but the heavy gunfire wouldn't allow it.

Over two dozen warriors hurriedly dispersed as they rode, crowding into alleyways and between houses and businesses for cover along the side streets. Sam saw Quetos slump on his horse's back, having been pelted by stray buckshot. But the leader still fought. He turned, looked at Sam and fired behind at him and the deputies as his horse pounded away.

Sam ducked down onto one knee and took aim with the double rifle. He didn't want to shoot Quetos, but the battle had commenced and Quetos had singled him out and fired at him. He was caught in the fight now; he had no choice. He took aim and fired back at Quetos. But he saw a warrior ride between them at the last second as he squeezed the trigger. The rifle roared like a small cannon. The hapless warrior, horse and all, went down as the big bullet flung them tumbling in the impact of its powerful thrust. They rolled sideways, knocking down another rider before sliding to a halt. Sam fired the second barrel and watched the middle of a warrior's back appear to break in half in a large looming mist of blood.

"Take cover!" Sam shouted at the two deputies, seeing the Apaches had taken positions and were now firing back what seemed an endless volley of repeating rifles. Fuller and Dukes, both reloading their shotguns, didn't have to be told twice. Bullets whistled past the two like angry hornets. They turned and ran, shotguns in hand, but drawing their Colts for immediate return fire. Sam ran too.

One of the warriors still racing along the narrower street flew sidelong from his horse in a spray of blood; another one leaped from his falling horse, grabbed another warrior's hand and swung up behind him. With the Apaches either gone from town or now behind cover, Sam realized that as long as the town kept firing the Indians had no choice but to remain there and keep fighting.

Running, Sam slid into an alleyway beside the two deputies and sprang to his feet against the side of a clapboard building. He saw Dukes squeeze his loosened bandanna against a bullet graze on his forearm, his shotgun reloaded now and in hand. Fuller began firing his Colt madly around the corner edge of the building.

"Stop shooting, Deputy," Sam said, leaning the empty double rifle against the side of the building.

"Like hell," said Fuller. "The only way I ever

heard of winning a gunfight is to shoot back." He fired as he spoke. "You know a new and better way?"

"Yes, I do," said Sam. He'd counted Fuller's shots. When the sixth one exploded, he reached over and clamped a hand over the Colt's barrel. Fuller gave him a cold stare and tried to twist the gun free. But Sam held firm. "Stop firing long enough to let them get out of here. You saw all those bandoleers. They can stay here a long time if they have to. But they want out. Let them go."

"I didn't see it that way," said Fuller. "If this Quetos didn't want a fight he shouldn't have thrown down the truce flag."

"The Ranger's right, Leon," said Dukes. "Apache don't want to fight in a place like this. How many times you ever hear of them doing it? They can't leave with us pinning them down."

"Oh, I see," Fuller said with bitter tone. "Everybody's turnt into a damn Apache expert now?"

"Listen," said the Ranger, directing their attention toward the lull of gunfire coming from the townsfolk as many of them had to stop and reload. With the firing from the storefronts and buildings waning, so did the fire from the Apaches.

"So what?" said Fuller. "All that means is . . ." He paused for a second as if searching for the rest of his answer. When he didn't find it, he said, "All right, maybe they do want out of here." He lowered his smoking Colt and opened the loading gate when the Ranger took his hand from around it. "I'm reloading anyway, in case you two *experts* are wrong."

As he reloaded, and the firing from the townsfolk

remained in a lull, Sam and Dukes looked toward the end of the alleyway at the sound of horses' unshod hooves pounding away on the desert floor.

"Easy, now, folks, let them go," Sam said under his breath as if speaking directly to the townsfolk. He looked back at Fuller and Dukes. "Let's give them a minute, let them wind down some," he said. The gunfire from the Apaches diminished even more; the townsfolk as well.

The three stood tense and listened as more hooves headed out away from town and gunfire from the streets lessened.

"All right," Sam said, leaning forward from against the building. "Maybe they can hear me now." He stepped just out of the alleyway onto the edge of the street. Holding his Colt high over his head, he waved it back and forth.

"Hold your fire," he shouted along a looming layer of gray gun smoke hanging in the air.

It took a moment for the townsfolk to all comply with his order. Sporadic rifle shots exploded as townsfolk joined in, shouting, relaying his command at one another until at length the street lay silent between two drifting clouds of smoke.

"They're gone!" a voice shouted. "We ran those heathens out of here! *Yahoooo!*"

Cheers rose along the street. Townsfolk ventured out. Sam and the two deputies hurried to the rear of the alley and watched the last of the Apaches disappear out of sight over a rise toward the desert floor.

"Figure they'll be back, Ranger?" Fuller asked, a little more willing to listen now that he'd seen the Ranger was right.

"Maybe, maybe not," Sam said, still gazing out, scanning the flatlands. "He said these men are part of the group. Maybe they'll go after the others first. They see this town is armed and not afraid to fight."

Fuller only nodded.

"I say they'll be back," said Dukes. "They won't leave this town alone as long as Erskine Cord and his men are here."

"Yeah, why didn't you hand them over?" said Fuller. "Nobody gives a damn about scalp hunters, except maybe some buzzards that's gotten attached to them."

"That's not how it works," Sam said.

As the two turned and walked back through the alley toward the street, a townsman appeared and waved his rifle back and forth.

"Ranger, you'd better come quick!" he shouted. "There's been trouble at the jail!"

Sam broke into a trot; the two deputies caught up with him, hurrying along a few feet behind him.

"What kind of trouble at the jail?" Dukes called back to the man.

The man continued waving his rifle back and forth. Two other men gathered beside him.

"It's *empty*! That's what kind of trouble," the man shouted. "The whole place is empty and the back end has been yanked out of it!"

"I'm glad we're not *really* lawmen," Dukes said quietly to Fuller as they trotted along behind the Ranger.

"Me too," said Fuller. "There ain't a way in the world I'd do this job."

As the three ran on toward the jail, Joseph

Curland walked across the empty, smoky dirt street and stood over the body of Denton Shenny. He held an unfired rifle in his hands. He studied Shenny's bloody body for a moment, then looked out toward the desert floor. Shenny's death was one more minor setback to be sure, he told himself. But it was nothing he couldn't work around. He just hoped the Apaches and the scalp hunters would ride off somewhere and kill one another.

Good riddance. . . . He took out a cigar, bit the end off and spit it away. Then he put the cigar between his teeth for later, turned and walked to the Old Senate Saloon.

"Fine work defending our town, everybody," he called out as he walked. "Come on to the Old Senate Saloon. The first round of drinks is *on the house!*"

That was that, he told himself. Erskine Cord and his idiot nephew were gone. He no longer had to worry about the Ranger connecting them to him. The Ranger wasn't foolish enough to go chasing seasoned scalp hunters, who just happened to have a band of Apache on their trail. He grinned to himself. "Adios, *Cord,* he murmured aloud, gazing out toward the distant desert hill line.

It was late evening when the fleeing scalp hunters lined their horses along the edge of a stone-lined water hole up on the bottom slope of a boulder-clad hillside. Erskine Cord and Sterling Childs had led the men on a hard ride on already tired horses. They'd had no choice. There were only four fresh horses in the livery barn and they hadn't found much to pick from at the hitch rails along the street while rifle fire filled the air. For the most part the men had ridden out on the same horses they'd ridden in on.

Bud Shank had led the four fresh horses out of the livery barn, but the Ranger's black-point copper dun had managed to rear up and pull free of the others' horses and make a run for it. There had been no time to chase the dun down. Instead the scalp hunters had mounted their tired horses, ridden behind the jail, tied four lariats to a barred window and yanked the entire frame out of the wall. They left the lariats lying in the dirt and had forced a trembling wide-eyed Harold Flake atop one of the three horses against his will.

"What about us?" Parker had asked Cord, seeing his and Atwater's chance to make a break. Cord had considered it for a second, then grinned.

"Sure," Cord had replied, "like you said when the Ranger jailed me, 'The more the merrier. . . .'"

Now, at the water hole, resting the horses and themselves for the first time since racing away on a back trail out of Mesa Grande, Cord and Childs leaned back against a boulder and slapped dust from their buckskins. Childs came up with a dusty bottle of rye, brushed it off with his hand, pulled the cork and handed the bottle to Cord.

"Let me buy you a drink, boss," he said as Cord took the bottle eagerly.

"I don't mind if you do, Sterling," Cord said.

Childs watched his boss raise the bottle to his parched lips and drink deeply.

"There's a bottle of whiskey in your hand, boss," he said, reminding Cord of what he'd said only a few days ago.

"Yeah . . . ," said Cord reflectively, lowering the bottle and staring at it, swirling it slowly. "You mean about Ozzie? Why I hold him so special? About the falling-out between his pa and me?"

"Yep," said Childs, "this is as good a time as any."

Cord let out a breath and spoke to the whiskey bottle instead of Childs.

"Ozzie's pa—my brother Grayson—used to be what you might call a backstabber. That caused our falling-out."

"I know that kind of kin," said Childs, "the kind who's always running their mouth, belittling a man when he ain't around to speak up for himself?"

"No," Cord said firmly, still swirling the whiskey. "I mean he *stabbed me*, three times in the back with a two-prong meat fork. Tried for my neck but missed. Nearly killed me."

"Whoa," said Cord, listening intently. "No wonder there was a falling-out."

Cord nodded and let out another breath.

"Once I was up and around, I waited my chance. When he wasn't expecting it, I tried killing him with an ironmonger's hammer. But he managed to duck when I swung it at him. His poor wife, Judith Belle, was standing behind him. Misfortune reared its head and I mistakenly smacked her right between the eyes. Knocked her cold as a gawdamn icicle—thought sure I'd killed her."

"Jesus . . . ," Childs murmured. He stared down and shook his head.

"She had Ozzie in her belly at the time I dealt

that hammer blow, but luckily she come to right before Easter when Ozzie was born," Cord said. "We always felt the incident marked the little fellow. . . ." He paused for a moment. "So I've always held the boy special, tried to make things up to him, I suppose you could say." He took another drink and passed the bottle back to Childs.

"That's a hell of a thing, boss," said Childs. He took a swig himself and corked the dusty bottle. "But I have to say, your hands were clean after what your brother done to you."

"I know, I know," Cord said reflectively. "I have reconciled it to myself, and between me and Grayson. Yet Poor Judith Belle and Ozzie . . ." As he spoke he looked over to where Ozzie stood beside Harold Flake, the two watering their horses. "They say she was never again to walk a straight line without it veering into a circle after so far." He straightened from against the boulder and stretched his legs and arms. "But enough of my bygone family troubles."

"What do you want to do with those three?" Childs asked, nodding at Parker, Atwater and Flake.

"Well," said Cord, "we both know Quetos will not rest until he kills himself some scalp hunters. He left town headed the other way, going for the ones of us who escaped in that direction." He nodded toward the distant hill line across the flatlands. "But he'll right his course once he knows we're out here."

"That's safe to say," said Cord. "It's safe to say he could be sniffing in our direction right now."

"True, he could, but we've got a contract for scalps we need to be filling. We can't back off.

Risk is part of the job. So we're going to dress these three daisies up and dangle them in front of him, see if we can't lure some Wolf Hearts and cut some hair," Cord said, looking the three unsuspecting men over, sizing them up as he spoke. "See if that'll sate ol' Quetos' thirst for blood and make us some money at the same time."

"Good thinking, boss," said Childs. He stepped forward and called out to the water hole, pointing from Parker, to Atwater, to Flake.

"You, you and you. Get over here," he said. He stood watching as the three handed their horses' reins to Ozzie and hurried over.

"Before you say anything," Parker said, holding up a hand. "Cero and myself just want to tell you how obliged we are, you bringing us along with you."

"Get your clothes off," Childs demanded abruptly.

"Get our *clothes off . . . ?*" Parker said. He and Cero looked themselves up and down as if they'd misunderstood him. Flake stood trembling, too frightened to fully understand anything.

"You heard me—get them off! Boots too!" Childs demanded, his Colt coming up from its holster cocked and pointed.

Beside Childs, Erskine Cord grinned cruelly at Harold Flake as he started undressing himself.

"We're going to have us some fun, townsman," Cord said, untying his buckskin shirt at the neck in order to pull it over his head.

"Oh no! Please no!" Flake whined, a sick look coming over his face. "I beg you, sir—"

"Shut the hell up, mister!" said Parker. "Can't you see they're going to trade clothes with us?"

As soon as he spoke he turned quickly to Cord with a questioning look. "That's all, ain't it?"

Ignoring Parker, Cord said to the trembling Flake, "Get them clothes off. I'm sending you three phildoodles on a little errand." He bent, raised a foot and pulled off a dusty boot and threw it to the ground in front of Flake. The frightened townsman jumped back as if it were a snake.

"Get them off, *fool!*" shouted Cord. "Do I have to undress you myself?"

Harold hurriedly peeled off article after article of clothes and piled them in front of himself. When he'd finished he stood in a one-piece pair of cotton undershirt shorts, his hands cupped soundly on his crotch.

Cord looked him up and down dubiously and shook his head. "If ol' Quetos falls for this he might not be smart enough to be an Apache," he chuckled.

"You're sending us out to get us killed, aren't you?" said Parker.

"Well, yes, 'More-the-merrier,'" said Cord. "What other use have I got for you?"

Chapter 12

It was after dark when the Ranger rode out of Mesa Grande on his copper dun. He'd loaded a canvas bag of supplies by lantern light and saddled the dun and strapped the bag on the back of a spare horse that the town blacksmith owned. Joseph Curland stood off to the side with two other gunmen who worked for him now and then, when he had dirty work he needed done.

"Ranger, what about the welfare of this town?" he called out in the lit open door of the livery barn. He spoke loud enough for the gathered townsfolk to hear him—like a man campaigning for office, Sam thought, listening as he prepared for the trail.

"What about it?" Sam said in a short tone.

"If the Apache come back, Mesa Grande needs you here, protecting its citizens, not traipsing around somewhere out in the hills between here and Mexico."

"I've got prisoners escaped, Curland," Sam said. "The Apache won't be interested in Mesa Grande once they realize the scalp hunters are gone."

"Quetos vowed to kill us all," Curland said.

"He wants the scalp hunters, Curland," Sam said. "Don't make this bigger than it is."

"If he strikes us in the night, how will he know they're not still here?" Curland persisted.

"I expect he knows it already," said Sam. "This is his country. He doesn't miss much."

"That's no answer, Ranger," Curland said. "I must insist that you stay here where we need you."

"Insist all you want, I'm going after my prisoners. Don't forget he's got Harold Flake as a hostage. How do you think that's going to turn out?" He gave Curland a grim look as he rolled the double rifle in his bedroll and laid it behind his saddle and tied it down. "Besides," he said, "you've got a fair gift for gab. If Quetos comes back, you can tell him they're gone. Offer them drinks on the house."

"What is that, some far-handed joke, Ranger?" Curland said, feigning anger for the sake of the onlookers.

"I don't get a lot of joke time, Curland," Sam said, checking his Winchester and shoving it down into his saddle boot. "You've got these two here. Use them," he said, nodding at Fuller and Dukes, who stood to the side watching everything. "I've seen they're stand-up gunmen." Fuller and Dukes both carried bandages from the gunfight. Dukes' forearm was in a sling.

"It's not just Mesa Grande I'm thinking about, Ranger," Curland said, taking another approach. "What about you? We don't want you killed out there." He gestured toward the two gunmen beside him. "At least take Buck and Willard with you."

Sam gave Fuller and Dukes a look. They looked away, which was enough to let him know what Curland had in mind.

"I'm obliged for all your concern, Curland," he said. "But I think I'll play this out myself." He looked Willard Sives and Buck Longhand up and down. "The two of you are warned here and now. I catch you on my back trail, I'll stop long enough to use you both for firing practice."

The short, sandy-haired Willard Sives stepped forward, a bristly air about him.

"That's a hell of a thing for you to say to us, Burrack. We're not bushwhackers."

"That's good to hear," Sam said. "You've still been warned. Don't let me see you out there. I might get the idea you lied to me."

"Why, you—" Sives wrapped his hand around his holstered Colt and looked ready to pull it up into play.

"Easy, Willard," said Curland. "This town has lost Bob Duckworth and our new deputy. Let's keep cool heads here."

"There's a voice of reason," Sam said flatly. He gathered the lead rope to the spare horse, a big strapping speckled barb. With the lead rope in hand, he gathered the dun's reins and swung up into the saddle. "I'll be back when I've got my prisoners," he said. He touched the brim of his sombrero toward the townsfolk, but he gave Curland a hard look. "It'll be interesting hearing what this assassin's got to say."

The Ranger traveled throughout the night under the assistance of a bright half-moon and a purple sky full of stars as bright as silver dust and diamonds. It wasn't hard to pick up the trail of the scalp hunters, his other prisoners and the townsman Flake. The hoofprints of that many horses, especially that many horses at a hard pace, had a way of taking over a trail and flattening all other prints beneath them. It was apparent that the scalp hunters were not doing what Sam decided reasonable men might do. They were not trying to get away from the Apaches as fast as they could.

No, these men were skirting the Apaches, toying with them. Getting away from Quetos and his warriors but staying close like buffalo hunters following the herd or big dangerous game, hunters whose prey they reconciled as merely one more challenge in their deadly profession.

Erskine Cord and his band of buckskinned, fur-clad miscreants had more to fear from white man's law than they did from the Indians. *If they feared anything at all,* Sam reasoned, stepping down from his saddle in the grainy dawn light at the edge of a cliff high where the horses bunched in close and turned almost single file from the high trail down toward the flatlands. The Apaches were a way of life for men like Cord. Dying by their hands must be as commonplace to him as a cave dweller dying from snakebite.

As Sam considered the scalp hunters and gazed down at the desert floor in the thin early light, he caught the faintest whiff of woodsmoke wafting on the morning air behind him. Knowing that the men he pursued would be on the desert floor most of the day regardless which direction they rode, he turned and looked off along the hill trail in the direction of the wood scent. Someone was along the hill trail, he told himself.

It was worth checking, he decided. Turning the copper dun and leading the speckled barb close beside him, he rode farther along the high trail, seeing it better now that all the fresh hoofprints had turned off and no longer covered it over. The hooves had obscured a set of wagon tracks that Sam immediately associated with Ison Prine.

Looking all around the rugged high trail terrain, he had to ask himself what the teamster had in mind. What would have made him choose taking this high dangerous trail instead of the safer trail that edged around the desert floor? Only one word came to mind: *Apache*.

Had Prine seen Quetos' Wolf Hearts crossing the desert flatlands, taking to this higher ground might have bought him some time, Sam thought. Especially since Quetos had already drawn his sights on Mesa Grande, knowing the scalp hunters were there.

Sam nudged the dun along the trail, leading the speckle, catching a stronger smell of woodsmoke now than he had only moments earlier. As he rode he instinctively reached his hand down, cocked the Winchester lying across his lap, lifted it away from under his reins and let it hang poised down the dun's side.

Wary of both scalp hunters and Apache Wolf Hearts, he followed the trail farther into the smell of smoke, noting that the smoke had taken on a smell of cooked meat. He stopped the horses and stepped down as the wagon tracks cut upward onto a terraced flat crown of wild grass and brush.

He led the horses onto the widened terrace and moved forward, seeing a slow rise of gray smoke a hundred yards ahead of him.

The sight of the smoke brought him no comfort. Nobody made camp in the open like this— nobody who wanted to stay alive, he told himself. Moving forward with caution, he kept a close watch on the waist-high grass and brush for any sudden movement. At the welcoming shelter of a large land-stuck boulder, he stopped long enough to judge the remaining distance to the woodsmoke.

Seventy-five yards, a hundred maybe . . . ? Thereabouts, he told himself.

He had started to take the horses forward when he heard a faint scuffling of boots atop the boulder. Luckily he'd heard the sound just in time. As he looked up twelve feet, he saw the figure of a man leaping out into the sunlight and down toward him like a mountain cat.

Sam managed not to take the full force of the attack, but he did fall backward as the man landed on the ground instead of him. Sam's Winchester flew from his hands. The two fell backward, grappling, rolling. Sam saw a melon-sized rock draw back in the man's hand, but he caught the wrist before the rock came down onto his face. Holding the rock and wrist at bay, Sam came up with his Colt and gave a hard swipe of the barrel across the man's bloody, dirt-streaked face. The blow didn't knock the man out, but it stunned him and sent the rock falling from his hand. As he wallowed facedown in the dirt trying to collect himself, Sam jumped back, crouched and looked around quickly for any other attackers, cocking his Colt in reflex. He hurriedly grabbed the reins and the lead rope to settle the horses.

As he reached out with the Colt at arm's length, he saw the man turn over onto his back.

"Don't make a move," he warned, keeping his tone low, not wanting to risk a shot up here, with Quetos and his warriors everywhere. He saw this man was dressed in mining boots, trousers and a bloodstained linsey-woolsey work shirt. Then he recognized the bloody face, the wirelike beard as the man faced him from on the ground. "Prine?" he said.

"Ranger . . . ?" said the teamster, both of them equally surprised. Prine let himself fall back on the ground in relief. "Thank God it's you." He closed his eyes for a second, squeezed them shut, then batted them open. "Thank God you seen me coming up there before I stove your head in," he added.

"Lucky for us both," Sam said. Uncocking the Colt in his hand, he lowered it to his side. He took Prine's hand and helped pull him to his feet. "What happened out here?" He gestured toward the thin woodsmoke. Even as he asked, he believed he already knew the answer.

"Apache, is what happened out here," said Prine. He dusted his bloody shirtfront as if dusting was all it took. "This is as far as I made it. I spotted them following me, got off the hardpan and made it up here before they got to me." He panted, trying to catch his breath.

Sam reached over, unhooked a canteen from

his saddle horn, took the cap off and handed it to him. Prine drank the tepid water like a man just back from hell. Then he poured a trickle on his bare, ragged head and let it run down his parched, bruised face.

"Why didn't they kill you?" Sam asked, taking back the canteen, capping it.

"No fault of theirs," Prine said. He managed a thin, grim smile with cracked lips. "I fought them off best I could. Seen I wasn't getting nowhere. I jumped off the bluff over there and let them have the rig and mules. Must've rolled and tumbled a hundred foot." He wiped his hand around on his wet, battered face. "The fall is what bested me, not the Apache," he added. He pointed toward the curl of smoke. "Come on, I'll show you what the heathens done." He started to turn and walk, but the Ranger stopped him.

"Get up on the spare horse," he said, "I'll lead you there."

"I can walk," said Prine.

"I know you can," Sam said. "So can I. But we're easy to see in this grass. If anybody spots us let's be ready to skin on out of here." As he spoke he picked up the Winchester, shook it off and handed it to the teamster. "Make sense to you?" he said.

"I didn't want to impose," Prine said, taking the rifle, then the barb's lead rope when Sam held it out to him.

The two swung up onto the horses. Prine adjusted himself behind the canvas supply bag and rode with the Ranger's rifle across his lap. As they rode, Sam took the double rifle from inside his bedroll, assembled the two pieces together, loaded it and carried it standing straight up from his thigh.

"Look what a damnable thing they've done here," Prine said when they stopped and looked down at a pile of charred wagon remains and roasted mules. Iron ribbing and wagon frame lay twisted from the heat and sticking up from a bed of smoldering embers. "I lay down over the edge there and heard them up here eating my mules." He spat in contempt and the two swung down off the horses and walked wide of the blacked circle of earth and wagon debris.

At the edge of a steep sloping hillside of rock, gravel and brush, Prine looked down as if recalling the hours he'd spent hidden down there in fear for his life.

Sam spotted a big Remington revolver lying among the brush a few feet from them. He walked over and picked it up and held it out to the teamster.

"Yours?" he asked.

"Holy cats, Ranger," Prine said, hurrying over to him. "You bet it is! I thought I'd seen the last of my ol' Remmy." He took the pistol, turned it in his hands and wiped dirt from its frame. "Much obliged," he said, grinning in spite of the pain it caused his battered face.

"The Wolf Hearts hit Mesa Grande—probably rode straight there from here," Sam said as Prine finished inspecting the Remington and shoved it loosely into his empty holster.

"Yeah, I figured as much," said Prine. With a

note of sarcasm he said, "After a good feast of mule meat and my jug of whiskey, what else did they have to do?" He paused, then asked, "Any townsfolk kilt?"

"No," said Sam. "They had good warning and took cover. Quetos rode in with a white flag."

"Ha, that's a good one," Prine said. "An Apache with a white flag." He shook his head.

"It was Denton Shenny's shirtsleeve," Sam said. "They threw Shenny's body in the street—him and some mine engineer."

"Albert Atz?" Prine said.

"Yep," Sam said, looking out and all around to the desert flatlands below.

"Now, that's a damn shame," Prine said. "Atz was a good man. Not to say that Denton Shenny wasn't." He paused and then said, "He didn't last long behind that badge, did he?"

"No, he didn't," said Sam. He looked Prine up and down. "I don't like asking you to do this, but you need to go with me for your own good. I can't get off Cord's trail, and I don't feel right sending you back alone."

"Then don't ask," said Prine. "I was going to offer anyway. As for riding alone, I've done that most my life, watching my mules' tails twitch. But I'd like to draw a bead on some of those bellies carrying my mules around in them."

"I'm looking for Cord and my prisoners, not Quetos," said Sam. "Cord and his men took Harold Flake with them."

"Jesus," said Prine. "In that case, I'd go even if I had to go by myself, on foot."

"That's what I figured from you," Sam said.

"Me and Flake ain't nothing alike, but he's been a pal for a long time. Seems more woman than man sometimes, but he's just overly excitable." Prine grinned flatly. "He never stands where he knows I'm spitting. I admire that in him." He turned as he spoke. "Let's go get him—these scalp-hunting sons a' bitches," he growled under his breath.

Chapter 13

———

Erskine Cord looked around the men, taking stock of them, formulating a plan. He didn't imagine there would be anyone on his trail. He'd broken jail, but so what? Who hadn't done that at some point or other? he told himself. Jails were made to bust out of. Nobody would be hunting him down for something like that, not with Quetos and his Wolf Hearts stirred into a frenzy over their dead squaws and their nits. He smiled to himself thinking about it. The shooting he'd done in Mesa Grande was over and done with. Leastwise until things cooled a little, he allowed.

When the time was right, he'd ride in and get his money from Curland, else he'd cure Curland's nut sack and make himself a tobacco pouch of it. His smile widened a little. Either way suited him, he told himself. He could use a new tobacco pouch, one with a little personal history to it. Behind him on the ground in the shade of cottonwood and cedar, his men lay tired and hungry. But that was all right. They worked harder when their bellies growled. It made them testy and mean, like feral dogs. He looked from man to man.

On the ground lay a Mexican-German, Emilio

Siebaugh. A foot from Siebaugh lay Eldo Berne, a Frenchman. Near Berne, Bud Shank sat sharpening a prized scalping knife he was most fond of. Leaning on an elbow in the dirt watching Shank lounged a Kansan named Early Doss, a man once hanged for rape and murder and tossed into a shallow grave for dead.

Four good men, Cord told himself, not to mention Ozzie and Sterling Childs. Seven men in all counting himself. One hard raid on Quetos and his warriors could net them a dozen scalps, maybe more if they caught the Wolf Hearts sleeping. It was time to get back to work. He looked over at Childs and gestured toward Atwater, Parker and the townsman, Flake. Then he and Childs stood up and walked over to where the three sat huddled close under a tree.

"It's getting late in the evening," Cord said down to his three buckskin-clad detainees. "Get on your feet. It's time you ride out of here and earn your keep."

Parker sat with a stick run up his buckskin shirtsleeve, digging the tip of it at reddened bites of some sort that the rancid odorous clothing had bequeathed him. He stood up, stick in hand, and looked at his own clothes now enclosing Sterling Childs. Atwater and Flake rose beside him, Atwater's fingertips digging at an itch on the side of his thigh. Flake stood with a sick look on his face, his skin crawly, the length of him badly chewed upon by some ravenous crawling species.

"Where—where are we going?" Flake asked. The front of his buckskin shirt was made up of scalp with human bones woven into it. He tried keeping his chest sunken to avoid the scalp touching him, but it did him no good. The other two tensed, expecting Flake to reap anger for asking the question. Yet Cord looked the frightened man up and down, and laughed out loud.

" 'Where are we going?' " he mimicked Flake, then laughed again.

Childs joined in. Finally the two scalp hunters stopped laughing. Cord leaned in close to Flake.

"You're going fishing, amigo," he said.

"Fi-fishing?" said Flake. He looked almost relieved, maybe a little *pleased* with the news.

"Right," said Cord. "Only we're fishing for Apache, and you three phildoodles are going to be our bait."

Flake stared at him, aghast. Parker and Atwater looked at each in fear. But they remained silent, knowing how little their lives meant to these men.

Under the trees, the men all rose stiffly and walked to their horses. The horses had found some meager grazing and were reluctant to give it up. But the men pulled them away from their pickings and adjusted their saddles and their guns, and in a moment the group had mounted the tired, hungry animals and ridden away.

At the head of the group rode Erskine Cord and Sterling Childs. Behind them rode Ozzie Cord with a lead rope connected to Parker's, Atwater's and Flake's horses, leading the three alongside him.

The party rode for two hours until they'd traversed downward diagonally and reached the lower slopes of a wide stretch of desert flatlands.

There they stopped, bunching themselves and their horses up behind the shelter of boulders and chimney rock. On the far side of the sand flats, a thick wavering veil of dust and heat hung low like a shroud over the rocky belly of the hills.

"They can't see us this time of day any more than we can see them," Erskine said idly, sharing information his men had known for years.

"Are we crossing here, Mr. Parker?" Flake asked Rollo Parker in a low whisper.

"I'm afraid we are," Parker replied, staring out blankly across the harsh world of sand, rock and cactus.

Atwater sidled his horse up closer to Parker, the lead rope drooping slack between their horses.

"We've got to make a run for it, before this crazy man gets us killed," he whispered.

Without taking his eyes from the distant shrouded hill line, Parker sat digging up under his sleeve with the same short stick he'd carried all day.

"Be my guest," he said quietly. "That's exactly what Cord wants us to do."

"Huh?" said Atwater, not understanding. Flake, frightened, kept his horse pressed up against Atwater's at every opportunity.

"You turds stop talking," Ozzie said before Parker could answer Atwater. He gave a fast yank on the lead rope.

Parker looked sidelong at him.

"We never mistreated you when the Ranger took you prisoner," he said.

"So?" Ozzie said back to him.

Parker looked away without further reply.

"Bring our bait on up here, Oz," Erskine Cord said over his shoulder. He sat looking at the three with a faint cruel smile as Ozzie led them forward and stopped. "I want the three of you to make a hard straight run across here. If you stop or slow down, you'll feel a bullet biting at your backs."

Parker looked at Atwater, who sat with a stunned expression on his dirty face.

"There," Parker said. "Any *more* ideas?"

"What'd you say?" Cord demanded of Parker.

"Nothing," said Parker. "I just told my friend here to kiss his ass good-bye."

The hunters laughed and chuffed at Parker's dark wit.

"I like a man with a sense of humor," said Cord. He took the lead rope from Ozzie and began untying each of the three horses from it. "Show me something here today. Tomorrow we'll see about making you a scalper with the rest of us."

Parker nodded toward the distant curtain of dust and heat.

"I'm not counting on *tomorrow*," he said. "I know you're hoping we draw some Apache down out of the hills over there."

"See? You might make a good scalper," said Cord. "Now get on over there. If you make it inside the rocks alive, lie down and wait for us. We'll be close behind. Then you'll have to do this all over again." He grinned. "Now get going."

"Must we?" Flake said shakily, drawing his horse back instead of tapping it forward.

Cord laughed.

"Must you?" he said, bemused. He drew his

big, long Colt from a saddle holster, cocked it and let it hang over his forearm. "Why, yes, indeed. I *believe* you must."

He pulled Flake's horse forward by its bridle and slapped its rump. The horse shot down the remaining few yards and leveled out across the sand flat. Atwater and Parker, seeing no use in resisting, booted their horses forward right behind Flake. As they raced out onto the sand and cactus carpet, Atwater glanced back over his shoulder, then looked at Parker racing along beside him.

"We might go unnoticed if nobody does any shooting!" he said to Parker through a swirl of Flake's blowback sand.

No sooner had he spoken than Cord raised the big saddle Colt and fired shot after shot straight up in air. The sound echoed around the hills and out across the flats.

"Damn it, Cero!" said Parker. "Can you just keep your mouth shut?" He slapped his reins back and forth across his horse's withers and rode on.

Behind the three riders, Cord lowered his smoking Colt and took out cartridges to reload it.

"Let's hope Quetos falls for this," Childs said quietly beside him.

"He will," Cord said confidently. "He wants to avenge his warriors' women and children so bad he'll fall for anything. If he's over there," he added. "If he is, we'll know it soon enough." He gave a shrug. "If he's not there, we'll go over, gather up our bait and try someplace else."

Across the desert flatlands, on a trail up on a craggy hillside, Quetos and men had heard the shots resound only moments earlier. He led his warriors to a higher cliff, which was hidden from the other side by the curtain of heat and afternoon dust. Along the trail the warriors dropped away one and two at a time and took position should the shots be a trick of some sort.

With a long, battered cavalry field scope, he lay behind a rock and scanned down onto the flatlands. He searched until he caught sight of the three grainy riders in the rising dust. Beside him a young White Mountain warrior, Sentoz Micabo, tried looking out with his naked eyes shielded under his hand. But he saw nothing save for the riding cloud of sand.

"Is it a scalp hunter's trick, Quetos?" he asked in ancient Mescalero Apache.

Quetos turned from the lens and gave the young warrior a pleased look for asking.

"Yes, it is only one more trick," he replied, turning the talk into English. "We must consider everything the scalp hunters do as a trick. They are all tricksters and liars." He gave a jerk of his head toward the dead scalp hunter bodies lying across their horses on the trail behind them. These were two of Cord's who had ridden in another direction when the Apaches raided their camp. "All but these scalp hunters," he added.

"Soon this man Cord and all of his scalp hunters will be like these two," said Sentoz.

Quetos nodded and looked out again at the three obscure riders racing across the flatlands. He looked farther back behind the riders along the barely visible hill line. Somewhere in the rocks there were scalp hunters hiding, waiting, watching. But he wasn't going to fall for it. He saw no supplies on the three horses crossing the flats— not even any guns, he reminded himself. And so it was a trick. Where were these men running to? What where they running from? This scalp hunter was good, but he left out many things when he made his plans. Men without guns, without supplies?

"No matter what the white man learns about us, still he thinks us stupid," Quetos said beneath the field lens, still scanning the other side of the flatlands.

"Yes, that is so," said the warrior. "But to kill these men for what they do to us, and to our women and children, will we let these three slip past us?"

Quetos lowered the lens and looked out for a second, gauging how difficult it would be looking in this direction even with the lens, with the evening sun stabbing them in their eyes.

"Yes, we will let the three pass. I will have you and some warriors follow and tell me what you see."

"Do you not want us to kill them, Quetos?" Sentoz asked.

"No, don't kill anybody, not yet," said Quetos. "We must keep the silence surrounding us. Come back and tell me what you see. When we are ready and they are deep into our hillside, we will kill them in silence."

"I will do as you say," said Sentoz. But Quetos saw the young warrior had a hard time accepting it.

"Your thirst for their blood is good, Sentoz," he said. "But there are plenty of scalpers running away from Hanging Pine. They too killed our people. We hunt them first and kill them. We will kill the leader and these other scalpers when the time is right."

"Will these men think the Wolf Hearts are weak if we don't strike right away?" Sentoz asked.

"When they look this way and don't see us or hear us attack, it will embolden them," Quetos said. "What would you have an enemy think when he hears only your silence? Would you have him think you are weak, or think you are *gone*?"

Sentoz only nodded.

"I want him to think I am gone," Sentoz allowed. He gave Quetos a respectful look. "I only ask these things so I can learn from you, Quetos," he said, almost as an apology.

"I know," Quetos replied, "and I answer for the same reason." He handed the young warrior the lens. "Here. Come to know how this world is when it is made bigger before your eyes."

When the young warrior took the lens, held it to his eye and scanned the flatland, Quetos stood and looked where his warriors lay strewn out, covering the trail in both directions.

It was hard for him to teach a young warrior like Sentoz patience and cunning, when he himself wanted to kill this scalper, Cord, so badly he could taste it. He not only wanted to kill him; he first wanted to watch him hang upside down above a fire and scream and twitch. He wanted to see, to hear the scalper's flesh fall away into the fire and sizzle.

Quetos took deep breaths while he thought such things. It cleared his head for a moment as he started walking forward, back to where his horse stood waiting, another of his warriors holding its reins. But the thoughts he'd had of Cord roasting over a fire were not through with him. They came back to him as he shoved himself up onto the horse and took its reins. He wanted to watch all the scalp hunters burn and scream. Not only these scalp hunters. He wanted to watch all the white men burn and scream. All the white men, and all their women and their children.

"Enough!" he shouted aloud at himself before he'd been able to keep himself from speaking. As soon as he heard his own voice, he looked all around, searching for something to blame his outburst on. But he found no reason.

His warriors sat watching him, stone-faced. He saw the question in their eyes, but he wasn't going to explain himself to them. He was the leader. His word was law.

He jerked his horse around roughly and batted his knee-high moccasins to its ribs.

The warriors looked at one another expressionlessly as he rode away.

"We should have burned Bloody Night to the ground and killed them all before we left," said one of the warriors.

They sat atop their horses in silence for a moment and watched as Sentoz stood up, closed the lens and came walking back to his waiting horse.

"The scalpers ran like elk from our arrows. What will they do now that we have guns?"

The warriors nodded in agreement.

"There will be a time to kill them all," one warrior said, breaking the silence. "When that time comes, let us remember how bad we felt riding away from Bloody Night."

Chapter 14

When Parker, Atwater and Flake reached the bare lower slopes of the hill line, they goaded and pushed their tired horses all the harder until they climbed out of sight into the shelter of boulder and chimney rock. With wary eyes on the hillside surrounding them, they jumped down from the horses and hugged close to the rocks. They lay searching the terrain all around them.

"I swear there is nothing natural about a man without a gun," said Parker in a hushed tone. "I don't even know what to do with hands without one." He opened and closed his hands nervously.

"I would trade my immortal soul for one of any size, right now, right this minute," Atwater gasped, out of breath, choking on hot, dry sand dust.

Flake ventured into the conversation.

"What if we just take off right now, refuse to play this insane game?" he whispered.

"Good luck," said Parker. "Either the Apache will torture and kill us up there, or the scalpers will ride us down and kill us for running out on them. I don't know which bunch would do the worse job on us. Neither side is much different."

Atwater looked across the boulders right behind them and up the hillside.

"How long you figure before Cord gets here?" he asked.

"Not long, I don't expect," said Parker. "He put his men into the dust close behind us, is my guess."

Looking up the hillside, Flake clasped a hand over his mouth and let go a muffled scream. Parker and Atwater both jerked their faces around at him, seeing his eyes bugged with terror.

"What the hell is wrong with you?" Parker snapped. Yet, as he and Atwater followed Flake's shaky finger pointing up the hillside, their eyes widened. Thirty feet away, between two rocks lying inches apart, they saw shiny black hair tied back at the forehead by a dirty cloth band. Two dark eyes stared in their direction.

"Jesus!" shouted Parker. "We're crawling with Apache! Let's get out of here!"

The three leaped to their feet and made a grab for their saddle horns. But before they could swing up into their saddles, shots exploded from the trail behind them and ricocheted off the rocks where they'd seen the leering face.

The three dropped back down quickly, seeing Cord's men thundering up the trail, firing just above their heads.

"Don't shoot!" Parker shouted, crouched, his hands raised above his ducked head.

The riders appeared not to even hear him as they raced past the three, still firing into the rocks.

As the gunfire continued, Cord and Childs veered their horses over beside the three and swung down from their saddles. Cord gave a dark chuckle.

"I told you we'd be close behind." He gave Parker a rough little shove. "Ain't you glad you didn't try making a run for it?"

"Yeah . . . yeah, I am!" Parker said, him and the other two still crouching as the gunfire roared only ten feet away, bullets pinging off the rocks and whistling in every direction.

Cord grabbed him and pulled him up straight.

"What's this?" he said, looking down at Parker's trousers. "Have you gone and wet your sorry self?"

Instinctively, Parker looked down at his trouser front. Catching himself, realizing Cord was only joking with him, he looked back up, red-faced.

Cord and Childs both laughed.

"You had to check and see, though, didn't you?" Cord said. He slapped a hand down hard on Parker's shoulder.

Parker let out a breath and looked at Atwater and Flake, standing near him. *What the hell?* he told himself, submitting to the dark joke.

"I came near it," he said, offering his own nervous little grin. "I'm glad you were close behind us."

"He's glad we was close behind them," Cord said to Childs.

They laughed again.

At the rocks, the shooting had fallen silent. Early Doss stood atop the rock and waved a hand at Cord.

"Three of them, boss," he called out. "They're not Wolf Hearts, though."

"Oh?" said Cord. "What the hell are they?"

"They're all three Mex, boss," Doss replied. "Want us to drag them out?"

"How's their hair?" Cord asked.

"Long, sort of," said Doss.

"Sort of long is long enough," Cord said. He gave Parker a wink and said privately to him, "This trade ain't always perfect." He called out to Early Doss, "Drag them out here, Early. We've got to make something for our trouble. Don't we, *More-the-merrier*?"

Parker straightened and saw an opportunity to redeem himself to the scalp hunter leader.

"About that remark I made," he said. "I never should've said it. I didn't mean any harm."

Cord laughed and slapped him hard on the back again.

"Hear that, Sterling?" he said to Childs, laughing as the other hunters dragged three dead Mexicans out of the rocks and across the dirt to them. "He wished he'd never made that *more-the-merrier* remark."

"I bet he does," said Childs, straight-faced. "Remarks can be ugly and hurtful. And once said, never, ever forgotten." He shook his head slowly, staring into Parker's eyes.

"I don't know what got into me . . . ," Parker said, sounding remorseful. "If I'd only—"

"Hush the hell up," said Cord. "Can't you tell when you're being joshed?" He and Childs both laughed as the scalpers flung the dead Mexicans at their feet. "I started thinking you're pretty swift. Don't give me second thoughts. I was going to put you two to riding with us. Remember I said I'd see how you do?"

"Yes, I do," Parker said, starting to see a way out of this deadly game. "I'd be honored riding with you. So would Cero here. Right, Cero?"

"As right as right's ever been," Atwater put in.

Cord turned and grinned at Childs.

"They'd both be honored," he said.

"As *right as right's ever been*," Childs said, repeating Atwater's words.

"So says I," said Cord. He pulled a skinning knife from behind his back, flipped it around in his hand and held it out to Parker, handle-first. "You and Cero get these boys haired down for us, we'll talk about this some more."

Parker took the knife and swallowed hard and looked at Atwater.

"What say you, fellows?" said Cord. "This is all part of the scalping trade. Just give a slash and a pull at the same time." He acted out the scalping process with his hands.

Parker looked down at the bodies, knife in hand. He saw the bandoleer of ammo across each of the men's chest—*bandits*, he told himself. Men just like Atwater and himself.

"What are you waiting for?" Cord said. "You want to keep being bait till the Apache wear your dried nuts for a necklace?"

Parker didn't answer. Instead he kneeled down over one the Mexicans, twisted a handful of black dusty hair in hand and gripped the knife firmly, held it against the skin just at the front hairline. *Here goes. . . .*

He gave a slash of the blade as he pulled hard, just the way Cord had shown him. The severed scalp made a wet sucking sound as it peeled up and back from the dead man's head. Parker stood up, letting the scalp fall from his hand. He swallowed hard.

Cord laughed and snatched the scalp up, slung it at the ground and looked it over.

"Not bad for the first time," he said. "It shouldn't tear back to a point here." He fingered the loose point the scalp came to as he laid in on his palm. "But you'll soon have the hang of it. For some reason Mexicans don't skin as well as Apaches." He handed the scalp to Childs as he spoke, and looked at Atwater as Parker handed the knife to him.

"Do it, Cero, damn it to hell," he insisted between the two of them, knowing this might be their way to stay alive among these ghoulish lunatics.

Atwater took the knife. Forcing himself to act quick without thinking about it, he stooped, grabbed a handful of hair and sliced under it. When he stood up, he held the dripping-wet scalp in his hand.

"Sling it," said Cord.

Atwater slung it at the ground and saw red-yellow matter splatter in the dirt. Sickness crawled in his belly, but he held it down.

"Now you, townsman," said Cord. He took the knife from Atwater and held it out to Flake. But the shaken townsman would have none of it. He recoiled, his hands clasped together at his chest. He shook his head violently. Tears flew.

"No! No! *Please*!" he begged.

"Don't want any, huh?" said Cord. "I didn't think so." He stooped and wiped the knife blade on the dirt and held it out to Parker, handle-first.

"What?" said Parker, Cord staring coldly in his eyes. Even as Parker asked he took the knife by its handle.

"What do you think?" Cord said with the same cold stare. Without taking his eyes off Parker, he spoke over his shoulder to the other men. "Anybody hungry here?"

"I am," said Childs.

"Lord knows I could eat," said another. The men all nodded in consensus, staring intently at Parker and Atwater.

"Take him over there and butcher him out," Cord said, gesturing a nod toward Flake, who had fallen to the ground on his knees. "Doss, gather some wood, build us a fire. We're here for the night."

Parker and Atwater stood stunned. Parker struggled and found words.

"You don't mean . . . ?" he said, his voice sounding shallow.

"I do *mean*," said Cord. "Nothing goes to waste with us. Horse is too valuable to kill. Go on, then, quarter him out." Childs stooped beside Flake and squeezed his thin arm. Flake kneeled with his face buried in his hands, trembling out of control. "He's skin and bones, boss, but tender, I'm going to guess." He stood and looked at Cord. The two nodded in agreement and turned to Parker and Atwater.

"Are you two going to be a part of this bunch or not?" Cord said.

Holy Jesus! God Almighty! Parker stepped over, reached down and grabbed Flake by his shoulder and dragged him to his feet. Atwater just stared, pale and stricken, as Parker gave the terrified townsman a shove toward the rock, the knife tight in his hand.

The scalpers all stood silent, watching as Parker continued shoving Flake forward every few steps. When Parker started dragging the sobbing man out of sight into the rocks, Cord grinned and shook his head and turned to Childs.

"Sterling, get over there and stop this crazy bastard before he goes on and does it," he said. He turned to the others as Childs loped forward, calling out toward Parker, "Men, let this be a lesson. Do not fall asleep around this one if he's gone to bed hungry."

The men hooted with laughter; Atwater slumped and drew his hand across his forehead.

What had he and Parker gotten into? He raised his head and put on a smile when Cord slapped him on his back.

"You two are going to fit right in," he said. They turned and watched Parker and Flake walking back toward them. Parker only raised a hand toward the scalpers when they laughed and clapped and cheered him for his willingness.

Atwater took a deep breath of relief.

Any way you cut it, this beats being dead, he told himself.

Chapter 15

———

The Ranger and Ison Prine had traveled hard and fast nonstop except to water and rest their horses. The night before, at a fork in a hill trail, they had come upon the mutilated body of a man dressed in buckskins and fur, wearing a necklace of pale sun-bleached finger bones and dried human ears. At the edge of the trail stood a large white paint horse that had managed to get away from the Apache warriors. The horse only ventured back and watched from the cover of trees while the warriors had concentrated on finishing the hapless scalper off with his own skinning knife. Three arrows stood spiked deep in the scalper's belly.

Slow death, Sam had told himself.

Standing over the body that night, Prine had looked down shaking his head as Sam raised the gruesome necklace on the toe of his boot, then let it fall.

"I'm surprised they didn't take all that homegrown *jewelry* off him," Prine said. "Like as not it's somebody's kinfolk."

Looking all around, seeing the paint horse watching them, Sam looked down at the scalp hunter's bloody eyeless sockets and a cavernous open wound where the man's once-working crotch had been.

"They must have been in a big hurry—so many scalpers on the run out here," he said. The top of the man's head, although hairless, had been nonetheless scalped to the skull bone.

"See any point in burying him?" Prine asked.

Sam just looked at him.

"All right," Prine said, "I'll just drag him off the trail so's not to scare any passing pilgrims."

"Any pilgrims coming this way need scaring," Sam replied. He backed away, double rifle in hand, and studied the fresh tracks of unshod horses. Beneath the flurry of Apache tracks he saw what was left of shod hoofprints. His eyes followed the Apache prints out along the trail to where the rocky trail disappeared around a switchback. "I'm speculating that this one might've spotted Cord and his band on a lower trail and was riding breakneck to join them."

"So breakneck he didn't see what was laying for him," Prine said, dragging the body off the edge of the trail. "Poor son of a bitch. Wonder what they done with his eyeballs." He looked all around on the ground, then stopped and straightened when he saw Sam walk away toward the paint horse.

The horse not only didn't shy away from the Ranger's hand; he stuck his nose out to it in curiosity. Prine watched the Ranger rub the animal's muzzle. Then without wasting time, Sam lifted the loose reins, gathered them and stepped around beside the horse's head. With his hand up close to the horse's muzzle, he led the animal forward as if the two had been friends for years. Prine nodded, knowing that was the way to lead a strange wary horse without it balking or causing an incident.

"He says for a handful of grain and water he'll haul our supplies for us," Sam said, handing the horse to Prine.

"Sounds like a bargain to me," Prine said.

Sam stood watching as the teamster grained and watered the paint, giving the other two horses enough to keep them busy chewing while the paint ate.

"Why do you suppose Quetos and his Wolf Hearts attacked Cord's men with bows and arrows when they had rifles and ammo?" Prine asked.

"Good question," the Ranger replied, watching him attend to the paint and the two other nosy horses. "Saving it up, most likely. Apache aren't keen on hitting a town or a settlement anyway."

Prine appeared to consider it, then nodded and shrugged.

"Yes, I suppose that's right," he said, putting the issue aside, accepting the Ranger's opinion. "Besides, they didn't waste bullets on that one when a few, couple arrows was all it took." He nodded toward the body in the rocks just off the trail.

"The worst trouble I get in is when I try too hard to think like an Apache," Sam said, watching Prine wrap the paint's reins loosely around its saddle horn and slip a lead rope on the animal. Prine nodded, organizing the animals, swinging the supplies from the speckled barb he was riding onto the big paint.

"I have a hard enough time thinking like a white man," he said, "let alone the Mescalero." He stopped and said in a more serious tone, "How'd you manage to get the drop on Wilson Orez and kill him?"

Sam thought about his answer for a moment before giving it. "Lucky, I guess," he finally replied. As an afterthought he added, "Besides, Orez was only half Apache." He gave Prine a slight, wry grin. "Ready to go?"

Atop their horses, they rode as hard and fast as before, the horses moving onto better, less rocky trail. After a few hours of hard riding, they stopped on a bare cliff facing out onto the flatlands. From that spot, the Ranger stretched out his brass-trimmed telescope and spotted the three scalper-dressed hostages crossing the sand flats, leaving a high swirl of dust behind them. Farther back, seventy yards, he'd seen the rest of the scalpers riding into the three front riders' dust. The first thing he'd noted had been the clothing on three of the following riders.

Not scalper clothing at all, he told himself. But then the riders fell away out of sight into the shifting, looming dust cloud.

"What is it, Ranger?" Prine asked, seeing the curious look on Sam's face when he lowered the lens from his eye.

"It's our scalpers," Sam replied, pressing the lens closed between his palms.

"Did you see Harold? Is he down there?" Prine asked. He stared at Sam intently.

"If he's down there I saw him," Sam said.

"Truth is I can't make anybody out in all the dust." He stood and dusted his trousers and shirt. "Cord and his men are up to something. Looks like he's got decoys crossing out in front of him. If he's running from Quetos, he's going about it in a strange way." He looked out across the sand flats. "Looks like he's back to work, scalping."

"These scalp hunters have got no sense," said Prine. "They don't care much more for their own life than they do the Indians." He spat sidelong in disgust. "Dang it, I just hope Harold's all right. Are we riding right up their shirttails, then, cross behind them while there's still daylight?"

Sam had turned to the horses, the big double rifle in hand.

"No," he said. "We're crossing tonight while the dust is still up some. Dust and darkness," he added. "It's all we've got going for us right now."

The two mounted the horses and rode away. At dark they reached the spot where the scalp hunters had crossed. They rested their horses and themselves for an hour while the last slim shadows of sunlight fell into blackness beneath a purple sky. Then they pulled the dusty but rested horses forward from among the rock and down toward the sand flats. And they rode on.

In the first clear light of dawn, the scalp hunters woke, some of them readying their horses for the hard, rocky trail. Others still sat around a pot of coffee that had been boiled over a fire, the low flames immediately extinguished. They had slept through the night in a dark camp with guards posted all around. Instead of fire they had wrapped themselves in their blankets around a cold spot on the ground.

Parker, Atwater and Flake had slept under the hawklike eyes of the Frenchman, Eldo Berne, who sat on guard atop a rock that afforded him a good view of both the camp and the wide sand flats below. Flake gave the Frenchman a cautious look before leaning over to Cero, who sat sipping coffee from a borrowed tin cup.

"I have a lot of money in Mesa Grande, Mr. Atwater," he whispered. "It is all yours if you and Mr. Parker will get me out of here and home safely."

Atwater just looked at him.

"I mean it," said Flake, "I've been saving for years. It's all yours, every dollar." His lip trembled a little. "Please get me out of here."

Atwater and Parker gave each other a look.

"Around how much money are we talking about, Harold?" Atwater said. He swirled the coffee around in the cup, watching it as if important information lay in the black steamy substance.

"More than either of you will ever make riding with these madmen," Flake whispered in reply, cutting a glance to Parker, bringing him into his secretive proposal.

"That sounds fine as wine," said Atwater, "but money's not money unless there's an amount attached to it." He looked away dismissingly and said, "Come back when you know what that amount is."

"No, wait," said Flake, his voice shaky. "Three thousand dollars. That's how much. My whole life savings."

Atwater gave him a skeptical look.

"You're whole life savings is three thousand dollars?" he said. "That won't cut it, Harold. We wouldn't save our own mothers' lives for three thousand dollars."

"Wait, ten thousand," Flake said, getting panicky, keeping his voice lowered.

"Whoa," Parker cut in, "we can save you for ten thousand. No doubt about it." He paused and looked Flake up and down. "But what did you do to save up that much money?"

"Never mind what I did," Flake said. "Get me out of here—get me to Mesa Grande and ten thousand dollars is all yours. Deal?" He reached out a hand as if to shake on it.

"Draw your hand back, Harold," said Atwater. "We ain't in church."

"But do we have a deal?" Flake persisted.

"We do," said Atwater, him and Parker both nodding.

"Shut up down there, you imbeciles," Berne said aloud. In the early sunlight they saw the Frenchman stand up atop the rock and look down at them. He cradled his rifle in his arm, and his blanket hung down around his broad shoulders. "I have listened to the three of you *wheesper* like little schoolgirls long enough—"

His words stopped short. The three saw his blanket spread wide on either side like the wings of some large creature of flight. But he did not bat his wings. Instead, some powerful unseen force picked him up and hurled him out off the edge of rock. He sailed straight out ten feet above them. Then he tapered down as in the distance a loud roar of powerful rifle fire echoed off along the hill lines and rolled above the desert floor.

The three men ducked to the ground as the Frenchman hit the ground a few feet away with a solid thud. Blood and shredded muscle matter rained and splattered down in his wake.

The scalp hunters froze, but only for a second as a deathlike silence set in. Breaking the silence, Childs jumped to his feet and ran for the cover of rock, his rifle in hand.

"Take cover!" he shouted as he ran. Cord had walked away behind a large shrub pine to relieve himself. He came running from behind the tree and fell in with Childs as he struggled to hold his trousers up.

"That's my rifle! I'd know that sound anywhere!" he shouted as he ran. He sounded outraged that his own rifle would be directed against him and his men. "Somebody find that poltroon bastard and kill him graveyard dead! I want my rifle back!"

The men, who had taken whatever cover they could, looked at one another as they ducked down. They knew as did Cord himself that there wasn't a rifle among them that could match the big Pryse & Redman double rifle. The thought of it being used on them was enough to give them pause.

"His rifle?" said Early Doss. "What does he think we're going to do?" He lay behind a rock beside Bud Shank. "We've got nothing that can match it. That shot could have come halfway across the flats or farther."

"Boss knows that," said Shank. "He just got caught with his pants down." He managed a flat grin even under the circumstances. "Come with me. Let's get these horses moved before whoever that is starts whittling away at them."

The two sprang up and ran to where the horses stood restless in a row, tied slip-style to a rope strung between two pines. Shank took one end and Doss the other. But as the two stood up and untied their end of the rope, Shank slammed and flattened against the pine as the whole tree shivered its length from the impact of the second shot.

"Bud!" shouted Doss in disbelief, seeing the loose rope fly from Shank's hand. Close to a full second passed before the powerful sound of the shot rippled across the hills and sand flats and followed the same trail as the first shot, out and away like two large terrible spirits fleeing the far edge of the earth.

"Grab them animals, Doss!" Cord shouted, seeing the spooked string of horses break up and all of them run away in every direction. "Don't let them get away!"

But Doss, having seen Shank's back explode in a violent torrent of blood, wanted no part of it. He raised himself just enough to fire two worthless rifle shots out across the sand flats and ducked back down before anyone could get a bead on him.

"How can anybody shoot that far?" he shouted.

Seeing the horses running away wildly, and seeing what happened to two of their own who'd been caught in the deadly sights of a precision rifle they were all too familiar with, the men stalled behind rock cover. They stole quick glances around rock and scrub pine, but they saw no sign of rifle smoke from the desert floor or from the distant hill line.

"No man can shoot a rifle that far," Emilio Siebaugh said, having slid in beside Cord and Childs. He lay prone, his rifle butt up against his shoulder, but of no use.

"Like hell," said Cord, judging the distance from the other side of the sand flats. "I've shot her that far and farther."

Siebaugh caught and corrected himself.

"I mean nobody but you, boss," he said. "I know you can shoot her that far. You can shoot her around the world if you wanted to."

"You're damn well told I can, Siebaugh." Cord sneered. He turned to Childs and said, "Sterling, you and Siebaugh work yourselves down around the lower trail—get closer. Watch for the next shot and kill this son of a bitch."

"What about the horses?" Childs asked. "We won't get anywhere without them."

"We won't get anywhere dead either!" shouted Cord. "Kill this son of a bitch *first*. Then we'll go after the horses." He stared out from around the rock toward the sand flats. "It's that damn lawman," he snarled aloud. "Who else would be fool enough to traipse around out here with the Mescalero on the warpath?"

Chapter 16

———

Prine had sat beside the Ranger with the field lens to his eye and watched both shots. The first had been simple enough. They had waited until the small figure stood up atop the rock with a rifle in his arms and walked over and stopped at the rock's edge, making himself a perfect target in the early sunlight. When the big double rifle fired, Prine was watching the targeted man through the lens.

"Holy Joe and Mary!" he said, watching the bullet fling the man away as if he were a thin strip of paper taken by the wind. "That ol' boy never knew what hit him."

The Ranger didn't reply; he'd barely heard him. He'd taken two strips of cloth and stuck the ends of them into his ears, knowing the shattering impact the powerful rifle loads would produce. He'd laid his rolled blanket atop the rock as a bed for his hand and the big Pryse & Redman. The recoil had jarred him soundly, but this wasn't the first large-caliber rifle he'd fired. He owned a Swiss Husqvarna himself. He was familiar with recoil and recovery. As soon as the first shot exploded, he rode the recoil easily and dropped back into position, ready to fire again.

"You're going to the horses now?" Prine said, the lens scanning the far hillside above them. The rock at the edge of the camp offered the only shooting angle Prine could see. He rounded a fingertip into his left ear, the ear nearer to the big rifle.

Again the Ranger did not answer. Instead he moved the high rifle sights slowly sidelong and aimed up a rocky ravine running up the hillside. He'd spotted it earlier as he settled into place and planned his two shots. From their angle, lying behind a twenty-foot-long upthrust of rock on the sand flats, he could aim straight up the jagged depression. The ravine ran narrow and deep, like stair steps in some places. And at the top of it stood the string of horses. Beside the horses, the tree, the rope—a natural-made target, the depression serving as gun sights. After the first shot he'd waited and watched.

"That's what I thought. All right, I've got it," said Prine, scanning over to the ravine with the lens.

The second shot he'd had to make quick, just as the figure stepped over to the tree to untie the rope holding the string of horses. He'd squeezed the trigger and he and Prine had watched the man slam against the tree and bounce off it as if made of rubber. He'd seen the horses scatter.

"Umm-umm." Prine shook his head slowly, the lens still up to his eye. "You have just ruint everybody's day, Ranger," he said. "There's a case against oversleeping if ever I saw one."

Sam had taken out two fresh loads and broken the rifle open to reload. He pulled the strip of cloth from his left ear.

"What?" he said.

"Nothing," said Prine, scanning the hillside above the ravine, hoping to see his pal Harold Flake. "I was remarking against late sleepers." He turned the lens over to the Ranger and sat scanning with his naked eyes while Sam checked the hillside for himself.

"There go the horses," he said to Prine, watching the spooked animals scatter in every direction, both up and downhill from the campsite. "They'll be a while rounding them up. We've done ourselves some good here." He assumed a crouching position even though they were unseen from the hillside in front of them.

"Still no sign of my friend Harold, though," said Prine, sounding concerned.

"Sorry," said Sam. "Maybe next time." He dusted himself and picked up the rolled blanket. "We've done all we can do here. Cord knows it's his own rifle out to kill him."

"Dang it, Harold, where are you . . . ?" Prine said toward the hillside, still searching the morning light with his naked eyes.

Sam looked down at him and nudged his shoulder.

"We'll find him," he said. "Right now let's go. I want to get us ahead of them while they're busy gathering horses."

"What about the Wolf Hearts?" Prine said, still giving one last search of the hillside as the horses continued to scatter. "They'll be watching the trail up there like hawks. They'll see us for sure."

Sam watched him as he rose slowly and dusted his trousers. There was no fear in his voice, only verbal speculation, a man planning his day's work.

"After those two shots, and the return shots," Sam said, "it'd be foolish to think they don't see us already." He paused, but only for a second. "All the more reason to get going, don't you think?"

"Oh yes, I *do think so*," Prine said, as if snapping out of despair. Forcing his thoughts off his hapless friend, he collected himself and turned with the Ranger. "I know we'll find Harold. I just hope it's sooner instead of later. I'm afraid my friend is too timid for his own good. It could cause crude people like this bunch to take advantage of him."

"I understand," said Sam.

The two walked to the far end of the twenty-foot rock upthrust where they had hitched their horses. In a moment they mounted and rode off diagonally toward the hill line, in the direction that would put them on the trail ahead of Cord and his scalp hunters.

As they rode out of sight, on the lower slope of the hillside where they'd started from the night before, two of Quetos' Wolf Hearts stepped out of the rocks. They watched in silence as dust rose and settled in the two riders' wake.

A seasoned warrior named Itza-chu turned to the younger Sentoz and looked him up and down, barely keeping from showing his contempt for letting the white men ride away.

"Do you feel courage swell in your chest watching them leave, Sentoz?" he asked with sarcasm.

Sentoz's nostrils flared. He clenched his teeth and his fists, a Winchester repeating rifle in hand.

"I do as I am told by our leader," he replied.

"But our leader is not here, Sentoz. If he were he would say something different," said another seasoned warrior, Norozo, who stepped out of the rocks leading their horses. "If he stood where you are standing, he would have us kill them both."

A fourth warrior stood off to the side, watching the flats should the two white men turn around and come back their way. He nodded, agreeing with the more seasoned warriors.

"He told me to come back to him and tell what we saw," Sentoz said firmly. "That is what we will do."

Itza-chu shook his head.

"Then you ride back and tell him what we have seen here," he said. "It only takes one warrior to speak for us." He looked around at the other two warriors. "The three of us will follow these two. One of them is the man from Bloody Night who drove the wagon we burned. The other is the lawman who would not give us the scalpers. These are not the three men Quetos had you to follow. So we kill them."

"No," said Sentoz. "Quetos said kill *no one*, not until he says so. These two are hunting the same men we are."

Itza-chu took a breath and settled himself.

"When two hunters pursue the same prey, one must become the other's prey as well. Quetos is not far away. Go to him wondering what you should do," he said. "We are Wolf Hearts. *Lupon* Warriors. We kill white men. Tell all this to Quetos. He will understand and he will come here. Tell him while we wait for him, I will go kill the man who killed Wilson Orez."

Sentoz stopped short.

"This is why you want to kill the lawman," he said. "Because he is the man who killed Wilson Orez?"

"Sentoz, you are still too young to understand such things as these," said Itza-chu.

"I am not too young to understand what I am supposed to do," said Sentoz. "I will tell Quetos what you say.

Itza-chu looked around coolly at the other two warriors.

"Go quickly," he said. "When you return with Quetos, I will give him the lawman's knife hand, the hand he used to kill the Red Sleeve warrior, Orez."

At noon the Ranger and Ison Prine pulled off the high trail and took a position among the rocks that allowed them a good view of the hill line in either direction and the wide desert floor below. They rested for two hours, taking alternate turns, one sitting up, alert, watching the trails and the sand flats while the other slumped and pulled his hat brim down over his eyes.

By his estimation, Sam decided that by now the scalp hunters had gathered their horses and were on the trail—this trail—headed straight toward them. With any luck, he would soon have his prisoners in tow, whether dead or alive; and he would have Prine out of peril.

He looked all around, knowing it would be hard to find a better spot than this for an ambush. They would remain here in the cover of the hillside boulders, rock and tall pine until they saw the scalpers riding up the trail. When they woke, Sam waited with the double rifle across his lap, and Prine sat at his right side. The two ate sliced jerked elk from a shank Sam had taken from the supply bag. They washed their meal down with tepid water from their canteens. The horses stood nearby behind a large boulder, each crunching on a handful of grain Prine had put on the ground before them.

"Quetos said the Mescalero call Mesa Grande Bloody Night," Sam said, swishing water around in his canteen. "That's the first time I ever heard of it."

"I heard they called it Bloody Night Hill years ago," said Prine. "Then it got shortened to just Bloody Night. But I haven't heard anybody call it neither for a long time." He sipped water from his canteen and turned his gaze back to the trail, making sure at least one of them had his eyes on it at all times.

"What's the story on Bloody Night?" Sam asked, capping his canteen.

"It's not a pretty story," Prine warned. "In fact, it's a dang gruesome story, even for a desert Apache."

"I've heard lots of those kinds," Sam assured him.

"I bet you have," Prine said. He took a breath, staring down at the trail. "The place we call Mesa Grande was once a trade center, long ago before

us white men set foot here. It was a place where
the Apache brought prisoners and traded them
off as slaves to other tribes. For the warring tribes,
it was a place to sort everybody out, so to speak.
Apache also brought Mexican hostages here and
sold them back to their people if their families
had any trade goods or mescal to offer for them.
If not, the prisoners were gathered and held
until a certain time of the year. If nobody claimed
them, or wanted them for slaves, or just plain
didn't like them . . . " He paused and looked at
the Ranger for a moment. ". . . Apache took them
out on a night with a full moon and slaughtered
them. Some of them had their throats slit and got
thrown off the cliffs. Story was the whole cliff
side was painted black with dried blood—still is
in places."

Sam shook his head slowly.

"But the ones who got thrown off with their
throats cut were the luckier ones," Prine continued. "The unfortunate ones were part of Apache
initiation. They had a hole cut in their bellies, and
the Apache pulled out a string of gut and wrapped
it around one of the young warrior's hands. He
would hold on to the length of gut and shove that
poor person off the cliffs—watch the person's
guts unravel like a knit blanket."

Sam let out a breath and uncapped his canteen
again. He held it up toward Prine as if in a toast.

"You're right, that is a gruesome story," he said.
He took a mouthful of water, rinsed it around and
spat it out in a stream. "How true do you think
it is?"

Prine considered it, still watching the trail below.

"Hard to say," he replied. "With the desert Apache you never know. I've heard of them doing worse. I've heard of the Comanche doing *lots* worse." He breathed deep. "Anyways, that's how Bloody Night got its name."

"And that's what Quetos and his Wolf Hearts call it," Sam reflected.

"The Wolf Hearts are a fairly new sect," Prine said. "A new bunch always wants to go back to the old ways, the old traditions, so forth. They think it calls in the spirits from those old times. Quetos and his bunch probably figure Grande Mesa is haunted by the ghosts of the bloody cliffs. I've even had whites, old-timers who lived here years ago, tell me they thought the place is haunted. That ever' now and then the spirits who roam Bloody Night have to have their measure of blood." He turned to Sam. "You believe stuff like that, Ranger?"

"I keep my hands full dealing with the living, leave the dead alone," he said, standing and dusting his trousers.

Prine stood up beside him, the two looking down onto the trail, rifles in hand.

"Same here," he said. "I never put much stock in stories I hear about the Apache. What I've seen with my own eyes is plenty—"

The teamster's words stop short as Sam heard the whine of an incoming arrow cut into Prine's back and rock him forward on the toes of his boots. He grabbed him to keep him from falling

face forward over the rocky edge of the cliff, and
another arrow whined in, and another. One stuck
out of Prine's chest through his right ribs. Another
sliced across the top of Sam's shoulder and slid on
out into the air.

Dropping down quickly, taking Prine with him,
Sam rolled onto his side. He swung the big Pryse
& Redman rifle up toward the rocks as three
warriors bounded down the rocks toward him.
His first shot picked one of the warriors up
and flung him backward in midair. Sam rose
to his feet and fired again. His second shot hit a
warrior in his upper shoulder and spun him
like a top. But with no shots left he barely had
time to draw the big rifle back and swing it as the
third warrior leaped out at him from atop the
rocks.

The rifle slammed into the warrior's midsec-
tion and knocked him sideways to the ground. As
he recovered and sprang to his feet, a war ax in
hand, Sam drew his big Colt and fired three times.
Each shot drove the warrior farther backward.
The third shot knocked him off the edge of the
cliff and sent him tumbling to the trail below.
Sam turned quickly, facing the rocky hillside. But
as he fanned his Colt back and forth, the land settled into its silence.

Sam stepped forward warily. He heard the
sound of horses' hooves racing away on the trail
below.

The scalp hunters? He didn't have time to stop
and check. Whoever it was, they'd turned and fled.
They knew he was here. Thirty feet up the hillside

he found the wounded Indian on the ground, the entire upper edge of his shoulder gone, torn away by the mighty blast of the big double rifle. The Indian lay gasping for breath, looking as if he had no idea what terrible fate had befallen him. He tried to mutter something in Apache, but Sam couldn't make it out. There was nothing he could do for the man even if he'd tried. Prine lay wounded in the rocks with three arrows in him. Prine's condition couldn't wait.

Sam only shook his head, leveled the Colt down, cocked it and pulled the trigger. The warrior bucked once, then fell limp onto the ground.

Sam turned and hurried back to where Prine lay on his side, the arrows stuck deep inside him.

"All the . . . danged luck," the desert-hardened teamster said. He tried dragging himself upright in a sitting position, but the pain in his abdomen prevented it.

"Lie still," Sam said, pressing him back onto this side, keeping the arrows from bending sideways and opening the wounds wider.

"Lie still . . . and do what, Ranger?" Prine said in a low, pained voice.

Sam had no answer. But upon examining the arrows closely, seeing that one appeared dangerously near Prine's heart, he said, "I've got to get you to Mesa Grande."

"I'm not going . . . to Mesa Grande," Prine said. "Not without Harold."

"Don't argue," Sam said. "I'll come back for your friend. You've got my word."

"What about your prisoners? We come . . . all

this way. It seems a dang shame. . . ." He strained to speak each word, and Sam saw he was having a hard time breathing.

"Stop talking," he said. "I'm going to have to break the shafts off these arrows to get you up in the saddle."

"Break them off, then," Prine said, giving in to the Ranger's plan. "I'm not . . . particularly attached to them."

Sam lifted him to his feet carefully and seated him on a rock, at the same time keeping an eye on the trail below. Looking back at the arrows, he said, "At least you're not bleeding a lot—not yet anyway."

"Lucky me," Prine said wryly, looking down at the arrow points sticking out of his chest.

Sam looked off down the trail where he'd heard the sound of horse hooves hurrying away in the opposite direction.

Everything changes here and now, he told himself. Whatever plans he'd made for an ambush just crumbled like a sand castle. He'd dealt himself the upper hand. But that hand played out when the arrows sank into the teamster's back. That was how quick things change out here, he reminded himself. Had the arrows killed Prine, he would have piled him over with rock and gone on. But Prine was still alive, and it was his first duty to try to keep him that way. He was still close enough to Mesa Grande to get Prine back there to the doctor—provided the ride there didn't kill him.

"This might hurt some," he said, gripping the arrow shaft between his hands. He wanted to snap it a few inches from Prine's back, leave the doctor room to work with.

"Oh? You think so?" Prine said, keeping his tough spirit up. He looked at Sam and gave a tight grin. "Break them off, Ranger. Let's get on with it."

Chapter 17

Without delay, Sam wrapped strips of cloth firmly around Prine, keeping each turn of it snug against the arrow stubs to suppress bleeding and help keep him sitting upright in his saddle. Once mounted, Sam led Prine's horse and the supply horse down onto the trail and turned the animals back in the direction of Mesa Grande. He kept a watchful eye for more Indians as well as for Cord's scalp hunters.

Two miles back along the trail, as Sam rode around a blind turn, he stopped quickly and raised the rifle from across his lap. Ahead of him he caught a glimpse of buckskin fur dash from the trail and leap over a rock. He raised the rifle to his shoulder but held his shot when he realized no one was going to fire at him.

"Hello the rock," he called out, deciding he'd waited long enough. "Come out with your hands high."

"Don't shoot, Ranger! It's us!" a nervous voice called out from the rock.

"Who's *us*?" Sam replied. Sam recognized Rollo Parker's voice, but he didn't know where that put things, Parker and Atwater being escaped prisoners, the same as Erskine Cord.

"Me and Cero," Parker said. "Don't shoot us. We've got Harold Flake with us."

This could be some good news, Sam told himself. He knew it would make a difference to Prine, seeing that his friend was back safe and sound.

"Show yourselves," Sam said. "Do it easylike."

Sam watched as Parker, Atwater and Flake rose slowly to their feet as one. No sooner had they stood than Harold Flake ran sobbing toward the Ranger.

"Oh, thank God! Thank God it's you," he cried loudly.

Sam moved his horse sidelong a step to divert the sobbing man, but Flake managed to grab his boot and cling to it. Sam, trying to keep an eye on Parker and Atwater, tried to pull his leg free.

"It was so horrible, Ranger," said Flake. "You can't imagine!"

"Take it easy, Flake," said Sam. "Keep quiet and back away. I've got prisoners to watch."

"Don't worry about us, Ranger," said Parker. "We're not going anywhere."

"We're just glad it's you instead of the Wolf Hearts," said Atwater.

"We were hoping you'd show up when you did," Parker said. "We told Harold we'd take him to you." He looked at Flake. "We've got a deal, right, Harold?"

Flake let go of Sam's leg and backed away, wiping his eyes.

"Well, yes, *sort of*, I suppose," Flake said.

"Don't go getting forgetful on us, Harold," said Atwater. "You know damn well we did."

Sam moved his dun around so he could watch the three of them. He reached over to Prine and nudged him carefully on his shoulder. Prine, who had taken a downturn, sat dozing, unconscious. But he opened his eyes and sat stiffly, looking down at Flake.

"Harold . . . ," he said weakly. "Are you . . . all right?"

"Yes, Ison," said Flake. "But my goodness, what's happened to you? I'm afraid you've been pierced!" His hands went back to both cheeks, covering his mouth.

Parker and Atwater just looked at each other, their hands still raised.

"I'm . . . all right now, Harold," said the wounded teamster, seeming to have gathered strength from seeing his friend alive and unharmed.

Sam, double rifle in hand, waved the two prisoners out from behind the rock.

"You both know if this is any kind of trick you and Cord have cooked up," he said, "I'll kill you both before Cord's men kill me."

"We understand," Parker said, stepping around from behind the waist-high rock.

"We sure do, and we respect you for it," Atwater put in quickly, stepping around with Parker.

"We all three wanted away from those lunatics," Parker said. "You wouldn't believe how crazy they are!"

"I bet I would," Sam said. "But what I want to know is, where are they?"

"Well," Parker said, "the fact is we were all riding

this way, looking for Apache. When Cord heard his big rifle go off, he pulled us all back, said he didn't want to spend the rest of the day rounding the horses up again. You need to know, Ranger, even though you kilt two scalpers back there, a half dozen more men straggled in on our way here—survivors of the Apache attack near Hanging Pine. So they're ready to do some damage."

"He's expecting more of his men to show up along the way," Atwater cut in. "Said if we waited back along the trail, you'd likely come back that way and we'd be set up waiting for you. Said we'd kill you when you rode through—he'd take his rifle back."

"He's real fond of that rifle, Ranger," said Parker. "Can we lower our hands?"

Sam looked down at Flake.

"They're not armed, Ranger," he said. "Cord took our clothes and put us in these filthy skins, told these two they were riding with him, but he was lying. He was only using us three for *bait*, as he called it." He paused and raised his hands to his cheeks again. "I don't mind saying, I was scared to death every minute of this ordeal. I even tried becoming friends with these two, hoping they would help me get away."

"Which *we did*, Harold," Parker said. "Let's not forget that part. We grabbed you and your horse when the others were turning back on the trail. If we hadn't gotten you out of there when we did, you'd still be their prisoner."

"I admit you were gracious, taking me with you when you made your getaway. But I consider that just human kindness—"

"What's going on here?" Sam asked.

"He promised us money once we got him away from Cord's scalp hunters," said Atwater. "Now he's trying to crawfish on the deal."

Prine perked up and stared down at Flake.

"Is that right, Harold?" he asked. "You promised these men money? How much money?"

Before Flake could answer, Parker cut in.

"Ten thousand dollars," he said. He looked from Prine to the Ranger. "He also said he knows the territorial judge, and he'd speak to him on our behalf."

Prine and the Ranger looked at Flake.

"All right, I said some things." Flake shrugged. "I feared for my life."

"Ten thousand dollars, huh?" said Prine, seeming to forget about the arrow stubs sticking out of his belly for the moment.

"I didn't mean it," Flake said. "I was desperate. I would have promised them anything."

"Why, you lying son of a bitch!" said Parker, taking a step toward Flake.

"Hold it, Parker," Sam said. "We don't have time for this. I've got to get Prine to Mesa Grande."

"You don't want to go this way," Parker said. "Cord will kill us all."

"Then we're not going that way," Sam said. "Where are your horses?"

"We hid them up on the hillside," Atwater replied.

"Let's go," Sam said. "We'll get the horses, find ourselves a game trail and swing up around Cord and his men."

"Sounds good to me," Parker said. He touched

his ragged hat brim to the Ranger. "I just want to say what a pleasure it is, being your prisoner again." He and Atwater both held their wrists out to be cuffed.

"No cuffs," Sam said. "You know everything that's waiting for you out here if you make a break for it."

Flake stepped over closer and laid a hand on Prine's boot. He looked up at Prine, then at Sam.

"Ranger, may I lead my friend?" he said. "I'll watch about him closely all the way to Mesa Grande."

Sam looked at Prine, who nodded.

"We're pals, Ranger," he said. "Harold will take good care of me." He looked down at Flake. "Else I'll break his fool neck for him."

Cord and his men had taken positions up among the rocks on the hill beside the trail. At the first sound of horses' hooves pounding toward them, Cord held out a hand steadying the men, keeping them from shooting right away. He knew what the big double rifle could do long-range with its tall sights up, and he wanted no part of it.

"Stay down, stay quiet until I give you a signal," he said. "When they're right below us, we'll rain hell down on that lawman and everybody with him."

"Yeah," said Childs. "Remember Berne and Shank. This is vengeance for them."

They lay waiting, watching. But to their surprise, when they saw the riders rounding the turn below, it was not the Ranger and posse of townsmen. It was Quetos and his Wolf Hearts.

"I'll be double damned," Cord whispered, his hand around the stock of a Winchester rifle, cocked, ready to fire.

"Jesus . . . ," Childs whispered, lying in the rocks beside him.

Seeing the Apache leader bringing his men into their well-laid ambush, Cord knew he had only seconds to decide what to do. Childs knew it too.

"Where the hell did my big rifle go?" Cord whispered, staring down at the Indians. "I figured for certain I'd get it back right here."

"What's it going to be, boss?" Childs asked in the same low whisper. "We ain't like to ever get this many Wolf Hearts on the same spot at once."

But Cord appeared distracted, his mind on another matter.

"I could just about see me walk up, kick that dead Ranger's hand aside, pick up my rifle and be gone."

"Tell me, boss!" Childs whispered. "Before it's too late. We've got a contract!"

The rest of the men grew anxious. They looked back and forth, at the Apaches riding below, and back to Cord, who just lay staring down at them.

"Come on, boss, tell us something!" said Childs, getting more and more anxious as the Apaches rode closer, almost straight down below them. "We've got a rope ready and waiting. All Doss needs is a signal to draw it. Are we going to let all this valuable hair ride away?"

Cord looked around at him and finally seemed to snap out of his disappointment. He gave a flat, tight grin and readjusted the Winchester.

"Not on your life, Sterling," he said. He raised

his voice and bellowed loudly to his men, "Kill these sons a' bitches!" And he quickly took aim at the Apaches and let the first shot roar.

The men fired before Cord got the words out of his mouth. They shouted and yipped and howled like hounds in ecstasy as they did so. As riders and horses fell on the rocky trail below, the scalpers were up and bounding down over rock and brush to get to them.

"Here's why I love this business!" shouted Childs, him and Cord remaining in the rocks, firing rapidly.

Quetos and many of his warriors managed to leap from their horses and take to the rocks themselves. But of those warriors still mounted, some dozen or more heeled their horses into a hard run out along the trail. They hoped to find relief from the deadly gunfire and regroup, yet instead they rode right into a taut rope that sprang up across the narrow trail.

"Whooo-iee!" Cord shouted and laughed. "Where else in the world can you witness such a sight as this!" He watched, seeing both man and horse topple and flip and roll in the dirt. The taut rope caught them, hooked them upward and backward and flung them about on the trail like leaves on a whirlwind. As the men and the stunned horses struggled to stand and get away, rifle fire from both sides of the trail cut through them, forming a red mist of blood in the roiling dust.

"Never say us ol' boys can't kill us some Mescaleros when we've a mind to," he said in a quieter voice, staring across at the opposite hillside where Quetos and his Wolf Hearts had formed together along a short wall of rock and begun firing back with deadly accuracy.

Across the trail, Quetos spotted Cord standing upright behind a waist-high rock. As his warriors' rifles roared all around him, he took careful aim and squeezed the trigger. But Cord spotted the Apache leader homing in on him and leaped away at the last second. Instead of Quetos' shot hitting him dead center, the bullet slammed into his shoulder and sent him twisting backward, his Winchester remaining in hand.

"You got him, Quetos! You killed their leader!" shouted Sentoz between firing rounds.

"No, he's not dead," Quetos said. He settled in for another shot as Cord, who stood unsteadily on his feet, took aim himself.

As a shot from Cord whistled in and skipped and whined off the rock at Quetos' shoulder, the Apache leader took close aim again and started to squeeze the trigger. But before he could get the shot off, Cord dropped back down behind the rock and raised his battered hat and waved it back and forth in defiance, taunting the Apache leader.

"He does not die easily," Quetos said. He kept his rifle on the rock where Cord took cover and waited.

Behind that rock, Cord tore open the cloth shirt he'd taken from Parker and looked at his wound. The shoulder wound was throbbing and bleeding freely, but it was numb, the pain having yet to set in. Cord pulled a grimy grease-blackened bandanna from around his neck, wadded it and pressed it to the open gunshot wound. He felt the blood running from the exit wound behind his shoulder, and he tried to crane his head around to look at it.

"Stop bleeding, you son of a bitch," he cursed the back of his shoulder. "I'm standing to make a lot of money here." He stuck the bandanna into the front wound deep enough that the wound held it in place. Then he tore most of his short sleeve off, wadded it and held it back over his shoulder.

As he sat leaning back against the rock, Childs slid in beside him.

"I saw you were shot, boss," he said, out of breath, covered with blood, his right hand gripping a scalping knife. "What can I do for you?"

Cord looked at him. He saw four bloody fresh scalps hung around Childs' belly, shoved down behind the waist band of Atwater's trousers.

"Do for me?" Cord said, annoyed at the suggestion that he needed any help. "Well, hell, stick this in my wound back there." He handed Childs the wadded sleeve and gestured toward the bullet wound behind his shoulder. "Then get me on my feet. We've struck the mother lode here, Sterling." He chuckled, but then winced as Childs buried the cloth deep into the back shoulder wound.

"You good now?" Childs asked.

"Never better," said Cord while gunfire blazed back and forth hillside to hillside. "Let's enjoy this upturn in fortune while it lasts."

On an upper game path far above the melee unfolding below, Sam stopped and looked down as the others rode slowly forward, keeping firm rein and attention to their animals. On their left, a straight drop of over two hundred feet lay as if in wait for the slightest stumble or turn of hoof. Hearing the gunfire and seeing long wisps of smoke seep upward through the tops of tall pines, Sam searched but saw nothing of the men locked in their death battle.

At the bottom of the two-hundred-foot sheer stone wall, a boulder-strewn stretch of hillside terraced out and dropped off again onto the high pine woodlands.

"Too bad, Cord," Sam murmured quietly to himself, thinking of what the scalp hunter had done to a good man like Winters. "I would have liked to see you die."

Beneath him the black-point dun shied to the side a little, not quite a misstep, but almost.

"Easy, Copper," Sam said, catching the reins firmer, helping the horse right himself. "I wasn't talking about you," he said in a settling tone. He patted a gloved hand on the tired dun's sweat-dampened withers. "You oughta know that. . . ." He touched the side of his boot to the dun and they surged forward. As the battle raged below, the tired band of men and horses rode on.

PART 3

PART 3

Chapter 18

———

At the end of the first day headed back toward Mesa Grande, the Ranger saw that Ison Prine was losing ground. When Parker and Atwater helped Flake lay the teamster in the sparse shade of an ironwood tree, Sam and Flake stooped beside him. In spite of the heat, Sam noted right away that Prine lay shivering as if in a bed of snow.

"He's—he's dying! Dying of the fever!" Flake said, once again pressing his hands to his cheeks in despair.

Parker and Atwater gave each other a look and shook their heads at Flake's outburst.

"No, he's not," Sam said quickly, giving Flake a cold stare. He turned to Prine, whose eyes had opened at the sound of Flake's wailing. "No, you're not dying, Prine," Sam said. "But you are taking a fever. We've just got to make better time getting back, is all."

"You don't have to . . . tell me nothing, Ranger," Prine said. "I have . . . imposed on you enough." He raised a weak hand and took the Ranger's gloved hand in it. "Leave me here. I'll catch . . . the next stage to glory." He paused and then gave a tired grin. "Or the gut wagon to hell . . . which-ever has the best whiskey."

"That's the spirit," Sam said. "If we don't stop we should be getting into Mesa Grande tomorrow night."

"I'm sorry, what I said, Ison," Flake offered, leaning in closer. He sniffled a little and wiped his eyes. "Death is just so frightening and ugly, up close like this, knowing the person's eyes you're looking into will soon see nothing but that great blackness—"

"All right, Flake," Sam said, cutting him off. "What's wrong with you? You're supposed to be this man's friend."

"Oh, I am, Ranger. Indeed I am," Flake said quickly. "I'm just saying how hard it is to see—"

Prine's hand, weak though it was, reached up and managed to clamp firmly around Flake's throat.

"Backhand him . . . for me, Ranger," he rasped.

"Hold it! We've got somebody coming, Ranger!" Parker said as he and Atwater crouched by the horses, unarmed.

"Jesus! It's Apaches!" said Atwater as two Indi-ans walked into sight around the edge of a broken boulder. One led a lank whip-scarred mule on a short length of rawhide. The mule pulled an empty travois of a sort used most by the northern plains tribes. The other Indian carried a four-foot-long painted stick that looked to have started out much longer years earlier. The paint on the stick was faded from the desert sun.

Sam swung around toward the two, the double rifle coming up waist-level, cocked and ready.

The two Indians made an abrupt halt. They stood staring at Parker, Atwater and Flake, the three still dressed in scalp hunter clothing.

"Don't shoot," said the one leading the lank mule. "We good people, not bad people." He nodded in the direction of the earlier gunfire. "We Pueblo people, not those bad peoples. We white man's friend."

"Oh, really, then," Flake said in a huff. He planted a hand on his hip as if exasperated with the two. "I suppose you 'good people' come to get your arrows back?" He flipped his free hand toward Prine, who had raised himself slightly and lay watching, wheezing with each breath.

"Shut up, Flake," Sam said. Seeing the two were unarmed, he lowered the double rifle a little. Parker and Atwater stood watching intently. The Ranger had noted all day how docile and cooperative the two outlaws had become.

The two Pueblos had no understanding of sarcasm, but they saw that the man under the ironwood had arrow points sticking out of his chest.

"He die," the one with the stick said flatly. "We don't fix him."

"Now, see here, you," said Flake.

"I said shut up, Flake," Sam said in a firmer tone.

Flake cocked his head to the side at a sharp angle.

"You're supposed to know better," Parker cut in.

Sam ignored Flake and Parker and stepped toward the two Indians, letting his rifle barrel lower a little more. He gestured toward Prine.

"What do you mean, you 'don't fix him'?" he

asked, speaking slowly, paying close attention for their reply.

The two Pueblos looked at each other and spoke in their native tongue as if sorting things out. The one with the mule, an older Indian, nodded and turned to Sam.

"He mean he die *if* we don't fix him," he said.

Sam nodded. He gazed harshly at Flake, then looked back at the two Pueblos.

"That's what I thought you meant," he said. He motioned them over to where Prine lay in the thin shade.

Looking down at Prine, the one with the stick studied the teamster's weathered face and nodded.

"Wagon driver," he said. As he spoke he pointed the tip of his stick against Prine's chest, between arrow stubs.

"Dang it," Prine said, shoving the stick away. He strained his feverish eyes and studied the Indian's face. He managed to stop shivering for a moment. "Yeah, I've seen you before too," he said. He looked up at Sam and said, "I might . . . be in luck here, Ranger. This man is . . . big medicine in these parts. Has a cure . . . for everything."

Sam stepped in closer to the Indians.

"You can get these arrows out?" he asked the Indian with the stick.

"Yes," the Indian said. "Pull them out, close them with mud." As he spoke he gestured the procedure with his hands, his faded painted stick leaned against his side. He patted a fist on his palm and held it up. "Three, four days."

Sam understood. The Indian was saying Prine

could travel in three or four days after his crude surgery.

"Can't spend three or four days," he said. He shook his head, knowing that his best bet was to get Prine on into Mesa Grande. He had no idea who would be coming up the trail toward them anytime now. He looked at the empty travois.

"You take," said the Indian, gesturing at the travois.

Prine cut in, leaning upward a little, the shivering coming back.

"Forget cutting the arrows out," he said to the Pueblo medicine man. "You got gumpsage?"

"Gumpsage . . . ," the Indian said, nodding, staring at Prine as if further diagnosing his condition. "I have gumpsage."

"All right, then, now you're talking," said Prine. He reached his fingers up and rubbed them together. "Get it out. Let me have it."

Sam watched as the Indian turned and took a woven cloth satchel down from the mule's back and rummaged through it. When he pulled up a leather pouch and opened it, he turned back to Prine, who had managed to rise a little more and prop himself onto his elbows.

"This very strong gumpsage," the Pueblo said, reaching the pouch out to show it to the wounded man. "Take this much." He held up the tip of his thumb to illustrate the proper dosage.

"Yeah, I got it," said Prine, jerking the pouch from the Indian's hand. "Harold, pay the men," he said to Flake.

The Indians both winced as Prine raised the

pouch to his lips and downed a large swallow of
the brownish green-and-red herb.

"He take too much," the Indian with the stick
said to Sam.

"Will it kill his pain, lower his fever?" Sam
asked.

The two Indians looked at each other.

"Then some," said the one with the stick.

Sam backed a step and watched as Flake pulled
Prine's leather coin pouch from his trouser pocket
and paid the Indian with two small gold coins.

The Indians looked at the coins, then at each
other. Satisfied, the one with the stick put the coins
away and stood for a moment studying Prine's face.
The other walked over and freed the travois from
behind the mule.

Prine seemed to settle and stop shivering almost
instantly. He reached a hand up toward Flake and
motioned for a canteen. Flake went and got one
from his saddle horn and rushed back with it. Prine
drank thirstily, then shoved the canteen away. He
stared up at the Indian with the stick as if in won-
derment.

"I feel all the pain leaving my body," he said
joyfully. "I feel the fever melting away!"

He looked at Sam, then at the Indians. He tried
to sit up and would have had not Sam and Flake
and the Indians pressed him back as gently as
they could. Prine lay back flat and stared up at the
sky though the spindly branches of the ironwood
tree.

"I can pluck these arrows out as far as that goes,"
he said, his voice sounding stronger, clearer, almost
happy. "There's no pain, no fever!" His voice grew

louder, stronger as he spoke. He wagged his boot toes back and forth. *"Woooo!"* he said. He gripped his fingers on the rocky ground as if to keep from flying off the earth.

The Pueblos looked at each other and nodded. Then they looked at Sam.

"We go," said the one with the painted stick.

Parker and Atwater stood staring down at Prine as the Indians turned and left.

"I have felt like hell all day myself," Parker said. His hand went to this lower back.

"Forget it, Parker," Sam said. He stooped and picked up the medicine pouch from beside Prine and stuffed it inside his shirt for safekeeping. "Get the travois rigged, get Prine on it. Let's get on to Mesa Grande, get these arrows out of him."

At the Pridemore Trading Post on the hilly northern edge of the desert flatlands, Turner Pridemore's elder boy, Lucas, looked up from an army of ants dissecting a large *Arctosa* wolf spider. The spider reached two of its spindly arms up as if pleading to the Pridemores for help. In answer to its plea, the dying spider received a blast of white cottony spittle from young Lucas' lips. Three of the spider's four eyes were gone. The lower halves of it legs were being carried away by a detail of purposeful worker ants. Turner Pridemore's shadow moved in over his son and his son's amusement.

"What've you got, boy?" he asked, staring down at the one-sided war playing out in the dirt. Turner had reconciled himself to the fact that his son would always be a little head-thick and easily distracted.

"It's a wolf spider, Pa. Look at it," the boy said, stirring a short stick around in the swarm of ants.

"I've seen enough blasted wolf spiders and ants to last a lifetime," Turner replied. "Did you skin them rattlers like you was told? Or do I have to get your brother, Fox, to do it?"

"I'm fixing to, Pa," said the boy, sounding too young and light-spirited for his eighteen years. "I want to see this all out. If I had me a *funning* glass I could see it all closer and burn up the lot of them after a time." He gave a dumb, joyous grin. If he weren't his elder son, Turner would have called it an *it's* grin.

"I don't know anybody gives a *funning glass* for shirking," Turner grumbled, "'less that person be a shirker himself. Which case he'll likely forgo a *funning* glass and anything else he seeks in this life."

Lucas looked up again. He had no idea what his father had said, or why.

"I'm just saying, Pa," he said quietly.

"I know you are," said Turner, sounding paternal. He brought the wide sole of his big miner boot down atop the ants, spider and all, and ground the scene down in a swirl of death. "Now go skin the rattlers 'fore they start stinking. I see them skins again, best be boards behind them."

Lucas stood and wiped his hands on his trousers. He stared down for a moment, as interested in the aftermath as he had been in the battle. Then he turned to leave, but his father stopped him.

"Hold on, boy," Turner said. Lucas saw his father staring out onto the flats toward the hill country where dust had roiled up suddenly on the still air.

"What, Pa?" he said.

"Go get Fox. Tell him I says load up," said Turner.

While Lucas started to turn again, the voice of sixteen-year-old Fox Pridemore called out from their trade shack.

"I'm loaded up, Pa," he said. "Brought ol' Dan Webster to you too." The boy stood in the open doorway of the shack, an ancient but still workable eight-gauge deck gun in his hands. A large Walker Colt stood at his waist, causing his striped trousers to sag on his wide black-and-white-checked galluses.

"There's a good boy, Fox," Turner said. He met his younger son halfway and pulled the big Walker Colt up from his trousers. Fox's trousers rose four inches with the weight of the gun gone.

"What do you want me to do, Pa?" Lucas asked, tagging along behind his father.

"Skin them rattlers, like you was told," Turner repeated, checking his big Walker Colt, "'less if you hear me and Fox holler out." He gave his slow-witted son a solemn look. "Then you take out of here, run like the devil. If it's Apache kicking up dust like that, they'll likely kill Fox and me, then you."

"Oh, all right, then," said Lucas. He shrugged and walked away to where three dead bull rattlers lay in a pile under a cloud of blowflies.

Turner shook his head, watching Lucas dawdle along stirring the short stick in the air as if rearranging objects unseen. Then he turned to his younger son.

"All right, then, Fox, let's see who we've got

coming here," he said in earnest. "We'll either have to fight them or sell them something." He turned and stared out at the looming rise of dust as it grew closer. "Either which it is, let's hope we come out ahead."

Chapter 19

The Ranger, his prisoners and Harold Flake had pushed on through the night traveling under a waxing moon and a purple starlit sky. They had only stopped for an hour to rest and water their horses at a stone-lined water hole. When they left the water hole they headed downward toward the desert floor.

The Ranger kept the two prisoners in front of him even though he believed they were done resisting the law. Flake rode at his side, leading the supply horse that pulled the travois with Ison Prine tied down on it.

Prine had babbled, howled and bellowed, laughed, flopped and wallowed vigorously all afternoon. Before dark the Ranger had Flake tie him down to keep him from rolling off the travois and opening his wounds. Or, worse yet, from rolling off the travois, out off the high trail and plunging to his death.

Now as they skirted diagonally along on the lower hillside slopes, Prine had stopped struggling against his rope restraints, but his howling and long bellowing sounds continued almost nonstop. The center of the travois was open down the middle, which kept the hallucinating teamster from goring the arrow stubs deeper into his back.

When the distant cry of a wolf called down from the hillsides as if answering Prine's persistent howling, Parker dropped back next to the Ranger and shook his head as he looked at the wounded teamster.

"Good Lord, Ranger," he said, "ain't there something that'll shut him up? He's got the wildlife all worked up!"

"I don't know of a thing," Sam replied sharply, a little put out himself. "At least his fever is staying down—his pain too, I have to think."

"He's givin' me the willies," Parker said. "I don't know that a little pain and fever is so bad." He saw Sam give him a look. "Just a little is all I mean."

Sam didn't reply.

"I had hoped the gumpsage would have worn off some by now," he said, "but he's still running full steam. He'll surely wear down soon, though. He hasn't had any more of it since before dark."

Flake looked over at the two as they rode. Behind them Prine howled long and loud, as if calling back to the distant cry from the hillsides.

"Huh-oh," Flake said in a hushed and guarded tone.

Sam saw the strange look on Harold Flake's face.

"What?" he said. "Did you give him *more*? While I wasn't looking?"

"Okay, *yes*, I might have," Flake said excitedly. "But it had nothing to do with whether or not you were *looking*. I wanted my poor friend to be comfortable. Is that so bad?" He clasped a hand to his face, his fingers pointed upward covering his mouth.

Sam shook his head. Prine continued howling. Another wolf replied, this one closer. Parker gritted his teeth. Atwater turned in his saddle and looked back at them. Then he dropped back next to Flake.

Atwater said, "Gumpsage will kill the pain and help the fever, but too much of it will get him graveyard dead."

"Oh, really?" said Flake in a sarcastic tone. "Now I suppose you're a medicine man?"

"All right, that's enough," Sam said. He looked sidelong at Flake, then at Atwater and Parker, who had gotten closer to him on either side. "You two step off, get back up there." As he spoke he laid his hand on his holstered Colt just in case. The double rifle lay across his lap. The two hurriedly pulled their horses away, then booted them forward. "He's right, Harold," Sam said. "Unless you want to see your friend in a pine box when we get to Mesa Grande, no more gumpsage."

"I'm—I'm sorry, Ranger," Flake said. "I only want to do what's best for him." He flipped a hand back toward Prine, who lay mumbling and laughing under his breath.

"All wheel—no wagon!" Prine blurted out. "All guns—no bullets!" He laughed insanely. "All thorn—no roses!"

"Please, Harold," said Flake. "Let's not show the Ranger how silly you can be."

The Ranger looked Flake up and down. On the

upper hills a mountain cat squalled out loud and long. The wolves fell silent, as if bested by the stronger voice.

"Give me the gumpsage," Sam said flatly.

Flake looked aghast.

"Well, I never," he said, offended. But he reached inside his stinking rawhide scalper's shirt and pulled it out and handed it over.

"Obliged," Sam said, reaching back, sticking the pouch up under the flap of his saddlebags. Then he reined his dun back a few steps and rode on, watching the party of four move along ahead of him in the moonlight.

Turner Pridemore stood in front of his trade shack watching Erskine Cord and five bloody, sweaty, dust-streaked riders slow down coming off the sand flats and finally bring their horses to a halt a few feet from him. No sooner had the men stopped than a long, weathered sign that had hung above the shack porch for four years pulled loose on one end and swung down with a crash onto a display of pans and pottery.

Turner, startled, threw his hands out to his sides, the big Walker Colt standing behind his belt.

"Hold it, now! That meant nothing!" he shouted as the six tired horses spooked and had to be brought under control. "The sign's been loose for a while!" He noted the string of wet-looking scalps hanging from each saddle horn.

The riders had brought up rifles and pistols as they collected the horses. But with a nod from Cord they lowered the weapons and settled their mounts.

"What brings you this way, Cord?" Pridemore said, only slightly relieved that it was scalpers instead of Apaches.

"Working for the Mexicans," Cord said.

"I can see you are," said Pridemore, eyeing the dusty, bloody scalps. "I hope you've got no Apache trailing you here." He looked off across the sand flats.

"It's likely I do," said Cord, swinging down from his saddle. He also looked back out across the flats toward the hill lines. "What's left of them anyways."

"Mescalero?" said Pridemore.

"Yep," said Cord. "A new bunch. They call themselves Wolf Hearts. Ever heard of them?"

"Oh yeah," said Pridemore. "Quetos' bunch. They come by the other day searching for bullets. I told them I had none, but they shook the place down anyway. Killed my last young goat, never paid for it."

"Tell them about it when they get here," said Cord. He looked at the doorway to the shack, where Lucas and Fox Pridemore stood peeping around either edge.

"You get Mescalero on your tail, they're hard as lice to shake loose," said Pridemore.

"They are indeed," said Cord. He swung down from his saddle and stood holding his horse, his rifle hanging from his hand. "Good thing you told me."

Pridemore's face reddened.

"Hell, I know you don't need telling. I was just reminding myself, is all." He gestured a hand off to the side toward a thin donkey hitched to a water wheel and slowly circling a stone well. "You and your men go water up," he said. "Kick that burro out of your way."

Cord raised a blood-blackened hand and motioned his men to the well. As the men moved their horses away, he looked all around at the shack, a lean-to barn and a weathered wagon with its wheels missing seated atop four piles of stones.

"You ever miss it, Turner?" he said to Pridemore, nodding back toward the string of scalps.

"Huh-uh, I don't miss it," Pridemore replied. Then he paused for a second and said, "Well, sometimes I reckon I miss it. Scalping gets in a man's blood just like panning for gold." He breathed deep. "But I got boys to watch about." He looked Cord up and down. "How long you figure?"

"An hour, maybe two," Cord said. "I know that's cutting it close."

"We're cooked," Pridemore said. "They'll kill us just knowing you was here." He looked out again, this time in regret, with his hand resting on the butt of his big Walker Colt. "I didn't wake up this morning wanting a fight brought to me."

"I had no choice but bring it here," said Cord. "We needed water bad. We knew you were here. You want us to leave when we've watered, we will. But weigh it first."

"I don't need to," said Pridemore. "I can't talk Mescalero out of killing me and the boys. I'm better off with you here, now that you are."

"That's how I see it," Cord said. He nodded toward the open doorway. "We can use your boys.

Anybody else you can send for? Anybody close enough, who'll fight?"

"Everybody'll fight. They fought to get here, they'll fight to stay. But there's no time to round anybody up," Pridemore said, shaking his head. "Anybody who happens to see Quetos' bunch on the trail will come here anyway. We've got a stage line trying to get a start out here. Looks like they're running late, though. They've got a Cherokee half-breed, Mickey Cousins, riding shotgun. He's a real fighting sumbitch. So's ol' George Lick, the driver."

"All right, but they're not here," said Cord. He looked at the shack sitting backed up against a huge stand of boulders. "How deep can you go in there?"

"Deep as you want to go," said Pridemore. "I keep some water and air-tights back underground in there for just such times as this." As he spoke he waved Fox and Lucas out of the shack. The two walked out warily, then stood before Cord and their father, Fox holding the eight-gauge. Lucas still held the stick.

"Boys, this is Erskine Cord. I used to work with him. Anything happens to me, you do like he says."

"Yes, sir," said Fox. But Lucas only nodded, distracted by moving the stick around in the air.

Cord looked Lucas up and down, then looked at Turner.

"I've got a nephew I'll put this one with," he said. Then he turned to Fox, seeing the wide-striped trousers, the polka-dot shirt and black-and-white-checkered galluses. "This one hurts my eyes," he said. He tugged at Fox's galluses and said, "You took these braces off a dead clown, tell the truth."

Fox looked at his father for support.

"We have to take whatever comes through here to us, Cord," he said defensively. "I expect you know that."

Cord only nodded.

Before he could reply, Sterling Childs called out to him from the well, "We've got a stage coming, boss. Coming fast."

Cord and Pridemore looked off at the stage rolling in from a different trail than the scalp hunters had ridden in on.

"This'll help," Pridemore said, watching the stage rock and bounce, hurrying across the flats from a set of lower hills east of the trade shack. The scalp hunter, the trader and his two sons stared out toward fresh dust billowing up where Cord and his men's distant dust still settled.

"Just in time. Here come the Wolf Hearts too," said Cord.

As the stagecoach drew closer, bouncing, swaying badly ahead of its own rise of dust, Pridemore and all the bloody, exhausted scalp hunters looked away from the approaching dust to the right and cheered and shouted loudly at the speeding stage. But watching it, they fell suddenly silent when the big Studebaker coach dipped down low on its front left corner and its left wheel went rolling out across the rocky ground. The coach's left front corner dug down into the dirt and sent the driver and shotgun rider flying off the seat in different directions. Their hats sailed away as they fell.

"Well, son of a bitch," said Cord. The men still stood watching, but all with sour, defeated expressions on their hollow faces.

The six horses twisted sidelong severely and almost fell as their harnessing broke free of the ill-fated coach. Yet they struggled and righted themselves and loped on toward the trade shack, recognizing it as their regular relay station.

Cord and Pridemore saw the shotgun rider rise running as dust billowed and roiled around him. The coach driver lay as still as stone. The scalp hunters grabbed the coach horses when they slowed and finally stopped near the lean-to barn.

"Somebody go get him," Cord said in disgust. "See if the other one's alive."

"I'll go," said Ozzie, already pulling his reluctant horse away from the wide well. He stepped up into his horse. "Want me to check for guns and bullets?" he asked, turning the tired animal.

"Yes, and check for *cannons and balls*," Cord said wryly.

"That's my nephew," Cord said to Pridemore as Ozzie rode away.

"Oh," said Pridemore.

They watched as Ozzie rode out and reached a hand down and the shotgun rider took it and swung up behind him.

Ozzie turned his horse and rode back to where the driver lay on the ground. The shotgun rider dropped and ran to the driver and bent over for a moment, then turned and swung back up behind Ozzie.

"We lost one before he even got here," Pridemore said.

They walked to the men who stood at the well as Ozzie and the shotgun rider rode in. All eyes went to the shotgun rider's long black hair as he stepped down from behind the saddle and dusted himself off.

"Lick is dead." He gestured toward the body lying out in the dirt. "We saw Mescalero on our way here. That's why the hurry," he said to Pridemore, eyeing the scalp hunters as he spoke. A two-inch-wide birthmark streak of white hair hung down one side on his face.

"We know it, Cousins," said Pridemore. He jerked his head toward Cord and his men. "This is Erskine Cord and his band of scalpers. They had it out with the Wolf Hearts. This is where the trail brought them."

"So, they're after you?" the half-Irish, half-Cherokee Cousins said, looking at Cord. He pushed the white streak of hair back off his cheek as he spoke.

Childs and one of the scalpers named Eli Banks, who had been separated from the men but straggled back in before their battle with Quetos, both looked at the rest of Mickey Cousins' long black hair, then at each other knowingly.

"They were and are after us," Cord said to Cousins coldly. "Careful what you say next," he added.

"The question is, no matter who they're after or why, will you stand with us?" Pridemore said.

Cousins looked around, then at Lucas and Fox, then back at their father.

"I don't need strong reasons to kill Apache," he said. He gave a shrug. "I'll stand with you. I hate Apache."

"Good for you," Pridemore said. He looked all

around at Cord's men. "I knew we could count on this one."

Childs and Banks looked at Cousins' hair again, then back at each other. Childs smiled slightly to himself and looked toward the approaching warriors.

Chapter 20

———

The number of Quetos' Wolf Heart warriors had grown in spite of the ones he'd lost riding into Cord's ambush. Blanket Mescaleros on both sides of the border had heard about the turmoil between the Wolf Hearts and Cord's scalpers, and many younger warriors had traveled from afar to join Quetos' sect. Members of other Western Apache tribes had also joined the fight. On the trail chasing Cord and his scalp hunters, seven new warriors had shown up and joined his Wolf Hearts.

When Cord and his men and the others looked out from behind the immobile wagon they'd carried out front and set up as a fighting barricade, they counted over thirty warriors bent on taking revenge.

"Jesus . . . ," Sterling Childs said under his breath. "There's enough hair here a man could buy a place and a woman to go with it, put his feet up awhile."

Beside him, Banks licked his fingertip and ran it along his rifle's front sight. Behind the men lined along the wagon, their horses stood waiting, watered and restless, sensing the tension of battle in the air.

"Got to first get it skint and dried," he said,

businesslike, examining first his rifle, then the sharpened skinning knife he'd taken up from his boot well.

"And so we will, Elias, so we will," said Cord, looking out through his telescope. He watched in silence for a moment, then said without taking the lens from his eyes, "Now, here's a good argument against getting caught by these heathens."

"What have we got here?" said Childs. He moved up close beside Cord and stared out, using his hand as a visor above his eyes.

In the circle of the lens Cord watched the warriors drag up in front of their ranks two naked scalp hunters they'd captured. The two men's wrists were bound behind their backs; each had a thick strip of rawhide tied around his neck. They were bruised and bloody all over. One's eye had been knocked from its socket with a war club and hung on its muscle, bobbing an inch down on his swollen cheekbone.

"Stiles and Johnson," Cord said, identifying the two. "We lost them, what, two days ago? I hate seeing this." He watched intently through the lens. "Sterling, get a couple of good shots up here," he said sidelong to Childs. He murmured to himself under his breath, "This right here's why I'm getting my big rifle back first chance."

Childs looked along the wagon barricade and motioned for Emilio Siebaugh and Early Doss. The two hurried to him in a crouch, their rifles in hand.

"Get your sights up and ready," Childs told them. "It's going to get ugly here."

"You got it, Sterling," said Doss, already lifting

the rear ladder sight on his rifle and tightening down the screw dial holding it in place. Beside him, Siebaugh had already laid out his rifle, raised the sights and leaned down and waited for Cord's order to fire.

In the circling lens Cord watched as warriors hurriedly set up two tripods made up of lodge poles the warriors had bound together with rawhide where the poles met near the top. Below, before the braves had even finished tying the tripods, other warriors, just young boys, hurriedly piled firewood on the ground inside the two tripods.

"Here we go," said Cord as the warriors scrambled down the long poles just as a fire began at the pile's base and long flames began to lick upward. "I hate this . . . ," he repeated.

Childs watched without benefit of a telescope. He winced when he saw one of the scalpers try to pull away from the warriors holding him. The warrior beat his ribs in with a rifle butt, careful not to do anything to make the man lose consciousness.

"Me too," Childs said. "All these ol' boys ever did was try to make a living. What we do is legal under Mexican law."

"Apache dogs don't give a damn about Mexican law or any other kind," said Mickey Cousins. "Heathen sons a' bitches. . . ."

Cord and his scalpers watched from afar as the fire raged and burned itself down. Finally, twenty minutes later, some of the warriors came in and smothered the flames down with blankets, leaving a glowing, wavering bed of red-hot coals. Cord shook his head behind the lens.

"Ready, boys?" he said to his two riflemen.

Siebaugh and Doss leaned into their rifle butts and took close aim.

Cord watched the warriors tie long ropes around the scalpers' ankles, the two ill-fated men kicking and fighting all the while. From as far away as they were, Cord and his men heard their comrades scream and bellow as the Apache raised them on long ropes they'd tossed over the tops of the tripods. The men were pulled upside down off the ground and hung helpless in the broiling heat.

"Shoot them now!" Cord said as both men pitched and bucked and swung wildly over the glowing coals, their hands bound behind their backs.

Siebaugh homed onto Lowell Stiles, the man with the dislodged eye. He swung his gun sights along with him as the man bucked and screamed, the hair on his chest, his head and his privates appearing to melt away. Then mercifully the man fell limp and swung back and forth easily as Siebaugh's shot resounded and the warriors hurried back away from the twin fires.

Doss' shot exploded at the same time. But instead of falling limp into a merciful death at the end of his rope, Doss' target, Aaron Johnson, crashed down, rope and all, into the coals, and his screaming and thrashing only got worse.

"Kill him, damn it to hell!" Cord shouted, already jerking up a Winchester himself and levering a round up.

Rattled, Doss fired again, but this shot missed Johnson and ricocheted off a rock on the other side of the fire, embedding itself in one of Quetos' warriors. The Indian jackknifed at the waist. Cord, levered and ready, took close aim with the Winchester on the thrashing ball of flames, smoke and tortured human flesh.

As Cord fired just as Doss and four other scalpers took aim again, Johnson's body fell limp and lay burning on the coals, stoking the red coals back into licking flames. As he fell silent in death, the injured warrior ran in short wild circles headlong into the fire, his pain so intense that he thrashed and flailed himself onto the dead man.

From behind the wagon, scalpers whistled and cheered and laughed aloud until Cord shut them up with a wave of his hand.

"Quiet!" he said. "I want to hear him scream."

As the men stared toward the Apache, a warrior atop his horse raised a rifle and silenced his burning friend. As the shot rang out, the warrior stopped thrashing in the fire and a deathly silence set in among the Apaches and scalpers alike.

Seeing the warriors mount and form up a line, Cord called out to his men along the wagon and to the others scattered here and there behind rocks or lying prone in brush and wild grass. They had forced their horses to stretch out down on the ground in front of them. Keeping the reins in hand, the men laid out their rifles across their nervous horses' flanks and lay in wait.

"All right, men," Cord said, "I needn't remind you how much Mexican gold these heathens' topknots will bring us." As he spoke he raised his skinning knife above his head and displayed it back and forth. "Any man who doesn't fatten his fortunes today will have to admit to the world that he was not wholeheartedly trying!"

From the gathered Apaches came a loud warbling war cry that sent the mounted warriors bolting forward toward the trade shack and the wagon barricade out front. Rifle shots resounded; bullets began flying, thumping against the wagon like rapid hammer blows.

"Steady, men!" Cord called out, stepping down and taking position himself. "Save your shots until they're close enough you can smell these bastards!"

"I've *been* smelling them for two days," called a voice along the wagon.

The men gave a laugh but did as they were told, standing poised and ready, watching the desert horsemen pound toward them, rifles up and firing. Cord watched and waited until he gauged the warriors to be within seventy yards.

"Fire!" he bellowed, and he started shooting round after round from the Winchester into the thundering mass of man and horse.

Until the rifle fire exploded from the scalp hunters, the attacking warriors had had their way, making a straight unimpeded run toward the trade shack. But upon suddenly facing a dark blanket of return fire wavering chest-high, man and horse stumbled forward and rolled dead and dying in the blood-misted dust surrounding them.

Cord continued firing, Childs firing right beside him. When the Apaches broke away, the dark blanket of fire now streaking around them red with blood, they began to veer away to regroup and form a firing circle in front of the wagon and its defenders.

"Pour it on them!" Cord shouted loudly above the sound of gunfire. "Remember Stiles and Johnson! Remember Berne and Shank!" He levered and fired, and levered and fired. Fighting in a fever pitch, he shouted, "Remember *Dixie*! Remember *the Alamo*!"

Behind a short pile of rock ten yards from the wagon barricade, Ozzie Cord and Fox Pridemore fired without letting up into the wide endless carnival-like circle of Indians. Return fire from the warriors dinged off the rocks and whined away in the air. A dead scalper lay in the dirt behind them. Lucas sat undisturbed by the raging battle, flipping the dead man's nose with the stick he still carried.

"If he don't pick up that rifle and do something with it, I'll shoot him myself," Ozzie warned, feeling senior and war-scarred to the Pridemore brother. But to his surprise and alarm, Fox swung the eight-gauge's barrel toward him.

"Touch a hair on his head, I'll splatter your guts out," Fox hissed in warning, his voice sounding as deadly as the melee playing out before them.

Ozzie was taken aback at the instant violent response to his words. Nobody reacted this way toward his uncle Erskine when he made threats to his men. His eyes went up and down Fox Pridemore as if seeing him for the first time. The checkered clown braces, the striped trousers high above his ankles, the dotted shirt.

"He's got to do his part, don't he?" Ozzie asked, his tone and attitude lowered by half.

"Shut up, you son of a bitch, he's doing his part," Fox launched back at him, the hammer drawn back on the deck gun.

"All right, all right," said Ozzie, raising a hand as a show of peace. "I didn't mean nothing."

Ozzie stared at Fox as if in fear and awe for a moment. Fox turned the eight-gauge quickly toward the passing circle of warriors and pulled the trigger. The blast sent a rider and his horse tumbling sidelong on the ground.

Ozzie turned away with his smoking rifle and resumed firing at the circle of horsemen. He heard Lucas behind him make a mocking sound, like a low cur that had just offered its belly to a bigger dog.

"You shut up too, Lucas," said Fox, turning toward his older brother, "and hand me that man's rifle." He'd loaded the eight-gauge and laid it aside to cool.

"It's his," Lucas, gesturing his stick at the body stretched out in the dirt.

"He ain't needing it," said Fox. "I am."

Lucas picked up the dead man's rifle with his fingertips and handed it to Fox.

"When do I get to shoot?" he asked.

"Real soon, Lucas," Fox said. He quickly checked the rifle and levering a round into its chamber. "Real soon. . . ."

As he turned and fired, two young warriors who had spotted the deck gun and seen what damage it could do rode wide around the battle and slipped into the brush and wild grass on foot behind the three young men.

As Ozzie and Fox fired on the circling horse-men, the warriors on foot snuck forward, rifles and war clubs in hand. As an act of courage they didn't want to shoot these three but rather bludgeon them to death face-to-face. They would return to their Wolf Hearts with the big deck gun and the fresh blood of their prey on their faces and chests.

Yet, as they had advanced to within twenty feet, Lucas looked and pointed the stick at them as if were a gun.

"Bang, bang!" he shouted. The two young war-riors hurried now, forgoing their plan for a face-to-face killing.

Hearing Lucas behind them, Fox and Ozzie both swung around and saw the two warriors raise their rifles. Ozzie fired wildly, missed and levered a fresh round, and Fox dropped the rifle, grabbed the eight-gauge, cocked it and fired all in one desperate motion. The powerful blast of bro-ken rock and scrap iron lifted both warriors off their feet as it bored and ripped its way through them. One got a shot off before he flew backward, leaving a fine mist of blood in the air.

Ozzie had tried again, but his bullet zipped past the falling warriors.

"That was close," he said in a shaky voice. Side-long, he saw Fox scramble over and kneel beside Lucas, who lay staring straight up at the sky. There was a circle of blood and brain matter in the dirt beside him.

"He's dead?" Ozzie asked, as if the gaping hole in Lucas' head required further explanation.

"Yes," Fox said flatly. He turned away from his brother, laid the eight-gauge down, picked up the rifle and turned back to the smoky dust-covered fray.

"I hope we make something out of all this," Ozzie murmured to himself, repeating what he'd heard his uncle Erskine say many times before. He looked out at the circle of warriors, seeing it had grown smaller by half. Dead littered the flats on either side of the horses' passing hooves. Looking along the wagon barricade, he saw dead scalpers lying strewn across the ground.

As he looked he saw his uncle and his men move back away from the wagon and grab their horses' reins. They swung up into their saddles in unison and rode away.

Atop his horse, Cord shoved his rifle into its boot and jerked his big Colt from his belly holster. Beside him Sterling Childs grabbed his horse and another horse whose rider he saw lying among the dead. He shoved the horse's reins to Turner Pridemore, who stood with blood running the length of his arm.

"Are you able to ride?" he shouted at Pridemore.

Pridemore only gave him a stare, swung up one-handed onto the horse's back, pulled his Walker Colt, ol' Dan Webster, from his belt, and kicked the horse out toward the warriors.

"I'll ride past hell and see you on the other side! Somebody look after my boys," he yelled. He jerked his horse's reins and rode away as other scalpers

mounted and formed up and raced forward squall-
ing like lions, firing at will.

"This is all going to my liking!" Cord shouted.
The men broke up the Apache firing circle and
rode inside it shooting in every direction as the
warriors fell back and kept firing. More dead fell
on either side. Cord glanced down at all the bodies and couldn't recall a time when he'd seen so
much hair for the taking.

Inside the smoke and dust and rage of battle,
Banks and Childs sidled up to the half-Indian
Mickey Cousins. Both of them fired at the remain-
ing warriors still inside the disbanded circle.

"Come on, Cousins! Stick with us!" shouted
Childs. He started to grab the half-breed's horse
by its bridle, but Cousins jerked his horse away
and stuck his smoking Remington in Childs' face.

"You ain't getting what you're after," he said
evenly. "Now back off."

"Look here, we're trying to *help* you, fool!"
shouted Banks on his other side, trying to get Cousins' attention turned away from Childs for just a
second.

But Cousins would have none of it. He swung
his Remington around at Banks without taking
his eyes off Childs.

"Help this!" shouted Cousins; the Remington
bucked in his hand and sent a bullet and a blast of
fire through the center of Banks' face. Banks' head
jerked sideways, slinging blood. He flopped off
his saddle as Cousins swung the smoking Remington around to Childs, cocked and ready. But
Childs had already started backing his horse
away, shaking his head.

"Let's get this thing done," he said to Cousins in his second-in-command tone of voice, nodding toward the battle.

Cousins nodded.

"Kill them all . . . ," he said evenly, batting his horse forward.

Chapter 21

It was midmorning when the two deputies, Leon Fuller and Tom Dukes, stood out in front of the sheriff's office watching the Ranger and his party of dusty haggard riders advance slowly into Mesa Grande from the southwest. Behind them inside the sheriff's office, workers were finishing up repairs on the rear wall. Sherman Geary sat at the sheriff's desk with his head in his hands. He'd gone back to drinking the night before and had no place to sleep off his whiskey while the jail was under construction.

On the street, the Ranger followed behind his two prisoners and Harold Flake, who led the horse pulling the travois where Ison Prine lay sleeping like a dead man. The blackened, blood-coated arrowheads stood out of Prine's chest, looking sinister and gruesome.

"Look at this . . . ," Fuller said under his breath. He and Dukes stood watching as the rider veered toward the doctor's white clapboard house. Dukes' arm was still in a sling from the town's Indian battle.

"Say what you will about the Ranger," Dukes responded in the same lower tone, "he takes this work *serious*."

"Yes, I'll give him that," said Fuller.

"Look over there," said Dukes, gesturing toward the Old Senate, where Willard Sives and Buck Longhand walked out onto the boardwalk and watched the Ranger and his party step down from their horses at the hitch rail out in front of the doctor's house. Dr. Young walked out off his porch wiping his hands on a white cloth.

"I see them," said Fuller. He gave a grin. "Curland is going to soil his johns when he sees the Ranger made it back here in one piece." He adjusted his gun belt. "Let's walk over to the Old Senate. I get the feeling things will get *real active* around here now that Burrack's back."

The two started off along the boardwalk toward the Old Senate Saloon.

"I have to say," Dukes offered, "the Ranger has done all right by me."

Fuller looked at him.

"Don't forget who's paying us here," he said. "This is the easiest work I've ever had—smack a drunk around now and then once he figures out Curland's new game machines have robbed him."

"I know," said Dukes. "Curland pays good. I'm just saying, the Ranger stood up with us against that Wolf Hearts bunch. He could have tipped his hat and said adios."

"He could have," said Fuller. "Or he could have made life easy for everybody and given over Cord and his scalpers."

"That's what I mean," said Dukes, "he didn't turn his back on them either."

"That's because he's got it in his head somehow that law is good," said Fuller. "I've done some scalping. They're the lowest, foulest men ever stood upright. When men are worse than I am, I want no part of them. That's why I got out." He looked sidelong at Dukes as they drew closer to the Old Senate. "You're not getting *lawful* on me, are you?"

"No," said Dukes, "my head's on straight. I'm just saying the Ranger was square with me, is all."

"That doesn't mean you won't kill him if Curland wants to, does it?" said Fuller. "I mean maybe even throws in a little extra bonus money for our trouble?"

"That could be a whole different thing," said Dukes. "A good cash bonus might go a long ways in swaying my opinion."

They stopped talking and stopped beside Sives and Longhand out in front of the Old Senate just as Curland stepped out of the doorway, a cigar in the fork of his fingers.

"Where have you two been?" he asked Fuller, sounding cross and testy.

"We're deputies, Mr. Curland," Fuller said evenly. "We've been at the sheriff's office, watching Sherman Geary, seeing over the back window being repaired."

Curland nodded as he looked over at the doctor's big clapboard house.

"Now that Geary's back to drinking, I want him to disappear," he said. "He's caused enough trouble here."

Fuller and Dukes looked at each other and nodded.

"You got it, Mr. Curland," said Fuller. He nodded at the dusty horses out in front of the doctor's house.

"What about all that?" Dukes asked.

"He means the Ranger," Fuller said on Dukes' behalf.

"I know what he meant," Curland said coldly. "I've got that problem taken care of, if need be."

Sives and Longhand gave Fuller and Dukes a smug flat stare, their hands on the butts of their holstered guns.

"All right," Fuller said. "That's what you want, then Dukes and I will keep busting heads and make sure everyone loses to your gambling machines."

Curland nodded.

"That's exactly want I want for now," Curland said. "Burrack can't stay here any longer. He's got too much badlands to cover." He took a draw on his cigar and blew out a stream of smoke.

Inside the doctor's office, Harold Flake stood on the Ranger's right in his odorous scalper's clothing. On the Ranger's other side stood Parker and Atwater. Sam had explained first thing about the heavy doses of gumpsage. Dr. Young had only grimaced and shaken his head. As he looked back down and examined the arrow stubs in Prine's chest, he sniffed the air and looked around at the filthy buckskin, interwoven hair and human bone the three men wore.

"For goodness' sakes, Harold," he said to Flake, "why don't you and your friends go find some clean clothes and burn this stuff before it makes somebody sick?"

"Good idea, Doc," Parker said quickly. He turned to Atwater and nodded toward the door.

"Stand still, both of you," Sam said, stopping

them. "These men are my prisoners, Doctor," he said. "They can't go anywhere." He looked at Flake and said, "Harold, you can go wash up and change clothes if you want to."

"No, thank you, Ranger," said Flake. "If it's all the same, I want to stay here and make sure Ison is going to be all right first."

"You mean you want to make sure you didn't kill him with all the gumpsage you gave him?" said the doctor.

Flake looked worried and ashamed.

"I will never forgive myself if something happens to him," he said, almost tearfully.

Hearing a coughing sound from the other room, the doctor looked around at Sam as he sorted through his surgical tools.

"Ranger, do you mind pouring some water for the sheriff so I don't have to stop here?" he said.

"Not all, Doctor," Sam said. "I need to talk to him some anyway, if he's up to it."

"He's getting better, healing a little more every day," the doctor said. "Sheriff Winters is as strong as any patient I've ever seen."

"I'll go with you, Ranger," said Flake as Sam started to turn toward the door.

"No," Sam said, "I want to talk to the sheriff in private. You stand here and shout out if these two try to leave."

Flake gave a tight little grin.

"I'll be your deputy, sort of?" he said.

Sam only gave him a look as he walked through the oak door connecting the two rooms. As soon as he shut the door he saw Sheriff Winters try to sit up on the side of his bed. He leaned the double rifle against the wall and hurried over to ease him back down.

"Unhand me, sir," the wounded sheriff said, his voice still weak from his ordeal.

"Easy, Sheriff, it's me, Sam Burrack," the Ranger said as he gently forced the sheriff to lie back in bed.

"Sam . . . ?" said Winters. His eyes looked puzzled as they moved over the Ranger's face. Then recognition set in. He relaxed onto the bed. "I kept thinking you were here off and on . . . while I was knocked out."

"I was here, Sheriff," he said. "I had to leave for a while to round up some escaped prisoners." As he spoke he noted the thick heavy bandaging on the sheriff's abdomen. He turned to a nightstand and poured water from a pitcher into a water glass and held it over to the wounded man. "I didn't get a chance to talk to you before I left. But I'm back now."

Winters nodded at the door between the two rooms.

"You brought somebody in . . . ," he said weakly. "Who is it?"

"Ison Prine," Sam said. "He went with me. He took three arrows in the back."

"Don't let him die, Ranger," Winters said, almost pleading. "He's a good man . . . no matter what we done. . . ."

Sam gave him a curious look. "If I'm any judge, he'll pull through it. You upcountry men don't kill easy."

Winters offered a weak smile; he sipped water as Sam held the glass to his pale, parched lips.

"I heard Harold Flake's voice," he said.

"He's over there too." Sam gestured toward the door. "He was taken hostage during the jailbreak. Some scalp hunters broke their leader out. There's been a lot going on, Sheriff."

"And you come here . . . to keep the peace for me?" said Winters. The Ranger could tell the man had not yet been brought up on all the events in Mesa Grande since his shooting.

"It's a long story," Sam said. "I was on my way here when you got shot. I ran into one of the men involved on my way here. There were two of them—both scalpers. One's an assassin." He held the glass to the sheriff's lips again and let him sip. "They're still running loose. I had to turn back and get Prine some help. But I'll catch them, Sheriff. They're out there now, them and some Mescalero, chewing each other up."

"But you saved Harold . . . thank goodness," said Winters, his voice growing weaker, talking wearing him out.

"Everybody's fine, Sheriff," Sam said. "You take it easy."

"You talked to Prine? And to Flake?" Winters said, his eyes falling closed. "They told you everything . . . ?"

Everything? What is this?

Sam just looked at him, hearing something in his voice.

"Pretty much, Sheriff," Sam said, weighing his words, watching the sheriff closely. He paused, then said, "I'd like to hear what you've got to say about it, though. . . ." He let his words trail.

"It was Curland. He hired the assassin," said Winters.

"I figured as much," Sam said. "I understand you were against him bringing in some crooked gaming machines?"

"The machines had nothing to do with it." He waved the notion away with a weak hand. "Curland's greedy. He wants a finger in every pie. . . ."

The Ranger saw his eyes drift closed again. He thought about letting him sleep, rest up some more. But Winters jerked his eyes open and batted them to keep himself awake. Whatever this was, the wounded sheriff wanted it off his chest, Sam decided.

"Curland wanted what Prine and Flake and I had set up with the Mexicans," said Winters. "He couldn't stand . . . us making money on something and him not. . . ."

The Mexicans?

Sam stood watching, listening close.

"Guns, Ranger," Winters said. "We've been selling guns to the Mexicans. It ain't illegal . . . but I'm not saying I'm proud of it."

"Legal to the Mexicans, but not to the Apache," Sam said, fishing now that he was getting an idea what all this had been about.

"We never sold guns to Apache," Winters said. "We'd have to be fools to do that."

"Curland wanted part of your enterprise with the Mexicans," Sam said. He shook his head. "It's legal, so why are Flake and Prine so tight-lipped about it?"

"Because I told them to," said Winters. "I told you it's not something I'm proud of," Winters said.

Sam saw him drifting again and knew this session was over.

He set the water glass down, left the room and closed the door again, the double rifle back in hand.

"How is the sheriff? What did he say?" Flake asked, keeping his voice low, sounding nervous, directing the Ranger off to the side.

Sam gave him a steady gaze, letting himself put some suspicion in it. He stepped even farther away from the two prisoners and the busy doctor.

"He was awake. We had a good talk," he said also in a lowered secretive tone. "But he's back to sleep now." He glanced away from Flake for a moment, to where the doctor stood bent over Prine's chest. One of the arrow stubs was out of the teamster's abdomen, lying in a pan heavily coated with thick, dark blood.

"A—a good talk?" Flake said, still nervous, even more so, Sam noted. "My, my, what did you have to talk about?" he asked.

Parker and Atwater stood watching the doctor intently as he worked on Ison Prine's wounds.

"We talked about selling guns to the Apache," Sam said. He was fishing again, wanting to hear Flake's reaction.

The townsman looked as if Sam had backhanded him in the face.

"Ranger, oh my God!" Flake said, bringing his hands to his face, his eyes darting back and forth. "Ranger, the poor sheriff must be out of his mind—his wounds, the pain!"

"No," said Sam, the same flat look on his face. "He told me about you, Prine and himself." His voice stayed lowered between the two of them as Parker and Atwater watched the doctor, engrossed.

"We never sold any guns to the Apache, Ranger!" Flake said, ready to blurt it all out now that he thought Winters had jackpotted him and Prine.

Here it comes. . . .

"I'm not talking about the three of you selling guns to the Apache," said the Ranger, going from fishing to bluffing, playing poker with the man. "Winters would never go along with that. Neither would Prine. I'm talking about Curland and you." He paused to study Flake's reaction again, seeing by the stunned look on his face that he had struck a chord.

Flake slumped, almost fainted. He would have fallen had the Ranger not caught him and led him out the main door. He held Flake by his buckskin collar as he looked back at Parker and Atwater and called out to the others, "I'm taking Harold right outside the door here. Do not try to leave."

Parker and Atwater just stared at him, then turned back to the doctor at the sound of another arrow stub plunking into the pan.

Chapter 22

Outside the surgery room, the Ranger turned Flake's collar loose and gave him a nudge toward a wood-framed sofa. Sam stood over him waiting as the tearful man collected himself and tried to control his hands by wringing them in his lap.

"It was all Curland's idea, Ranger," he said. "I was all for it at first—you know, bringing in a man like him as a partner. He has all the where-withal to finance more guns and ammunitions for the Mexicans."

"But that wasn't good enough for him, was it?" Sam asked, digging deeper.

"No, it wasn't enough," Flake said. He shook his head. "He told me that there was a whole other market among the Apache. Said they would rob mines on both sides of the border for the gold to pay for guns. Said they had no understanding of prices, that we could charge whatever we wanted, they'd pay it."

"But Prine wouldn't go along with it?" Sam asked, sorting it out, wanting to know just who was involved and who wasn't.

"I knew he wouldn't, so I didn't even bring it up. Curland said leave Prine to him. He set it up with the Apache to ambush Ison while he was taking a load of rifles to the Mexicans. It was a ruse, about bringing back more gambling machines. Prine was delivering rifles to the Mexicans—or so he thought. It was an ambush all along. The Wolf Hearts were supposed to kill Prine. But he got away. I suppose they were happy enough getting all those new, shiny repeater rifles." He paused, then said, "But they had no ammunition."

"'All guns, no bullets,'" Sam said, repeating what Prine had said when he was babbling on the gumpsage.

"Yes, that's what he meant," said Flake. "He must've realized Curland had set up the ambush— he knew that at least the Indians had no bullets."

"Where *did* they get the ammunition?" Sam asked.

"From Willard Sives and Buck Longhand," Flake said. "They drove a buggy-load of bullets out to the Quetos' warriors in the middle of the night. That's why they weren't here when Quetos' men hit Mesa Grande."

"Sives and Longhand made it all possible." Sam mused for a moment. "Did Fuller and Dukes have anything to do with it?"

"No, they work for Curland," said Flake, "but Curland was clear about keeping them and everybody else out of the gun venture." He tossed a hand. "Sives and Longhand are just gunmen, Ranger, nothing else.

"Am—am I going to jail?" Flake ventured. "I mean, all I did was try to make some money for myself."

"Seems that's all anybody tries to do, starting

out," Sam said. "I've got a sheriff hanging on to life. I've got Prine shot full of arrows." He looked Flake up and down. "But no, Harold, you won't have to go to jail. Not if you had nothing to do with selling the guns to the Apache. You might have to tell it all to the judge when he gets here—"

Flake cut him off.

"Oh, I didn't have anything to do with it," he was quick to point out. "But do you suppose the judge will believe me?"

"Probably so," Sam said, "especially since you'll be willing to tell all about Curland, Sives and Long-hand."

"I will, Ranger, I swear I will." Flake looked relieved.

"The judge will scold you, maybe slap your hands," Sam said. "But that's about all if you're telling me the truth."

"My hands!" Flake's eyes widened; he looked at his hands, turned them back and forth. "You don't mean—?"

"That's just a figure of speech, Harold," Sam said. "You need to settle down some."

"I will, Ranger," Flake said, already taking a deep breath. He gave Sam a hesitant look.

"What is it, Harold?" Sam asked.

"Well," Flake said, "I was just wondering. Will those prisoners of yours be going to Yuma for a long time?"

"I can't say," Sam replied. "This is their first time arrested and charged. They're only charged with providing horses for some robbers. Judge could go easy." He looked at Flake closely. "Why do you ask?"

Flake shrugged his thin shoulders under the smelly buckskin clothing.

"I'm afraid those two may think I may owe them some money," he said.

"Now, why would they think that?" Sam asked, having already heard parts of the story listening to Flake and the two prisoners bicker back and forth about it.

"Because I'm afraid I *may* have mentioned something about paying them, *should* they, or perhaps I might say *would* they help me get back to Mesa Grande. It's not as if I *actually* said it, although indeed they may have thought I said—"

"Harold," the Ranger said, cutting him off, "you need to talk straight if you want people to believe anything you've got to say. People won't always say when they know you're lying, but they do."

Flake fell silent.

"Here's what I understand happened," Sam said. "You were afraid the scalpers would kill you. You offered Parker and Atwater ten thousand dollars to get you away from Cord and headed back to Mesa Grande. Isn't that the whole of it?" He stared at Flake.

"Well, yes and no," said Flake.

Sam shook his head. "There's no such thing as 'yes and no' here, so pick one and stick to it."

Flake slumped under the Ranger's insistence.

"Okay, I did tell them that," he said. "But—"

"No buts either," said the Ranger. "If you owe them the money and they are not in jail, I can see them doing whatever they think it'll take to get it from you." He paused, then said, "Your life was worth that ten thousand dollars when you thought you were about to lose it. Is it worth it now?"

Flake looked confused for a moment. He sniffled and wiped his nose between his thumb and finger.

"So you're saying I should pay them?" he said.

"I'm not saying one way or the other," Sam replied. "I'm just laying out the question. You have to decide."

"All right, I think I understand," he said with some measure of resolve in his voice. "I suppose I should stay in Mesa Grande until after the territorial judge has come and gone?"

"It would be a good idea," Sam offered.

"Yes, then." Flake nodded. "And I suppose you don't want me telling Curland what you and I have talked about?"

"Makes no difference to me, Harold," the Ranger quietly. "I get the feeling Curland knows he and I have a reckoning coming. He'll do what his nature requires of him, whether you tell him or not."

"All right, then, I'm not going to tell him," Flake said, chin forward. "I don't care what he says, or how much he threatens." He paused with a determined look. But Sam watched it fade as the man began to second-guess himself. "I mean, unless you feel it's all right that I do." He paused again. "Or if it's not all right, that telling him might somehow jeopardize—"

"Harold. Hey, Harold!" Sam said, sharply cutting him off, having to raise his voice to cut through Flake's verbal sprawl. "I don't want to see your face the rest of the day. See how clear I said that?" He touched his fingers to the brim of his sombrero and nodded Flake toward the front door. "Get going."

He watched as Flake left; then he took a deep breath and listened to the sound of the nervous townsman's footsteps hurrying away across the front porch.

As he turned to open the door, the door opened from inside and Parker almost ran into him. But the big outlaw halted, even took a step back, seeing the double rifle barrels pointed at his chest.

"*Whoa*, Ranger! Don't shoot," he said. His hands went chest-high. "I'm not going anywhere. The doctor sent me to get you, said the sheriff's in a bad way."

Sam hurried along behind Parker through the room where Ison Prine lay unconscious, the arrows out of his chest, a bloody cloth lying over the wounds.

"I'm afraid he's dead, Ranger," said Dr. Young as Sam and Parker hurried into the sheriff's room. Atwater stood to the side, his ragged fur-trimmed scalper's hat in hand. "I've been expecting it," the doctor continued. "He's been hanging on as if to make sure he got something off his chest before leaving us."

Sam stopped and let out a breath.

"I think I understand what it was, Doctor," he said. Even as he spoke he realized the news about the sheriff dying would get out quick.

As if reading the Ranger's thoughts, the doctor stepped over close and said quietly, "Should I keep word of his death under our hats, give you some time to make plans?"

"Obliged, Doctor," Sam replied, "but I've an idea how things need to go from here. Tell who you need to tell. The rest of this will work itself out."

"Ranger, are you sure?" the doctor asked. His eyes searched the Ranger's intently.

Sam replied with only a nod of his head.

It was time to settle with Joseph Curland. Hearing about the sheriff's death, Curland would realize he was getting closer and closer to facing a murder charge for hiring an assassin. Once Flake told Curland about the conversation they'd just had, and Sam was sure he would, Curland would have no doubt the Ranger was coming for him.

Sam knew that dealing with men like Curland, men who paid others to do their killing for them, could turn into a long, drawn-out court proceeding. That might have been something Sam could have abided had the sheriff stayed alive. Winters was the kind of man who would have taken it all back to Curland and settled it man to man. No court, no trial. But now that Winters was dead and Sam knew he had no witnesses and no hard evidence against Curland, there was only one way to settle things for the dead lawman.

And there it is. . . .

Sam looked at Parker and Atwater and nodded them toward the door.

"Let's go get you two a scrubbing and a change of clothes," he said.

Fuller and Dukes had watched from the boardwalk of the Old Senate Saloon as the Ranger and his two prisoners led their horses from the doctor's house to the town mercantile store. After a few minutes they'd watched the three leave the mercantile and lead their horses toward the sheriff's office. Parker and Atwater each carried a bundle of new clothes under his arm. Sam looked over at the saloon as the two deputies walked out into the street and fell in alongside him.

"Good to see you made it back, Ranger," said Dukes.

"Even got the men you went hunting for," said Fuller. "Two of them anyway."

Sam gave the two a nod.

"I expect your boss knows I'm back by now?" he said. As he spoke his eyes went across the front of the saloon.

"Yes, he does," said Dukes. "Harold Flake went up the side steps like a jackrabbit, stinking to high heaven. Whatever he had to tell, he couldn't wait to tell it." He looked at Sam evenly. "You must've known he would."

Sam only nodded again.

"What become of the idiot, Ozzie," Fuller asked, "and my ol' pal Erskine Cord?"

Sam just looked at him.

Fuller clarified himself.

"I should have said my ol' *used-to-be pal* Erskine Cord," he said. "That was a long time ago. These days I have no more use for scalpers than you do, Ranger."

"I understand," Sam said. "Cord, his nephew, the whole bunch were fighting Apache last I heard them. They could all be dead by now."

"They don't die easy, that bunch," said Fuller. He nodded at the double rifle in Sam's hand. "If

Erskine's alive, you'll know it soon enough. He
don't give up stuff like that. He'll come looking
for his rifle, if he knows you've got it."

"You think?" Sam said, glancing sidelong at him.

Fuller gave him a bemused look as they walked
along.

"You already figured on that, didn't you?" he
asked, looking the Ranger up and down.

Sam didn't answer. Instead he took a deep
breath, knowing what the next words out of his
mouth would initiate.

"Sheriff Winters is dead," he said flatly.

A silence set in for a moment. Then Fuller and
Dukes looked at each other and Fuller let out a
breath.

"It's no surprise, the shape he was in," he said.
"Where does this put things with you and Curland?"

Sam gave him a cold look as they walked on.

Fuller shrugged.

"All right, we work for Curland," he said. "It's
not a secret. Curland's money runs this town.
That's not a secret either. That doesn't mean he
owns Dukes and me. We don't run to him with
everything we hear." He paused. "Anyway, it looks
like Harold Flake's already done that," he added.

Dukes cut in, saying, "We don't have to do
everything he tells us to either. We're deputies. We
work for you until someone is appointed sheriff."

"I don't expect that will be very long, once Curland gets the news," Sam said.

"Who do you suppose will be appointed acting
sheriff?" Fuller asked, almost jokingly. "Sives or
Longhand?"

"I've got five dollars that says Willard Sives," said Dukes.

"You'll get no bet from me," Fuller said. "Willard comes from a long string of shootings and killers, some for the working for the law, some of it for gun money."

"Well, right now we're still working for you, Ranger," Fuller said. "What do you want us to be doing?"

"When we get to the jail, get each of these prisoners a bucket of water to wash off with," Sam said. "They smell like wet buffalo hides." As Parker and Atwater looked back over their shoulders at him, Sam said to them, "No offense intended."

"None taken, Ranger," Parker said.

And they walked on.

Chapter 23

In Curland's office above the Old Senate Saloon, Harold Flake stood shaking and nervous as he explained to Curland what he and the Ranger had talked about. When he'd finished he took a long drink of water from a tin dipper that Willard Sives handed him. When Flake took the dipper, Sives stepped over beside Buck Longhand. They stood to the side, listening, their thumbs hooked in their gun belts.

"What you're saying, Harold, is that you've spilled everything you know to the Ranger," Curland said flatly, a disgusted angry look on his face. He bit down hard on his cigar.

"What? No! Absolutely not!" said Flake. "The Ranger already knew everything! The sheriff told him!"

"Don't lie to me, Harold! It will get you killed quick!" Curland slammed his palm down on his desktop.

"I'm not lying, Mr. Curland, I swear!" Flake said. "He came right out of the room from talking to Winters, and told me everything I just told you."

Curland thought about it for a second, working

his cigar around in his mouth. He looked at Sives, then at Longhand, then at a younger gunman named Louis Burdell who stood at the door.

"What say you, gentlemen?" he asked the three.

Sives shook his head and chuffed under his breath.

"The Ranger got him rattled," said Burdell. "Flake here started talking and couldn't shut himself up."

Flake stared at the young gunman, stunned.

"Sounds about right to me," Longhand agreed.

Flake's mouth dropped open.

"Well, *I never!*" he said.

Curland looked at Sives as if concluding the census.

"I'd say the Ranger just played our boy Harold here. Had him jumping through hoops like a Mexican carnival dog."

"Pl-played me . . . ?" Flake said, edgy and nervous. He looked at Curland pleadingly. "Mr. Curland, he knew everything! He had to get it from Winters."

Curland let out a breath and tried to calm himself.

"That's what I think too," Curland said. He leaned back in his chair and folded his hands behind his head. "Lawmen have a way of making you think they know more than they know. It gets to a man. Makes him want to find out what it is the lawman knows. The more he tries to find out what he knows, the more he ends up telling him."

Flake thought about it for a second and shook his head, rejecting the notion. "I just don't think that's what happened, Mr. Curland. With all due respect, I believe Winters told him all about us selling rifles to the Mexicans."

"That's nothing, Harold," Curland said. "Selling guns and bullets to the Apache . . ." He let his words trail as he shook his head. "That's the bad part. Burrack will be all over the three of us for that." He looked at Sives and Longhand knowingly.

"Then I did all right, Mr. Curland?" Flake asked, his voice trembling.

"Yeah, we can work it out, Harold," Curland said in a more friendly tone. "Burdell is going to walk you to your place and keep watch while you get yourself cleaned up and get a good, long rest." He offered Flake a sympathetic smile. "You have been through an awful lot, my friend."

Flake slumped with relief. "Mr. Curland, it was terrible, simply terrible."

"Let's go, Harold," said Louis Burdell. He ushered Flake toward the side stairwell.

Curland, Sives and Longhand stood listening in silence until they heard the footsteps stop and the downstairs door close.

"I expect that'll be the last we'll see of Harold Flake," said Sives, "standing upright on his own anyway."

"Yes, I expect it will be," said Curland. He stood up from his desk, reached down with a key and unlocked a bottom drawer. He took out a gun belt wrapped around a big holstered Colt. "Want to know what Burdell whispered to me when he came in a while ago?" he asked, reaching the gun belt around his waist and buckling it as he spoke.

The two looked at him curiously.

"Yeah, sure, I'd like to know," said Sives, "if you feel like telling us, that is."

"He said Winters is dead," Curland said flatly. "He saw him through the window. Said he saw the doctor pull up a sheet and cover Winters from head to toe."

"Then that's that," said Sives. "No more worrying about what Winters is going to say, crooked gambling machines or anything else."

"I never gave a damn what he thought about the new gambling devices," said Curland. "But selling rifles to the Apache was a whole different story. He would never have gone along with it." He shrugged and gave a smug grin. "So he had to die. It was just good business, simple as that."

"Too bad it took so long for it to happen," Sives commented.

"Yes," said Curland, "and too bad we've still got this Ranger sniffing around. He's got enough from Harold to keep him around here a little longer."

"You still going to wait him out, just avoid him until he leaves town?" Longhand asked.

"No," said Curland. "It's gone past that now that Flake told him about the gunrunning." He adjusted the gun belt at his waist and raised the Colt and checked it. He spun the cylinder and shoved it back into its holster. "I'm through with this Ranger. He's going to die tonight. Let the town think that whoever killed the sheriff came back and killed the Ranger too—some crazy cowboy that held a grudge against them both."

Longhand grinned and gave Curland a curious look. "If you can get this town to believe that, you ought to think about running for Congress."

"Oh, it shouldn't be too hard," Curland said. "I'm respected here. Once folks respect you, you can tell them anything. They won't doubt it."

"Kill him today," Sives asked, "after Burdell gets rid of Flake?"

"Tonight," said Curland, "while the Ranger is at the sheriff's office watching his prisoners with Fuller and Dukes."

"I don't know that I trust those two anymore," Longhand said.

"I don't trust them at all," Curland said. He puffed his cigar and blew out a stream of smoke. "That's why I'm making sure they don't know anything about it." He grinned again. "Any other questions?"

"That'll do it for me," said Sives.

"Me too," said Longhand.

"Tonight, then, gentlemen," Curland said. "We meet here at midnight. Show up with all your bark on. We're going to finish with this Ranger once and for all."

It was getting late in the afternoon when the Ranger heard the creak of the front door opening. In the doorway he saw Sherman standing there in the evening sunlight. Fuller and Dukes looked up from their wooden chairs leaning back against the wall. Geary was sweaty and out of breath. It took him two tries to get his voice and breath to work together without cutting each other off.

"Jesus, Geary, are you drunk again?" Fuller said, having dragged the man to the jail the night before rather than leave him lying in the dark street.

"Yes . . . I am drunk," Geary said. "But not that . . . much. I'm out of breath. . . . I ran all the way here from . . . Harold Flake's house." He gasped, adjusted his glasses and continued. "Harold Flake is . . . hanging dead . . . from a rope in his kitchen."

"Easy," said the Ranger, "don't pass yourself out." He stood up, bone-weary from all the time on the trail chasing prisoners and ducking Apaches and scalpers.

"I'm . . . all right," said Geary. "But you'd best come see . . . he is sure enough dead. I didn't want to leave him hanging . . . but I had no way to get up and cut him down."

Sam picked up the double rifle from against the desk and put on his sombrero. As he turned to the door, Fuller and Dukes both stood up from their chairs.

"Want us to come along, Ranger?" Fuller asked.

Sam looked over into the shadowy cell where Parker and Atwater lay snoring, wrapped in their blankets on the two cots.

"Yes," he said, "but only one of you. We need one of you here to watch the prisoners."

Fuller sat back down; Dukes walked to the door and followed the Ranger and Geary out onto the street.

"Take your time," Fuller said as they left. He sat down and leaned back in his chair.

Outside, Sam and Dukes followed Geary to a modest house off one of the side streets at the far end of town. Once inside, Sam saw an oil lamp sitting on a table. He picked up the lamp, lit it with a match from a tin container and carried it through the house to the kitchen. The first thing he saw was the dark silhouette of Harold Flake hanging from a rope thrown over an open kitchen rafter, still wearing the filthy scalper clothes.

"I came to see what he might be able to tell me about the sheriff dying," Geary said, having caught his breath. "I never thought I'd find him like this. I always knew he was peculiar and crazy, but he never struck me as suicidal."

Sam looked all around. He couldn't picture how someone would manage to take his own life here. The rope was thrown over a rafter and tied off around a big iron kitchen door hinge in a large-loop slipknot. There was not even a chair turned over under Flake's hanging body. Sam looked at the filthy clothes Flake still wore and shook his head. One of the oversized boots lay on the floor beneath Flake's body. A pale toe stuck out of a hole in his sock.

Sam didn't buy it.

"Flake didn't do this to himself," he said. "I don't think he would have been caught hanging here dead in these stinking scalper clothes." He looked at Geary. "Do you?"

Geary studied Flake's dead bulging eyes.

"No, come to think of it," he said, "I sure as hell wouldn't myself, and Harold was more particular than me." He fanned a hand back and forth against the stink wafting off the filthy buckskins.

Dukes dragged a chair over and stepped up on it. "Want me to hold him, you pull the knot loose?" he said.

"Yes," said the Ranger.

Dukes slipped his forearm out of the sling and tested his grip.

Geary stood near Dukes. As Sam pulled the knot and let the rope give way to the weight hanging from it, Dukes steadied Flake's body and gently laid him on the kitchen floor.

"I want you to both keep quiet about this until morning," Sam said. He gestured toward the darkness outside the window. "There's nothing can be done for him tonight anyway." He looked at the two and saw them both nod in agreement.

"We're not going to leave him lying here, are we?" Geary asked quietly.

"No," said Sam. "We're going to put him in his bed and cover him up until morning. Then we'll send for the undertaker and let him take it from there."

"But we're not going to say Harold went and committed suicide, are we?" Geary asked, poking his slumped glasses back up on the bridge of his nose.

"No," Sam assured him. "If I get the man who killed him, we'll call it murder."

"If you don't get him?" Geary asked.

Sam didn't answer. Instead he nodded down at Flake's body, its blue-purple face and its bulging eyes.

"I've got his shoulders," Sam said. "One of you get his feet."

It was well after dark when the Ranger, Sherman Geary and Tom Dukes walked back into the sheriff's office. Fuller, sitting leaned back in the chair, pushed up his hat brim and barely opened his eyes when the front door closed.

"What about Flake?" he asked Dukes. "Is he dead, or is Geary here still drunk enough to be seeing things?"

"Flake is dead, sure enough," said Dukes, his forearm back in the sling. "We found him hanging from a kitchen rafter."

Fuller tipped his chair forward and pushed his hat farther up on his forehead.

"Hanged himself, huh?" he said.

"No," said Dukes, "but it looks like somebody wanted us to believe he did."

"See?" said Geary. "Just because I'm a drunk doesn't mean I don't get some things right." He turned his gaze to the Ranger. "You mind placing me under arrest tonight, let me sleep in the other cell?"

"Are you still that drunk?" Sam asked.

"I still don't trust myself going very far on horseback," Geary said.

"Go ahead, then," Sam said. "But get settled in for the night and don't go wandering around. Some of us might be a little tense with all that's going on."

"You won't notice I'm here," said Geary. He adjusted his thick glasses on his eyes and stepped away.

As he walked over and stepped inside the cell, Sam looked over at where Parker and Atwater lay in the other cell under air heavy with loud and seamless snoring.

"I can't sleep with all that wood-sawing going on," he said. He looked at a closed door down a narrow hall. "What's in there?" he asked Fuller and Dukes.

"Extra blankets, some supplies, a cot," said Fuller.

"Good," Sam said. "I'm going in there and sleep till dawn. Don't wake me for anything less than an Indian attack."

"You got it, Ranger," said Fuller.

The two stood watching as Sam walked away down the hallway. They looked at each other. Fuller shrugged, tipped his chair back against the wall and pulled his hat down over his eyes. Dukes sat down in the chair beside him. Their rifles leaned against the wall between them.

Chapter 24

At midnight Willard Sives closed the side stair-well door of the Old Senate Saloon without a sound. In the light of a full moon, he turned and walked to where Buck Longhand and Curland stood waiting in the alley behind the large clap-board building. Music from a player piano still rippled from inside the Old Senate as the three checked their rifles. The only words spoken were those said by Curland before they turned and walked up the shadowy alleyway leading to the sheriff's office.

"Let's get this done, quiet-like," he said barely above a whisper.

Willard Sives drew a big knife from its sheath behind his back and turned it in the grainy light.

Curland and Longhand looked at the big knife. Curland nodded.

"We'll have you covered," he said.

The three turned, rifles and knife in hand, and walked along the alleyway in the moonlit night. When they reached the shorter alley that led alongside the side of the sheriff's office, Longhand stepped over small scattered debris workers had left while repairing the damage Cord's men did to the rear of the jail and slipped inside.

The other two walked quietly around the front corner of the building and stood at the front door of the sheriff's office. Without having to knock, they watched the door open just enough for them to slip through one at a time. Inside, they looked at Tom Dukes in the grainy moonlight through the front window. Dukes only nodded toward the hallway and the single rear door to the supply room. Then he took a step back and stood watching as the three crept away on soft cat paws. From his chair against the wall, Fuller raised his hat brim, reached over, picked up his rifle and laid it across his lap.

When the three assassins reached the small door, Curland and Longhand stood on either side. Sives waited, knife out and ready. When Longhand reached around and opened the door, Sives slipped inside the dark room as silent as death.

Dukes stood staring down the hallway, watching, also waiting. After a moment he watched the three slip back out of the room and walk back down the hall toward him. "Damn it *to hell!*" he heard Sives whisper viciously. He saw him gripping his right hand by the wrist.

Fuller stood up from his chair. He and Dukes stood watching the three.

"Did you kill him?" Dukes whispered as the three stopped and stood staring at him.

"No, we didn't *kill him*," Curland whispered back. "He's not there." He glared at the two.

"He was there," Fuller offered, his voice still

lowered against the snoring from the cells. "We saw him go in."

"Then he went out the gawddamn window," Curland said, his voice rising equal to Fuller's. "He must've suspected we were coming!" He glared harder at the two in the grainy light.

"My hand's bleeding bad," Sives said, still gripping his right wrist.

"Here, then, damn it," said Curland. He reached inside his coat, yanked out a folded handkerchief and handed it to Sives, who immediately laid it on his palm and squeezed his fist shut.

"What happened to him?" Fuller asked.

"What does it look like happened?" Curland snapped at him. "He's cut the living hell out of himself."

"Jesus!" said Fuller, staring at Sives, who stood half-crouched holding his bloody fist. He looked at Longhand, then at Dukes and back to Curland. But before he could say anything, Curland reached out and swung the door open in a huff.

"Don't you dare *ever* waste my time again," he said, "or you will be the next one who dies around here!"

As Curland stomped out onto the boardwalk, Sives, stooped a little at the waist, stomped out right behind him. Longhand stopped and looked at Fuller and Dukes.

"This ain't funny, not by a damn sight," he said in a slow-boiling tone.

"The hell did he mean by that?" Fuller asked Dukes as the door slammed shut behind Longhand.

"I don't know," said Dukes. "I was wishing you'd ask how Willard cut his hand so bad."

"I didn't think it was the right time to be asking," Fuller said.

The two looked all around in the grainy darkness.

"The Ranger knows we jackpotted him," Dukes said, "one of us anyway."

Fuller gave him a look.

"It wasn't me. Was it you?" he asked.

Dukes saw what he was doing.

"No, it wasn't me," he said.

"It wasn't you, it wasn't me," Fuller said. He grinned. "I wonder if we'll ever know for sure who it was."

"I'm with you," Dukes said. "Curland and those two stormed in here so fast, there was no stopping them. We didn't even *hear them* for all this snoring!" He gestured a hand all around at the cells.

"I like how you think, Tom," said Fuller. "We might be some good lawmen given a little more practice."

The three men walked purposefully along the shadowy street. Overhead, a golden full moon reigned supreme over a purple starry sky. Above the town on the high cliffs, moonlight glistened black on the sheer wall of stone where once at this time of year and turn of the moon, blood had spilled over rock for reasons too arcane to know. Yet, on the ground, on the street, Joseph Curland only glanced up at the moon and cliffs in passing as the shadow of his boots reached out in front of him, as if guiding him.

"He knew we were coming. That's all there is to it," he said over his shoulder to Sives and Longhand, flanking him. "I'm sick of figuring him out, and I'm sick of him being alive. I want him found and I want him dead!"

Hearing Curland's voice grow louder as he spoke, Longhand looked all around. Sives walked along with his hand wrapped in Curland's bloody white handkerchief.

"Boss," Longhand said, "we ought to keep quiet here. He's prowling around somewhere. He's not a damn fool. Could be watching us this minute."

Sives looked all around with Longhand.

"It's true," he said. "Burrack's no fool. This might not be the best time to stop figuring him. This might be the best time to *start*."

"Indeed, you say!" Curland said. "What am I, then, an idiot?"

"No," said Sives, "all I mean is—"

"Find him, gawddamnit!" Curland cut him off and began deliberately outwalking the two. "There's five hundred dollars waiting for you! Can you even count that high? I wonder if the Ranger can!"

Longhand whispered to Sives as Curland stomped away from them toward the saloon, "Tell him you can count to a *thousand* just as easy."

"Shut up, Buck," Sives said, gripping his wrist against the bleeding. "He's in one of his killing moods. I've seen him like this before." He called out to Curland, "Where'll you be, then, Mr. C?"

"At *my* saloon," said Curland. "Do you suppose you can find your way there without stabbing yourself?" He stomped on.

"Son of a bitch . . . ," whispered Sives to himself.

"Why does he think it's safe in the Old Senate?" Longhand asked.

"I don't know—why didn't you ask him?" said Sives, getting testy himself from all the verbal abuse Curland had heaped on him, ready to pass some of it along.

"All's I mean is, the saloon might be the *first* place I'd look for a saloon owner—"

A blast from the big double rifle cut his words short. Longhand and Sives both ducked instinctively, seeing Curland flying jackknifed backward, crashing out through the door of the Old Senate. Spinal bone fragments and stringy innards exploded from his back and streaked the dirt, as if marking a spot before he even landed.

"Jesus God Almighty!" Sives shouted, slamming both hands to his ears in afterthought. He and Longhand heard the big bullet that had torn Curland apart thump like a hammer blow into a post supporting an overhang on a building thirty feet behind them. The overhang shook violently; dust billowed along its roof. The sound of the shot echoed and rolled, seemed to even *squall*, out along the hill lines and across the flats.

"Okay, I'm done," said Longhand. He raised his hands high.

"You damn fool," shouted Sives already turning away. "He's not going to *arrest* you!"

Longhand stood dumbfounded for a second, the rifle shot ringing in his head, watching Sives race away on foot toward the far end of town.

"Oh . . . *yeah!*" he said, finally getting it. He turned to run himself. But before he could get

started, the big rifle roared again. The shot lifted
him, his feet pumping hard, flung him ten feet
and slung him onto his side. His feet pumped a
few more waning steps and fell in a running position. This time Sam heard the bullet whine away
out across the flatlands, sounding almost disap-
pointed as it disappeared into the night.

Stepping out the door of the Old Senate, Sam
broke the big rifle open and reloaded it as he
walked to the middle of the street and kneeled
and took aim at Sives fading away into the night.
When all he could see was a pale, white dot—the
handkerchief—batting up and down with Sives'
running footsteps, he let out a breath, lowered the
rifle and stood up. He dusted his knees and stood
up as lamplight swelled inside windows.

He raised a cupped hand to his cheek for volume.

"This is Ranger Burrack," he called out loud
and clear. "*Do not* come out of your homes. Stay
indoors until I tell you it's safe."

"Ranger, are you all right?" a voice replied from
the grainy darkness.

Sam let out a patient breath and instead of
answering raised his hand to his cheek again.

"*Do not* come out here until I say it's safe," he
called out again.

"Don't worry, Ranger. We're coming!" another
voice called out farther up the street.

Sam turned his head, hearing doors open and
close. He turned back to the Old Senate and as he
walked inside he heard Fuller shouting in an
angry voice.

"Get back inside, damn it! Before you get yourselves killed!" he bellowed to the townsfolk. "Are

you all deaf, you bunch of blockhead sons a' bitches?"

"Inside, now!" shouted Dukes.

Sam walked across the floor of the saloon and pulled out a porcelain handle that would pause the player piano until an inside spring ticked down quietly and released it. He heard the slightest ticking inside the piano as he walked behind the bar. He laid the double rifle lengthwise on the bar, on the shelf holding the bartender's scatter-gun. He stood with his arms spread, his hand resting on the bar edge. Fuller and Dukes walked warily through the door; he just stared at them.

"All right, listen to me, Ranger," said Fuller, his and Dukes' hands chest-high as they crossed the floor to the bar. "We're not here to fight." Dukes' forearm was out of the sling; the dirty cloth hung down his chest.

Sam just stared at them and remained silent, keeping his hands spread and in sight.

"We never denied working for Curland," said Fuller. "So you knew what you could or couldn't count on us to do. And that's the truth, huh?"

Sam stared.

"I mean, when it come to the Apache, to us protecting this town, didn't we run right in there for you like a couple of darts?"

Sam only conceded the point with a slight shrug of a shoulder.

Fuller and Dukes relaxed a little. Fuller looked at Dukes for approval.

"Tom, it's all right with me if you want to go ahead and tell him," he said. He gestured Dukes toward the Ranger.

Dukes considered it and said, "Okay, Ranger, here it is." He let go a breath and said, "We told Curland you was there, sleeping in the stockroom."

"Jesus, *Tom!*" said Dukes. "That ain't what I meant you to tell him!"

Dukes grimaced but recovered and said, "Then you should've made it more clear."

Fuller turned back to the Ranger quick and said, "All right, there it is, Ranger Burrack. We did wrong. But something we both come to know is how good we felt protecting this town. Am I right, Tom?"

"Yeah, you're right," Dukes said. "The fact is, had it not been for Curland offering—"

"But why don't we stop right here, Tom?" Fuller said, giving him a cold stare. "Sometimes the less said—"

They both stopped talking as the Ranger's hands went down under the bar. But when he came up holding two empty beer mugs, Fuller and Dukes relaxed a little. They glanced at each other when the Ranger held the two mugs down in one hand, filled them and slid them a few feet down the bar. Then he kept his hands down out of sight and stared at them again.

"You're pouring us a beer?" Fuller said with uncertainty.

Sam cut his eyes to the beer mugs, then back to the two men.

"Drink up," he said flatly.

"Now, wait a minute, Ranger," said Fuller. He reached a hand out and stopped Dukes from stepping forward. "Are you saying that like 'this might be the last beer we ever drink'?"

From the open doorway the voice of Erskine Cord filled the saloon, saying, "Drink up, you damn cowards. Else I'll drink it myself after I splatter this law dog all over the wall."

The two gunmen spun toward Cord and saw him and four of his scalp hunters step through the door and spread out a few inches apart. Two of them threw Sives' body on the floor.

"Look what we run into," said Cord. "Saw his hair wasn't dark enough, but we went ahead and killed him anyway." Seeing Fuller and Dukes, their hands on their gun butts, badges on their chests, he grinned. But his grin went away as he turned his eyes back to Sam.

"I come here to get my rifle . . . and to kill you, Burrack, for ever putting your hands on her. Don't deny she's here. I heard her crying out from down the trail, on the flats—*come get me, come get me*," he said in a strange voice, that of a speaking rifle.

"*She's* right here under the bar," said Sam, personifying the rifle, the same as Cord. "We've gotten to know each other pretty well, the two of us." He stared at Cord.

"Watch your ugly mouth," Cord warned. "Reach down easylike and hand her over."

Sam looked at the four scalp hunters flanking him, one of them, Mickey Cousins, a bloody bandage covering half his head. Around Cord's waist hung four scalps, one of them with Cousins' long, white birthmark in it.

Seeing Sam look at the half-scalped man, Cord said, "Yep, it was his. Childs scalped him and this man killed him for it." He grinned again. "But we don't let nothing go to waste."

Sam nodded as he reached down slowly and raised the big double rifle and laid it along the bar, the hammers already cocked, ready, waiting.

Cord looked at the cocked rifle and said, "You ain't using her on me, Ranger. There ain't nothing going to jump up at the last minute and save you." He said to his men, "Cover me good, boys. This one's tricky."

Sam stood staring as Cord stepped forward and picked up the rifle and kept the hammers cocked.

"Say when, boss," said one of the scalpers. "Kill all these jakes and get back to the others waiting." He held his hand on his gun butt.

Sam cut a glance to Fuller and Dukes; they stood ready, tensed, waiting.

Cord stepped backward, bringing the rifle up toward the Ranger.

"Hate to kill and run," said Cord. "But we lost lots of men to Quetos." He looked down the rifle sights at Sam and added, "Sweet dreams, Burrack—"

But as he squeezed the trigger, the porcelain pause handle made a loud click, like a gun cocking. Cord swung the rifle toward the sound just as music burst loudly to life—a tinny rendition of "Oh! Susanna."

Before Cord could stop himself, the rifle bucked in his hands, blowing a huge hole through the piano. At the same time, Sam grabbed the shotgun and went to work. He fired one barrel into Cord's face and saw it blow away. He swung the second shot at Cousins, sending him backward in a cloud of blood.

Dukes and Fuller fired as one, repeatedly,

dropping two remaining scalp hunters as the third one turned and ran out the door. But no sooner had he run out than he came flying back in and flopped dead atop the bodies. Behind him, Sherman Geary walked in cautiously, fanning a rifle back and forth.

Sam stepped over to the piano that was trying to play in spite of the hole it. He pulled the pause handle again.

A silence set in under a cloud of black smoke.

Without a word Sam stepped over to the double rifle and picked it up. Wiping blood from its stock, he nodded toward the piano.

"I don't know how to turn it off," he said. "It'll start again, so don't let it surprise you."

Fuller and Dukes stood loading their guns. Sherman Geary walked to the bar, picked up a mug of beer and swallowed over half of it in a single gulp. He let out a breath and finished it in another drink, then pointed at the other mug.

"Go ahead," said Fuller. He looked at Sam as he finished loading his Colt and slid it into its holster.

"Where were we, Ranger?" Dukes asked, seeing Sam walk toward the open door.

"I don't know where *you* are," Sam said over his shoulder. "If you'll take care of this mess, I'd like to lie down for a couple of hours—maybe till daylight. It has been a while since I got any real sleep."

Dukes followed him out the door and stood on the boardwalk.

"What about us, though?" he called out as Sam walked back toward the sheriff's office. "We've got more to talk about. We want to know where we stand—"

"Shut up, Dukes, and get back in here," said Fuller.

"But I want to know if we're squared up with him—don't you?" Dukes said, stepping back inside but looking out at the Ranger as he walked away.

"I already know," said Fuller. "Now stay in here and keep quiet." He gestured a hand at the dead lying about on the saloon floor. He looked at Geary, who stood with the second empty mug in his hand.

"Tell him, Geary," he said. "Tell him where we'd be right now if we weren't squared up here."

Geary gave a little belch and raised the mug as if in a toast.

"He'll figure it out," he said. And he swirled the beer, raised the mug to his lips and drank it down.

Arizona Territory Ranger Sam Burrack rode his copper-colored black-point dun past a broken hitch rail, over toward a short, wind-whipped campfire fifty feet away. He led a chestnut desert barb beside him. Over the barb's back lay the blanket-wrapped body of the half-breed named Mickey Cousins, who had died in Mesa Grande in a shoot-out with the Ranger and two town deputies at the Old Senate Saloon. Cousins had been a shotgun rider on a desert stage route before falling in with a band of scalp hunters who were under contract with the Mexican government to kill the desert Apaches when and wherever they found them.

The leader of the scalpers, Erskine Cord, and his nephew, Ozzie Cord, had been paid to lie in wait and gun down the sheriff of Mesa Grande. While the Ranger was convinced that Erskine had done the actual shooting, Ozzie was with him, side by side. Erskine, whom Sam had left lying dead on the floor of the Old Senate in the same gun battle that had taken Mickey Cousins' life, had been waging a private war with a particular band of Mescalero Apache known as the Wolf Hearts, led by the seasoned desert chief Quetos. A bad enough hombre in his own right, Sam reminded himself.

He had been on the scalpers' trail now for what . . . a week? he asked himself. Yes, he believed it had been a week now since he'd loaded Cousins' body and struck back out on the trail. Time passed quickly, while you were chasing down scalp hunters and assassins while a band of Mescalero warriors was busy killing any white man foolhardy enough to be out here along the border badlands.

What does that say for you? he asked himself wryly.

He looked all around the abandoned trading post when he stopped and stepped down from his saddle. The wooden part of the structure had burned unobstructed for days. All that remained standing were two of the original stone walls that had been here since the days of Spanish rule. The charred remnants, strewn utensils and bits of leather shoe and clothing were signs of yet another generation who'd come and gone through the portal of time. Recent bullet holes dotted the stone walls; arrows stood slantwise in the sandy ground.

Twenty feet in front of him past the blackened adobe walls, a man with dark bloodstained bandaging wrapped around his chest sat in the dirt, staring at him. Sam saw the shotgun lying across the wounded man's lap. Two Mexican women busied themselves preparing an evening meal over a wind-driven fire.

"Hello the camp," the Ranger called out, stopping at a respectable distance.

The wounded man continued staring at him as he spoke sidelong to the two women.

"Keep . . . cooking," he murmured under his waning breath. A few yards behind the man, a two-wheel mule cart sat with one side propped up on a stack of rocks. A removed wheel leaned against its side. A mule stood tied to a stake by a lead rope, crunching on a small mound of cracked grain.

The Ranger started to step forward and say something more. But he stopped himself as the shotgun came up quickly in the wounded man's hands and pointed at him.

"Easy there, mister," Sam said in a calm but firm tone. "I mean you no harm." He reached a hand up slowly and drew back the lapel of his riding duster. Late-afternoon sunlight glinted on his badge. "I'm Arizona Territory Ranger Sam Burrack."

"What's that mean to me?" the man asked bluntly. His voice sounded weakened and halting. He looked around and off toward the distant hill line. "Is this Arizona?"

Sam didn't answer right away. He looked at the women, noting for the first time that one was not much more than a child. They only glanced at the Ranger and continued their work.

Finally, "It is, just barely," the Ranger said. He lowered his gloved hand from his lapel and ventured another step forward.

The man eased the shotgun back onto his lap and stared.

"Besides," Sam said, "it wouldn't matter if it's not. I'm in pursuit of a killer. We have an agreement with the Mexican government—"

"Ha! The Mexican government," the man said, cutting him off with a sharp tone. "Where was the Mexican government when I was being kilt by Injuns?" He eyed Sam bitterly. "Where were you, for that matter?"

"I expect I was somewhere between here and Mesa Grande," Sam said, keeping his voice civil. He walked closer, leading the two horses, until he stopped and looked down at the man. "How bad are you hurt?"

"I've been stabbed deep," the man said. "I fit back a whole band of wild heathens—had 'em leaving too. Danged Injun boy no bigger than a pissant ran out of nowhere, stabbed me twice with a spear bigger than he was." He shook his head in reflection. "And that's how I, Vernon Troxel, died . . . out here, the middle of nowhere, stuck to death . . . by a stinking little nit."

"Take it easy, Vernon Troxel," Sam said, hearing the man's breath and voice getting weaker, shallower as he spoke. He reached out toward the edge of the bandaging, to take a closer look at the wounds. "Maybe you're in better shape than you think."

But the man jerked back away from him.

"Keep your hands to yourself, Ranger," he said. "Only one's going to touch me . . . is my *esposas*." He wagged his head toward the two women.

Sam looked around at the women, the young one in particular.

"Your wives," he said, still looking at the younger of the two women as they straightened and looked over at Troxel.

"That's right. . . . What of it?" Troxel said, his voice growing a little stronger.

Sam didn't reply; he sat watching Troxel, listening, getting an idea what kind of man was sitting before him.

Troxel coughed up a glob of black blood and spat it away and wiped the back of his hand across his mouth. The young woman, seeing him motion for her with a weak bloody hand, hurried over with an uncapped canteen.

Troxel swiped the canteen from the young girl's hand with a malicious stare. The girl flinched and shied back in a way that told the Ranger she had more than once tasted the back of this man's hand.

"I bought them both down in Guatemala, outside Cobán. They're mother and daughter." He gave a weak sly grin. "Made them both my *esposas*, legal-like," he said. "Legal as you can get . . . in Guatemala anyway."

A slaver . . .

Sam only stared flatly, but Troxel had seen that same stare in many places across both the American and Mexican frontier.

"You see anything wrong in that, Ranger?" he said, blood bubbling deep in his chest.

"I enforce the law to the best of my calling," Sam said. "I don't judge the laws of another nation." He took the canteen from the man's faltering hand to keep him from spilling it.

"That's . . . no answer," Troxel said, coughing from deep in his chest.

"It's all the answer you'll get from me," he said. He didn't like slavers, legal or otherwise. He looked up and all around the pillaged and charred trading post as he capped the canteen. He handed it away to the young girl, who took it hesitantly, then hurried back out of reach. "I'm tracking some mercenaries, white men who rode through here on shod horses," he said, nudging his head toward the wide sets of tracks across the trading post yard. "Looks like the Apache were tracking them too. Were you here?"

"No," Troxel said, "but damn their eyes . . . for getting these Injuns stirred up." He gave a bloody, rattling cough. "I got caught here smack . . . between the two. Damn my luck."

Sam saw his point. The scalp hunters were going to leave bitter feelings between the whites and the desert Apache for a long time to come.

"Can I wheel your cart for you before I leave?" Sam asked.

"I won't be needing a cart come morning," Troxel said with finality.

"You might," Sam said. "Either way, the womenfolk will."

"Yeah . . . they will," Troxel said as if in afterthought. His eyes took on a crafty look. "I'd make you a good price . . . for the two of them."

Sam just stared at him for a moment.

"Don't look at . . . me that way," the man said, struggling with his words. "What good will they do me . . . when I'm dead?"

"As much good as the money I'd be giving you for them," Sam replied.

Troxel closed his eyes and sighed.

"Obliged if you'd . . . wheel my cart," he said. "Obliged if you'd spend the night too. Keep these desert critters . . . from chewing on me before I'm gone."

"I'll fix the cart. Then I've got to go," Sam said.

"The womenfolk will see to you. It's only another day's ride to Iron Point."

"Punta de hierro. . . ." The wounded man translated the name Iron Point into Spanish, then spat as if to rid his mouth of bad taste. "What might I find . . . in Iron Point?"

Sam didn't answer. He started to stand.

"Your womenfolk will see you through the night," he said.

In spite of Troxel's waning strength, he grasped the Ranger's forearm.

"No, wait!" he said. "My womenfolk will take pleasure . . . watching critters drag away my bones." He sounded desperate. "Stay the night. Bed down with either of them—bed them both . . . I don't mind. They need a good going-over. But don't leave tonight!"

The Ranger pulled his forearm free.

"Don't say such a thing," Sam said quietly, seeing both the mother and her daughter look over at him from the fire. "I'm on a manhunt."

"Shoot me, then . . . before you leave," the man pleaded. "Shoot them and me. It's best all around." He broke down sobbing. Sam saw the man's mind had taken all it could and was ready to snap. What would he do to the women when he finally snapped, before he turned the double barrels up under his chin and squeezed the trigger?

Sam reached down and picked up the shotgun while he had the chance. The man stopped sobbing long enough to make a futile grab for it.

"Take it easy," Sam said, moving the shotgun out of reach. "I'll wheel your cart. We'll load you on it and ride on to Iron Point tonight."

"Tonight . . . ?" The man sniffled and wiped a ragged sleeve under his nose. "I—I can't go tonight. I'll never make it to Iron Point."

Sam let out a patient breath and propped the shotgun over his shoulder. He looked over at the slaver's mother-and-daughter dual wives and felt something ugly turn in his stomach. The two stared at him; the mother tried to smile, putting herself out in front of whatever bargain Troxel might have struck for them.

"I'll fix the cart," he said to Troxel.

Turning away from the woman's feigned smile and dark hopeless eyes, he led the two horses to where the mule stood crunching its meager handful of grain. The animal looked up and brayed and pulled back its ears, grain clinging to its lips. As Sam walked the horses closer, the mule plunged its bony head down and ate hurriedly.

When the last of the sun's light had sunk below the curve of the earth, the cart and the mule hitched to it stood in black silhouette against the purple sky. With the spare wheel in place and the broken wheel cast aside into the rocky sand, the Ranger and the mother and daughter gathered the remaining cooking utensils and piled them into the cart alongside the wounded half-conscious slaver. The Ranger noted how the woman tried to keep herself between him and the young girl.

"I speak *inglés*," the woman said quietly. "But my very young daughter does not. So, you will speak to me, *sí, por favor*?" she asked hesitantly.

"I understand," Sam said. "Tell your very young daughter to take the seat." There was something about these two he wasn't buying. He gestured up at the front of the two-wheel cart where a rough board lay crosswise front to side as a makeshift driver's seat.

"*Sí. . . ?*" the woman said, looking at him in cautious surprise.

"*Sí,*" the Ranger replied. "She can ride up there. You can ride this one." He nodded at the barb. The woman only stared as he pulled the blanket-wrapped body of Mickey Cousins from across the chestnut barb's back and carried it to the rear of the wagon and secured it down on a narrow board with dangling lengths of tie-down rope.

"My name is Ria Cerero," the woman ventured in a hushed tone of voice. "My young daughter's name is Ana."

"Arizona Territory Ranger Sam Burrack, ma'am," Sam said, touching the dusty brim of his pearl gray sombrero. "If the two of you are ready, we need to mount up and move on out of here." He nodded toward two shadowy wolves who had circled in closer over the past hour, drawn in by the scent of fresh blood. "Get your husband somewhere off the desert floor."

"*Sí,* I understand," Ria said. "But he is not my husband, this one," she said in an ever-more hushed voice. "He purchased me and my daughter from my dead husband's brother."

Sam listened as he ushered her up into the barb's saddle.

"My husband's brother, Felipe, took Ana and me in when my husband died from the fever. But Felipe could not take care of us and his wife and children as well. So he sold us to King Troxel."

"King . . . ?" Sam asked as he settled into her saddle and he swung up atop his dun.

"I meant, *Vernon* Troxel," the woman said, correcting herself quickly. She sidled the barb over to the dun and said under her breath, "He has the two of us call him *King* when he is drinking his whiskey and we are . . . all three alone." She lowered her dark eyes in shame. "Please do not tell him I told you this—I only say this to you because you are a man of the law." A fearful look came over her face.

"I won't tell him," Sam said. Letting out a breath, he looked out across the darkening desert flats. "You can talk as we ride, ma'am," he offered, knowing there was more to come.

"*Gracias,*" she whispered. "I know I must ask God to forgive me for what I tell you now, but I wish he would die before this night is through." She immediately crossed herself for saying such a thing. Tears glistened in her eyes.

Sam nodded and leveled the brim of his sombrero.

Before he'd scooped Troxel up into his arms and carried him to the cart, Sam had seen the wispy figures of the two wolves circling farther in the waning evening light. They were growing bolder, more brazen in their quest for food. He did not want to fire a gun, he told himself. Gazing off into the encroaching darkness, he saw other black forms appear as if out of nowhere and move about, falling onto the wide circling pattern as he and the woman and the mule cart moved forward at a slow pace.

"Careful what you wish for, *señora,*" he said quietly. "A night like this, you just might get it."

S909